TURTLE BOY

TURTLE BOY

BOY

M. EVAN WOLKENSTEIN

A YEARLING BOOK

This is a work of fiction. Names, characters, places, and incidents either are the product of the author's imagination or are used fictitiously. Any resemblance to actual persons, living or dead, events, or locales is entirely coincidental.

Text copyright © 2020 by M. Evan Wolkenstein
Cover art copyright © 2020 by Ellen Duda

All rights reserved. Published in the United States by Yearling, an imprint of Random House Children's Books, a division of Penguin Random House LLC, New York. Originally published in hardcover in the United States by Delacorte Press, an imprint of Random House Children's Books, a division of Penguin Random House LLC, New York, in 2020.

Yearling and the jumping horse design are registered trademarks of Penguin Random House LLC.

Visit us on the Web! rhcbooks.com

Educators and librarians, for a variety of teaching tools, visit us at RHTeachersLibrarians.com

The Library of Congress has cataloged the hardcover edition of this work as follows:
Title: Turtle boy / M. Evan Wolkenstein.
Description: First edition. | New York : Delacorte Press, [2020] | Audience: Ages 10 up. | Summary: Seventh-grader Will's Bar Mitzvah community service project, visiting an incurably ill older boy in the hospital, leads to a friendship that is life-changing for both them and those around them.
Identifiers: LCCN 2019041080 (print) | LCCN 2019041081 (ebook) |
ISBN 978-0-593-12157-3 (hardcover) | ISBN 978-0-593-12160-3 (library binding) |
ISBN 978-0-593-12158-0 (ebook)
Subjects: CYAC: Friendship—Fiction. | Face—Abnormalities—Fiction. |
Bar mitzvah—Fiction. | Terminally ill—Fiction. | Middle schools—Fiction. |
Schools—Fiction. | Jews—United States—Fiction.
Classification: LCC PZ7.1.W633 Tur 2020 (print) | LCC PZ7.1.W633 (ebook) |
DDC [Fic]—dc23

ISBN 978-0-593-12159-7 (paperback)

Printed in the United States of America
10 9 8
First Yearling Edition 2021

Random House Children's Books supports
the First Amendment and celebrates the right to read.

Penguin Random House LLC supports copyright. Copyright fuels creativity, encourages diverse voices, promotes free speech, and creates a vibrant culture. Thank you for buying an authorized edition of this book and for complying with copyright laws by not reproducing, scanning, or distributing any part in any form without permission. You are supporting writers and allowing Penguin Random House to publish books for every reader.

NOW IT'S OVER, I'M DEAD,
AND I HAVEN'T DONE ANYTHING THAT I WANT
OR, I'M STILL ALIVE AND THERE'S NOTHING I WANT TO DO.
—THEY MIGHT BE GIANTS, "DEAD"

PART ONE

PROLOGUE

"HEY, WILL," SAID JAKE. "GOT YOUR CHIN!"

He snatched at my face, pinching his thumb between the knuckles of his pointer and middle fingers.

His big, dumb friend Spencer guffawed "Hwah-hwah-hwah," and the two of them walked off together, leaving me with my PB and J sandwich.

Got your chin? What did that even mean? I had no one to ask. I always sat alone at lunch. At the opposite side of the table, some fourth graders were building a catapult out of drinking straws.

I forgot all about Jake's little taunt until a few weeks later, when I was sitting at my desk, waiting for fifth-grade social studies to start. He walked into class, hands cupped like he'd caught a grasshopper.

"I found it!" he announced, peeking between his hands. "Will's missing chin!" A bunch of other kids laughed, and I could feel my face burn with shame, but at what? What was so funny about my chin? As soon as the tardy bell rang, I grabbed a hall pass and went to an empty restroom to look at my reflection. It was my usual face: glasses, big front teeth, chubby cheeks. My chin seemed very uninteresting.

•••

That night, everything became clear.

I was brushing my teeth when Mom's makeup mirror caught my eye. I grabbed it and peered at my reflection. It magnified everything; my nostrils and nose were monstrous. My eyes were large and looming. Then I held the mirror out to the side. From this new angle, I could see myself the way others did.

I'd seen my face in the mirror a million times, but I'd never noticed. I knew it hadn't grown that way overnight.

Now I know that bad things can happen a little at a time.

•••

That Saturday night, I was holding the makeup mirror to my face. I'd been checking it at least twice a day. If my chin had shrunk, maybe it could grow back.

"What are you doing with my mirror?"

Mom's voice startled me. She was standing behind me in her old nightgown. I slammed the mirror down on the counter so hard, I nearly broke it.

"Will? What were you looking at?"

"Nothing," I said. I pushed past her into the hallway, but she followed me.

"Stop," she said. I turned and glared at her. "What were you doing?"

"Looking at my face," I said quietly.

"Why? What's wrong with it?" she asked, coming closer.

"Something's wrong with my chin," I said. "Look, see?" I turned my face to the side. "It looks weird."

"Who told you that?" she demanded. "What idiot said there's something wrong with your face?"

"A kid at school," I said reluctantly. I didn't want her to know I was getting teased.

"Will, don't you ever let anyone tell you how you look." She sounded angry, though I knew it wasn't directed at me. "Except your mother," she went on, her voice softening. "And I'm telling you, the only thing I see when I look at you is a handsome young man who looks a lot like his dad."

"Are there pictures of Dad without a beard?" I asked.

She shook her head. "No, but I promise you, there was nothing wrong with his face. I loved his face."

She took a big breath, as if she'd just climbed a hill, and told me it was way past bedtime.

"It's only eight o'clock," I objected.

"Past *my* bedtime," she said.

She drifted off to her room. I don't have any brothers

or sisters, so the house suddenly grew quiet. I went down the stairs to the living room, then to the kitchen and back up to the hall, reviewing each of the framed photographs: Dad and Mom on their honeymoon in Hawaii. Dad and Mom at the hospital after I was born. A grainy selfie of Dad and Mom and me with a blurry playground in the back. I'd looked at these pictures a million times, and in each one, the face beneath Dad's beard was a mystery.

• • •

A few weeks later, Mom told me she'd had a chat with my doctor about my chin. I was going to meet a surgeon.

"A *surgeon*?" I shouted. "No! No hospitals! You know how I am!"

"Yes, I do know how you are," she said. "And his office isn't *in* a hospital. It's in a *clinic*."

As if that made a difference. I hate hospitals and anything that has to do with them, probably due to the fact that Dad died in surgery when I was four. He was only getting a hernia fixed—a tiny tear inside the abdominal cavity—but something went wrong and he never came home. Even now I get jittery and jumpy when I go to the doctor, even when we drive by a hospital. But it's not like I have a bunch of traumatic memories. I can barely remember the room, the bed, the monitors.

The next morning over breakfast, Mom looked awful,

like she hadn't slept. She apologized for making the appointment without telling me.

"I do think your face looks absolutely fine," she added. "Let's have the doctor tell us that too."

But that's not what happened.

The surgeon, Dr. Haffetz, stuck his gloved fingers into my mouth and pulled my cheeks—side to side, up and down—yanking my upper lip up toward my nose, and my bottom lip down to my chin so hard, I thought he was going to rip my face off. After a few minutes, he pulled off his gloves and turned to Mom and me.

"There's quite a gap between the mandible and maxilla," remarked Dr. Haffetz. "That's the lower and upper jawbones. I don't know what your father looks like, but maybe you take after him?"

"He does look a bit like his father," Mom said firmly and decisively, steering us around a heavy topic. "And his father looks perfectly fine."

I appreciated that Mom wasn't revealing any more than necessary about Dad.

"Maxillofacial conditions like this can go in all sorts of directions," Dr. Haffetz explained, balling up his gloves and throwing them into the trash. "They can be minor and purely cosmetic, or they can develop into more serious conditions. They can make it hard to eat, hard to speak—sometimes they contribute to sleep apnea."

"What's that?" I asked quickly.

"Oh, like snoring," Mom interjected. "Your father's snoring could wake the dead."

I noticed that Mom had switched from the present tense to the past, but Dr. Haffetz didn't seem to pick up on this.

"Snoring is a symptom of sleep apnea," he corrected, "but apnea itself is caused by a blockage of the airway during sleep. It can strain the cardiopulmonary system, which can lead to heart damage. It's definitely not something to play around with."

He went on to explain that there wasn't much to be done—not at my age, not while my bones were growing. I'd have to wait at least a couple of years for my face to finish developing.

"And then what?" I asked.

"It's too soon to tell," he said. "Sometimes occlusion can be treated with orthodontic appliances. Sometimes it requires a reconstructive surgical procedure."

The only thing I hated more than my chin was the hospital. The idea of getting any sort of operation made my stomach churn.

Mom must have picked up on what was happening inside me, because she put her arm around my shoulders.

"Don't worry, Will," she said. "You're only in fifth grade. You'll be in seventh grade before you even need to think about the next step. That's two full years away."

CHAPTER 1

ALL THAT HAPPENED TWO YEARS AGO.

Now it's the first day of seventh grade. Mom is driving me to school because I missed the bus.

"Is it possible you *tried* to miss the bus?" she asks, her eyes on the road. "Sometimes you're late for things—you know, accidentally on purpose."

Truthfully, it isn't the bus's fault. It's my feet's fault. Halfway to the bus stop, they froze. They *would not move.* I stood there, riveted, until the bus cruised past my stop, barely slowing down before gliding on its way.

I get these mini-panic attacks sometimes. Like at the start of summer, when I went to volunteer at a soup kitchen. Mom dropped me off outside an old church, and the receptionist pointed the way to the cafeteria. Halfway down the hall, I could hear the laughter of the other volunteers and kitchen staff. All I could think was *What will they think when they see my chin?*

My brain said *Go,* but my feet said *Nope, no way.*

I was at the soup kitchen because of Rabbi Harris. He was making all the kids who were starting the seventh-grade Hebrew school class do forty hours of community service—something to do with us having Bar and Bat Mitzvahs and becoming adults in the Jewish tradition, that we needed to take on responsibilities and give back to the community. The thing is, I didn't want to do anything on the list. All the options involved meeting new people or going somewhere I've never been before, and I really, *really* like my routines.

We have a sheet of paper that an adult is supposed to sign each time we volunteer, and I totally could have forged the supervisor's name—Mom wouldn't have suspected anything—but I'm not like that. I'm not a liar.

Over dinner that night, I confessed that I'd hidden in the church parking lot for two hours instead of going into the cafeteria. Mom dropped her fork on her plate with a loud *clank* and went and got Rabbi Harris's list.

"We're going to find you a new place to volunteer," she said. She went down the list of Rabbi Harris's suggested volunteer opportunities: tutoring, senior home, community center, backyard or basement cleanup.

"No," I responded after each one. "No, no, no."

"Will!" she finally said, nearly shouting. She took a deep, exasperated breath. "You can't go through life turning down every opportunity that comes along. You need to get out there and *do* something."

"Why should I?" I asked back. "You never do anything."

"We are not talking about me," she said harshly. "We're talking about *your* Bar Mitzvah responsibilities, which require you to do more than sit in your room all day taking care of your turtle collection."

I resented the phrase "turtle collection," but that's pretty much what I did for the rest of the summer: I hung out in my room and read books and took care of my specimens. I have four kinds: a box turtle, a painted turtle, a musk turtle, and a small snapping turtle. I don't know anyone else who loves turtles the way I do. I'd much rather be in my room, taking care of my turtles and their habitats, than doing anything else—with one notable exception: walking the trails of the Back 40.

The Back 40 is the nature preserve behind school. Some trails I've walked a hundred times. Some I've barely seen. In the Back 40, with the sun and the breeze, I can move freely, taking big steps and scanning the sky for soaring hawks, or I can inch along, searching the ground for herps. "Herps" is a nickname for reptiles and amphibians. It comes from the Latin "to creep." I love looking for herps: toads and frogs and tiny garter snakes and especially turtles. In the Back 40, I'm alone but I'm never lonely.

When my science teacher, Ms. Kuper, first brought us out there in sixth grade, she explained that it was called the Back 40 because in the 1800s, farmers in Wisconsin used to be granted plots of land: forty acres in front of their homes, and forty in back. Our Back 40 isn't forty acres, she explained, it's more like four—and it was never part of a farm. It's too marshy and full of cattails and trees. But that's the nickname the Prairie Marsh School gave it when the county lent the land to the school a long time ago, Ms. Kuper said, when some of our grandparents were probably sitting in that very classroom.

My parents weren't from Horicon: Dad grew up in California, and Mom grew up in Milwaukee. They met and got married in Berkeley. That's where I was born. We only came to Wisconsin because my aunt Mo lives an hour from here, and after Dad died, Mom wanted to be closer to her sister.

At first, I hated Marsh Madness. That's what Ms. Kuper called the class excursions into the Back 40. We were supposed to be looking at the flora and fauna. I only noticed the mosquitoes and mud. But then I realized that no one ever went out there after school. That meant it could all be mine.

I spent more and more time there, spotting red-winged blackbirds flying overhead, listening to the whoop of the whip-poor-will camouflaged in the trees. One by one, as spring turned into summer, I caught my turtle specimens. I didn't tell anyone about it—not even Ms.

Kuper. You could say that I secretly brought the Back 40 home with me and kept it in four large rectangles of glass in my room.

. . .

Mom and I drive in silence. There may be no way to escape going to school, but I've invented a way to keep people from seeing my face. I've started wearing an extra-extra-large hooded sweatshirt, even when the school is hot and stuffy, so I can draw the strings and close it around my face. Also, I fill my backpack with big books, partially so I have something to read when I eat lunch alone, but mostly so I can set up a wall in front of me.

On the bus, the front seat is mine. Nobody can turn and see my face except the driver. Last year, my best friend, Shirah, would get annoyed because her volleyball friends sat way in the back and she wanted to sit with them, but we had a deal: I copied her math homework and she copied my science homework. To do that, she had to sit in the front with me. We didn't see it as cheating—we helped each other.

I hope we'll continue that routine this year. I hope we're over our rough patch. Back in third and fourth grades, Shirah used to come over every Saturday after synagogue, and we'd play hide-and-seek or we'd invent new snack recipes, like Nutella, Cheerios, and marshmallows, microwaved into a steaming blob.

In sixth grade we weren't how we used to be. Shirah made the volleyball team and got a million new friends. Now we only hang out at Hebrew School and on the bus.

"You're awful quiet," Mom says. "Nervous?"

"No," I say.

"Not even a little?" she asks, a hint of a smile in her voice.

I shake my head.

"Okay, so what are you feeling?" she asks.

"Nothing," I say.

"Nothing at all?" she presses. When I don't answer, she adds, "Will, I wish you'd talk to me. I want to be helpful."

"If you want to be helpful, let me be homeschooled. You don't even have to do anything, I'll read my own books."

Mom laughs, even though I'm not really joking.

We pull up to the curb outside school. "Have a great day, Will," she says. "I think seventh grade is going to be much better than sixth."

"I don't," I say, getting out of the car. "I think it's going to be a living nightmare." I slam the door.

"Beep!" she calls, leaning closer to the open window. "Will? Beep!"

This "beep" thing started a long time ago, just after Mom and I moved to Horicon from California. I hadn't met Shirah yet, and Mom didn't have any friends, so we would go to the budget theater on weekends—they showed reruns and oldies for five dollars. In one movie, a bunch of secret agents were synchronizing their watches before a mission. Mom and I started doing the same thing whenever we were going separate ways. She'd say "beep" and touch her watch and I'd answer "beep." I loved it.

But that was when I was little. I think it's totally stupid now. I don't want to tell her that, though. I don't want to hurt her feelings.

I muster a grumpy "beep" and turn toward the school. Once Mom drives away, I draw the strings on my hood and push through the school's glass doors. The lobby and halls are empty.

This is bad. This is very, very bad. The receptionist sees me through her sliding window, standing there, frozen.

"Hello, young man," she says, and points to the double doors. "Go in quietly; the assembly has started."

CHAPTER 2

THE FIRST THING I SEE IS A WALL OF KIDS TO MY LEFT and a wall of kids to my right. Everyone's sitting in bleachers while Dr. Monk, our principal, stands in the middle of the gym, droning into a microphone.

I hitch my backpack a little higher and begin my walk past the sixth graders, heading toward the seventh-grade section. The entire school is looking at me. My heart is pounding so hard, I'm not even sure I'd hear the Turtle Boy chant if it started.

You'd think I'd love being called Turtle Boy, but they don't call me that because I love turtles. That's just a sick coincidence. In fact, no one knows I have turtles at home. They say I look like one. They call me that to humiliate me.

"Will! Will!"

I flinch, as if I've been kicked, but I turn and it's Shirah! She's about five rows from the back, sitting with all her volleyball friends. It's impossible to miss her: she has huge, curly hair and braces and freckles and kind of looks like a lion. She waves for me to join her. I start to climb the bleachers, but the moment I take my first step up, I hear another voice: "Hey, look! It's Turtle Boy! Turtle Boy, you're late!"

It's Jake. He's pointing at me. He and Spencer start pumping their fists, chanting rhythmically, and one by one the rest of his lacrosse friends join in. *"Tur-tle Boy! Tur-tle Boy!"*

My face burns with shame. I drop down to sit alone on the lowest bench, push my knees together, and bury my face in my lap.

A teacher picks up on the commotion from my section and comes over to stand in front of us, arms crossed, feet apart. The chanting stops.

Dr. Monk continues his list of announcements, but I'm not paying attention. I'm trying not to be here. In my mind, I'm at home, with my turtles. Or walking the trails of the Back 40, the breeze against my cheeks, all alone. But then Dr. Monk says something that brings me back to the gym.

"And now," he says, "a few words from Ms. Kuper."

There's a friendly round of applause, and I look up to watch Ms. Kuper, my favorite teacher, clump-jog to the microphone in her duck boots. She's shorter than Dr. Monk, but her Afro sticks up a few inches, making her almost as tall as him. She stands there in baggy corduroy pants and a flannel shirt and waits a minute for the noise to die down before speaking.

"Hi, everybody," she says. "I have only one quick announcement, and it's concerning the Back 40."

I lean forward in my seat.

"Unfortunately, the Back 40 is going to be off-limits to students for a while," she says. I feel my jaw drop.

"For your own safety," she continues, "we ask that you not try to climb or go beyond the new fence."

Did she say "fence"? Off-limits? For how long? And why?

I push my face back down into my lap and leave it there for the remainder of the assembly.

CHAPTER 3

FINALLY, DR. MONK DISMISSES EVERYONE TO OUR FIRST class, and the mob surges to the double-doors. I hang back as the seventh graders flood around me. Shirah climbs down the bleachers, and I see her say goodbye to her volleyball friends.

"Hey," she greets me, coming closer. "Are you okay?"

"Why wouldn't I be?" I reply.

"Because you had your head shoved way down between your knees for the past fifteen minutes," she says. "That doesn't seem 'okay' to me."

"Well, I do that sometimes," I say.

"You shouldn't let that stupid Turtle Boy thing bother you so much," she says. "It's a dumb name, and they're idiots. Sticks and stones, right? Ignore them."

"Easy for you to say. No one calls you names."

"You don't know that," she says firmly. "Maybe they do. Maybe I choose not to make a big deal about it.

"Okay, changing the subject. How was your summer?"

"Fine," I say.

"And did you do anything?" she asks brightly. "Did you go anywhere? Did anything happen?"

"No, no, and no," I say.

"All right." Shirah barely conceals her annoyance. "How about I just tell you about my summer?"

We start walking toward our first-period classes. She goes on about volleyball camp: It was hot, the food was bad, she got athlete's foot, and yet, she had a great time! To me, it sounds like a bad dream: being surrounded by hundreds of kids all day and then sleeping on a bunk bed in a cabin with total strangers? Torture. Still, it's way better than my summer.

I also had my appointment with Dr. Haffetz, the surgeon; the appointment I'd been dreading since fifth grade. He took X-rays and a bunch of blood tests and bigger, fancier X-rays. I finally learned the scientific name for what was happening to my face: a condition called "micrognathia, with aplasia of the mandibular condyles."

Micrognathia sometimes starts during puberty, which is a really cruel joke of nature. It's the reason my chin has continued to shrink; it's why I've developed a lisp and why I've had more and more trouble eating. I can't take bites like a normal person; I have to grab my food with the side of my mouth and tear off chunks. Dr. Haffetz concluded that there would be no way to correct my occlusion with braces alone; I'd need surgery.

"What kind of surgery?" I asked, frantic. Mom put her hand on my back and rubbed gently.

Dr. Haffetz grabbed the plastic skull model from his desk and pulled off the removable jaw, showing Mom and me how they would break the hinge, move the jaw forward, and add bone from my hip to build up my chin. Then they'd wire my teeth together so the bones could heal. I'd have to eat my food through a straw. He suggested I do the surgery a week before winter break to allow maximum time to recover at home.

The rest of the appointment passed in a blur.

• • •

"What if I decide not to have the surgery?" I asked on the way home. I'd been Turtle Boy for almost a year. I hated it, but I was used to it. If living with the humiliation got me out of surgery, I'd take it.

Mom turned down the radio and spoke to me very gently, both hands on the steering wheel. "Will, remember how Dr. Haffetz explained that this condition can affect your breathing? We need to take care of this. And you're not alone. I'll be with you every step."

That evening, Mom went on with normal life; making dinner, doing some work for the *Dodge Gazette,* where she's a copy editor (that means she takes other people's bad stories and uses a red pen to make them better). But I was on summer vacation, and I had nothing to distract me. I'd be watching TV, and see a toothpaste commercial and remember . . . *Teeth wired together.* Or I'd be eating a frozen pizza . . . *Food through a straw.* Or I'd be walking the paths in the Back 40 . . . *Break the jaw hinge. Bone from my hip.*

Eventually, I stopped going to the Back 40. I stayed in my room, shades down, and let the sliver of light around my window turn bright, then blue, then dim with the evening. I thought about turtles, how they overwinter. When it starts getting cold out, they burrow under the mud, under ice, and their heart rate slows down. It's more than sleeping. It's almost dying. It would be nice to overwinter my year away and wake up when the surgery is over.

"Hey, Will," Shirah finally says, looking me in the eye. "Are you *really* okay? Besides those idiots and the Turtle Boy thing . . . is something going on?"

I wish I could tell her about my diagnosis, that I need major surgery to correct it. But we're not the friends we used to be. I can't tell her my secrets. Not because I don't trust her . . . but because I'm too embarrassed. She's turned into a popular girl. I've turned into Turtle Boy.

"I'm completely fine," I say flatly. "Have a good first period."

CHAPTER 4

I'M WALKING ALONG THE CENTER AISLE IN THE CAFETE-
ria, between the two rows of tables. About halfway down,
I see Jake and Spencer and the other lacrosse kids. I don't
want to go anywhere near them. Besides being the first
to point out my deformity, Jake was the one who gave me
that stupid, awful nickname.

Last year, I was eating lunch, minding my own business, when he and Spencer walked by. Jake looked at me
with his little weaselly eyes, pointed straight at my face,
and said, "Hey, look! He eats like the turtle in the bio lab."
Spencer—who's built like a big, dumb bear—snatched
one of my carrots with his giant, fleshy paw-hands and
nibbled at the tip, imitating a turtle. There was nothing I
could do. From that day on, a bunch of kids started calling me Turtle Boy.

I tried to ignore it. I hoped it would go away. But it
stuck and it spread. Whenever we played kickball and I
dropped a pop fly, someone would say, "Nice job, Turtle

Boy!" And whenever I got up in front of the class to do literally anything—sharpen a pencil, hand in my homework, do a presentation—somebody would start that stupid Turtle Boy chant, and then the others would join in, quiet enough that the teacher couldn't hear it.

"Tur-tle Boy! Tur-tle Boy! Tur-tle Boy!"

They thought it was hilarious, but it made me want to climb into my backpack and zip it up. Sometimes I'd get so upset, I'd take the hall pass, go to a bathroom, and just sit in a stall until the bell rang.

So no, I won't sit anywhere near Jake and Spencer. That cuts off the entire back half of the cafeteria.

I'm watching Shirah eat lunch with her volleyball friends. One of them is talking excitedly, making big gestures with her hands, while the others laugh. I wish I could sit with them.

I'm starting to think I should go eat by myself in the library when something drills between my ribs.

I cry out in surprise and whip around.

Max Rosenberg-Chan!

Max moved here last year and joined the carpool with me and Shirah to Hebrew school. Pretty much he's ruined one of the few times Shirah and I still hang out. She seems to like him, but he's the most annoying person I know. At school, I stay as far away from him as possible.

"Dude!" he says, practically panting with excitement. "Look at my arm! You gotta sign my cast!"

Max's arm is strapped into a plastic brace, the kind you wear for a sprain. He's taped a long strip of masking tape along one edge, where it's signed by two people: *Mom* and *Mikey,* his little brother. Also, he's written *L'Art du Déplacement* several times around the edge of the tape, whatever that means.

"This is a brace, Max," I say. "You sign a *cast,* not a plastic brace."

"Whatever," Max says, trying to hand me a marker. "Just sign it."

I grab the marker and scrawl my name.

"Where are you sitting?" he asks.

I don't want to admit that I've been in the cafeteria for five minutes and still don't have anywhere to sit, so I point to the nearest table. It's occupied by a small group of sixth graders, except the two seats on the end.

"You wanna know how it happened?" he asks excitedly, holding up his brace. "I was executing a dive-roll down an entire flight of steps. My cousins in Chicago taught me a bunch of maneuvers this summer, and I've been practicing nonstop."

"And your cousins are ninjas?" I wonder skeptically.

"First of all," he says, "ninjas are Japanese. That side of my family is Chinese. Not the same. Second, for your information, it's called *parkour*. Climbing, diving, rolling—it's urban movement."

"I know what *parkour* is," I say. "You sent me You-Tube videos all summer."

"It was originally gonna be the whole flight of steps," he continues, "but I bailed at the last second, so it was only about half, but it was still *awesome*! My idiot brother was supposed to get it on video, but he's such a doofus, all you can see is me running. Then the camera's all jumpy and it's over. Here, you wanna see?"

He digs his phone from his pocket and shows me. He's right. I can see Max running toward the camera, but then it's chaos: a thud and some loud groaning.

"I landed too hard on my arm and had to go to the emergency room," he says, sounding almost happy about it. "We were there for, like, five hours. Now I have this cool brace, and I'm a full-fledged *track-ee-ur*."

"A what?"

"Track-ee-ur," he says. He spells it out: "*T-r-a-c-e-u-r.* It's French."

"I think it's pronounced tray-*suhr,*" I say.

He ignores me, admiring his brace with a smug expression, as if the injury were a small price to pay for an honorable French title.

"Once the brace is off," he says, "maybe you could come over and we'll make a video, but this time I'll nail it!"

"Hey, Turtle Boy!"

Before I can stop myself, I've looked up. It's Spencer and Jake, standing behind Max, grinning at me. They both pump their fists and chant: "Tur-tle Boy! Tur-tle Boy! Tur-tle Boy!"

Max registers what's going on and seems upset. I look down, my eyes glued to my sandwich. Finally, Jake and Spencer turn and walk away, still doing the Turtle Boy chant.

"That is so unfair," says Max. "Why should you get a nickname and I don't?"

"What?" I ask. "Are you kidding?"

"In parkour, you get to pick a nickname," he says. "I'm *Aero*! But no one else calls me that. I wish I had a cool nickname people actually used."

"Turtle Boy is not a cool nickname," I say coldly.

"Why not?" he says. "It's a superhero name . . . Turtle Boy! Like Batman."

Max often seems to live in a world of his own, where everything is super awesome and nothing bad happens and people aren't cruel. Sometimes I wish I could live in that world.

CHAPTER 5

RABBI HARRIS FOLLOWS THE LAST KID INTO THE CLASS-room, closes the door, and plops down on the edge of the desk. As usual, he's wearing a huge T-shirt that drapes down over his substantial belly. This one has a bunch of pine trees on either side of the word YOSEMITE, which is a national park in California. Except there's a space between the O and the S, so it really says "YO SEMITE." I have no idea what the T-shirt is supposed to mean, but it suits Rabbi Harris perfectly: his giant frame, his bushy beard, and the thick, chunky-knit kippah on top of his mostly bald head make him look more like a lumberjack than a rabbi. I've known him since I was six, when Mom and I moved to Horicon and joined the synagogue, but rarely have I talked to him one on one.

The class is a dozen kids. Half are from nearby towns that are too small for synagogues, and the other half go to Prairie Marsh. Shirah is friends with almost everyone, but I keep to myself.

"This is it, *chavreim*," Rabbi Harris says with a big smile on his face, calling us by the Hebrew word for "friends." "Bar and Bat Mitzvah year," he continues. "We've been working toward this goal for a long, long time. Soon it won't be me up at the *bimah*, leading prayers and chanting from the Torah—it'll be you! Dena, your date is already this weekend! And Shirah is next week. I get *farklemt* just thinking about it."

I look over at Shirah, and she looks back at me with a little eye roll. Even though she's pretending to be all casual about it, I can tell she's excited. She's bouncing her knee. That's what she does when she's nervous or excited.

"The rest of you have dates a bit later in the year," Rabbi Harris goes on. "That gives you longer to practice leading the prayers, to polish up your speeches, and to memorize your Torah portions."

Memorizing a Torah portion isn't like memorizing lines of poetry for English class or learning song lyrics for school musicals. The actual scroll is only in Hebrew, and there's no punctuation, no way to tell where each verse stops and starts. You sing the Hebrew to a melody—again, with no marks to remind you. It's both repetitive and unpredictable.

"The thing is," Rabbi Harris continues, "I've been doing this long enough to know that you'll be tempted to say bye-bye to Hebrew school once your Bar or Bat Mitzvah is done."

He hops off the edge of the desk and folds his arms. "But this isn't a thing you're doing alone. On your big day, the whole congregation, your friends and family, are all gonna be there. As you take your steps into adulthood." It's a *community* celebration.

He draws a bit closer to us and pauses, scanning the room and looking us in the eyes.

"And that's why I expect to see every last one of you at Dena's Bat Mitzvah this weekend. The party *and* the service."

I know other kids would think it's weird that I want to miss a party, but for me, a party is not a good time. I can't dance, I never know what to say to anyone, and I don't like to eat in front of other people because of the way I chew. To me, parties are hours of feeling gross and different and weird, and there's nowhere to hide. I stand around with my hands in my pockets, hoping no one is looking at me.

I don't care what Rabbi Harris says. I'm skipping it.

• • •

Rabbi Harris ends class almost ten minutes early, and we all grab our bags and stampede the door before he changes his mind.

"*Shmarya ben Baruch v'Gittel*," he says as I pass by, calling me by my Hebrew name. He calls all of us by our

Hebrew names except Shirah, whose name is already in Hebrew.

"Can we chill a few minutes? Let's go to my office."

We head down the hall to his office. It's cluttered with tons of books. Some of them look like what you'd find in a typical library: paperback books, hardcovers, periodicals in plastic organizers. But also, he has shelves and shelves of gigantic tomes that look like they belong in a wizard's laboratory.

Posters cover most of the wall space: oldies rock bands and a huge laminated sign of a rainbow, with the words LGBTQ SAFE ZONE. That same sign hangs on the door of the guidance counselor's office at school. There's also a shelf full of Star Wars action figures, which strikes me as unrabbi-like and very weird but *very* Rabbi Harris.

"I hear you had a little trouble over the summer with your community service," he says. "Care to share what happened?"

"I guess I'm not a soup guy," I say.

"I wonder if you gave it a fair try," he says. "Sometimes we experience something called 'productive discomfort' when we try something new. You need to give these experiences a fair shot."

"I gave it a fair shot," I say.

"Have you looked at other stuff on the list?" he asks. "Anything there float your boat? Or something not on the list? The list is just to get you started. If you're going to spend forty hours doing something, might as well be something you're passionate about."

He continues to watch me for a minute, but not with judging eyes. I've seen that look. It's the way Mom trains her gaze on the road when she drives on a rainy day—all quiet concentration.

"Is there something holding you back?" he asks.

Seeing I'm not going to respond, he nods with some finality. "Well, you don't have to worry," he says. "This Sunday afternoon, you're going to visit someone really special. His name is Ralph and he's sixteen, but he's been in the hospital for a long time and could use the company of a great guy like yourself."

Did he say "hospital"?

"No, no. I can't," I say definitively. "I don't do hospitals."

"Hospitals can be scary places," he says. "But you'll love Ralph. And I'll be right there to support you."

I'm filled with cold terror. He can't support me. He doesn't understand. He doesn't know that I need to stay as far away from hospitals as possible.

I glance and see that Rabbi Harris is still looking at me. Gone is his usual scraggly, dopey look, and instead, he has only the shadow of a soft smile in his eyes, something I never would have seen if I weren't sitting right in front of him. He looks at me—without staring, without judging—and it makes me want to tell him everything, to share the burden I carry around all day on my back, in my face. I remind myself, I don't really *know* him. I don't *trust* him.

I decide to deploy one of my most trusted tactics.

"I'll have to talk to my mom first," I say.

"As a matter of fact, I've already mentioned this to your mom," says Rabbi Harris, surprising me. "She's cool with the plan."

"Can I go now?" I ask, my throat tight and aching.

"Absolutely," he says, standing up and opening the door for me. "And I'll be seeing you at Dena's Bat Mitzvah. Right?"

I head into the hallway without answering, without looking back.

CHAPTER 6

OTHER FAMILIES HAVE TACO TUESDAY. MOM AND I HAVE this vegetarian dish she discovered online. It's called "nut loaf." I don't mind the taste, but it's the worst name imaginable. Whenever she makes it, I make a point of asking unnecessary questions about it: "Ooh. Is the nut loaf ready?" "How many servings of nut loaf do I get?" She's usually good-natured about it, but tonight, she's ignoring me. Clearly, something's on her mind.

"So," she finally says, pulling the nut loaf out of the oven. "Did you end up having a conversation with Rabbi Harris today?"

Mom and Rabbi Harris talk pretty often. She says he helps her keep a positive outlook on life, but I can tell when they trade notes about me.

"We talked about how I'm going to write a paper on world hunger," I say.

"Really? That's the opposite of what he told me." She puts the nut loaf on the counter and bends down to peer under a pot on the stove. "He told me there's a young man in the hospital he wants you to visit."

"Rabbi Harris won't listen to me," I say. "Can you please talk to him? You know how I am with hospitals."

Mom takes a deep, unhappy breath.

"I do know how you are with hospitals," she says, scooping two steaming slices of nut loaf onto each of our plates. "And you're going to need to get over it by December, anyhow. That's when your surgery is scheduled. Might as well start now."

We sit down, and she starts eating. I pick up, then immediately put down my fork and draw my elbows toward the swirl of nausea forming in my stomach.

"I don't see why you can't just write a note to get me out of it," I say. Mom keeps a pad of paper and a mason jar full of red pens near the phone for memos. "You got me out of running four hundred meters in gym class. You got me out of playing violin recitals. Last year you got me out of giving that speech in English class. And that stupid—"

"I know," she interrupts. "And maybe that wasn't the right thing to do."

"Are you kidding?" I say. "Why should I have to do those things? They're pointless."

"They're not pointless," says Mom. "You should be out doing things. Trying stuff. You can't sit in your room with your turtles all day. You can't hide from life."

"And you're really living life," I say. "How many times has Aunt Mo tried to get you to go to La Crosse and meet her friends? And she's always trying to set you up on dates. How many have you gone on?"

"That is none of your business, Will," she says, all patience and humor gone out of her voice. She goes back to eating her nut loaf. "And by the way," she adds flatly, "you're going to Dena's Bat Mitzvah. Rabbi Harris said you might try to ditch it, but you're going."

"What?" I yell, outraged.

Without eating another bite, I get up, dump my plate and silverware into the sink with a loud clatter, and go up to my room. Mom and I don't exchange another word for the rest of the night. I stay in my room with the door closed.

CHAPTER 7

THE NEXT DAY, I'M WAITING ON THE FRONT STEPS OF school when an old white Volkswagen Beetle comes down the long driveway and pulls up to the curb. It has stickers all over the back window: skulls and rainbows and dancing bears. The same designs appear on Rabbi Harris's T-shirt.

"Ready to do a *mitzvah*?" he asks brightly.

I know a mitzvah is a commandment or a good deed. But I'm not doing this because I'm commanded by the Torah. I'm doing it because I'm being coerced by Rabbi Harris.

"I didn't realize this guy is Jewish," I say as we pull into traffic.

"Okay, let's review something," says Rabbi Harris. "The Mishnah, one of our sacred texts, tells us about the importance of every *mitzvah* of loving kindness. To make peace when there is strife. To make people happy.

To welcome the stranger. To visit the sick. All of those are *mitzvot*."

He glances at me. "It's not just helping your own tribe. It's reaching out to anyone in need. When I'm not at temple, I'm the chaplain for the whole hospital. I spend time with people who are scared, people who need hope, people searching for the strength to forgive someone . . . people who just need company. Long as they don't mind hanging out with an old hippie, whatever their religion, I'm their rabbi."

We drive for a while, and then, just as we pass a sign with an arrow pointing the way to the hospital, Rabbi Harris says, "Now, before your visit, *Shmarya*, there are a few things I want to speak with you about." His voice startles me—maybe because it's serious, almost cautious. "I want to talk to you about Ralph." He pauses.

Hearing this, I start to tense up. I get very still.

"Ralph has something called a mitochondrial disease. It affects the organs in the cells that produce nutrients."

"Mitochondria are *organelles*," I say. "Not organs."

"That's right," he says. "And if these organelles don't work right, the body can start to lose function. Some people can live with it for a very long time, and other people . . . Their organs—liver or kidneys or heart—can get damaged, and that can be fatal."

My heart is starting to pound. Maybe because of this information, maybe because we're pulling into the hospital parking garage.

"There are medicines that can keep the organs working as long as possible," says Rabbi Harris. "But I want you to know up-front that what Ralph has won't ever go away."

"Is he going to die?" I ask. The words leave my mouth, and the moment they do, I wish I could call them back.

"Well, Will," says Rabbi Harris, "we're all going to die, right? But yes, Ralph is going to die sooner than we will."

...

I manage to walk into the hospital and a nurse looks up at me from behind a desk.

"Are you Will?" she asks. "Rabbi Harris said you were coming. I'm Roxanne."

Standing here, with the weird hospital smells, the sound of buzzers and beeping, I'm already feeling queasy and dizzy, like when I visited Dr. Haffetz with Mom over the summer. I wish I could leave.

The nurse comes around the desk and leads me a ways down the hall to a closed door. She knocks. There's no answer. She knocks again, louder. No answer.

"Maybe he's sleeping?" I ask. "How about I come back another time?"

"He can't hear us," she says, "but trust me, it's not because he's sleeping." She bangs on the door with her fist. "RJ!" she yells.

She sighs and turns to me. "He doesn't like it when I barge in," she says, "but he's not giving us a choice." She turns the door handle, and a strange sound—quick clacking, like hundreds of fingers on keyboard keys—pours out from the crack in the door.

The door swings open. Rabbi Harris's description of Ralph's illness made me picture lots of machines, sad bouquets of flowers, blankets pulled up to a pale patient's chin. I didn't expect a teenage kid wearing a tropical-colored shirt with a string of little shells around his neck. He's thrashing his shaggy hair around and banging with drumsticks on a disk of rubber and plastic, about a foot in diameter, sitting on the bed in front of him. He has no idea we're standing there.

He clacks and hammers with his drumsticks, and his expression is all fury and intensity, as if he's trying to beat down a door with his sticks alone. He has thick eyebrows that bunch over his squinted-shut eyes. But he isn't smashing savagely; each drumstick's tip strikes its own precise spot, blurring in a perfect pattern, like the buzz of a bee's wings.

His head bobs to whatever's in his headphones, and finally, he increases the tempo and explodes into a finale. Both sticks smash the rubber disk at once with a final *shka-back!*

Then silence. He pushes his headphones back onto his neck and looks up, noticing us for the first time.

"You're supposed to knock first," he says.

"I *did*," Roxanne says.

"You're Will," he says to me.

"Yeah, you're Ralph?"

"No one calls me Ralph," he says. "Except my dad and Rabbi Harris. It's RJ."

He reaches for my hand and shakes it, which feels weirdly grown-up. That's when I notice he's wearing a mass of bracelets—brown woven string and colored threads; five or six of them. The bracelets don't hide the fact that his wrist is so thin I can see long bones through his skin. He may be three years older than I am, but he's barely any bigger.

"I'll leave you two to get acquainted," says Roxanne.

She shuts the door behind her. I shift back and forth on my feet and wait for RJ to say something. He catches me peering down at the rubber disc on his bed.

"It's not polite to stare," he says.

"Oh, sorry," I say, taking a step back.

"Just kidding," he says. "It's called a 'practice pad.'"

"What's it for?" I ask.

"I'm banging on it with drum*sticks*," he says. "It's shaped like a *drum*. What do you think it's for?"

At first I think it's a rhetorical question—one of those questions you're not supposed to answer—but he's glaring at me.

Say something, idiot, I tell myself.

"Practicing drums?" I ask.

"Very good," he says. "Here." He holds the sticks out to me. "Try it. Let's see what you got."

"Oh, no, that's okay," I say.

"Try it," he says more insistently.

I shake my head and step back again.

He pushes his headphones over his ears again and bangs on his practice pad, this time more fiercely. His eyes are fixed on an invisible spot on the bed in front of him.

He doesn't show any sign of stopping. At first, I feel like it's my fault. Maybe I said something wrong. But as the minutes pass and he continues drumming on his pad, ignoring me, I begin to feel angry. I don't want to be here. And if this guy doesn't want me here, then I should just walk out the door and go wait for Rabbi Harris in the lobby. The only problem is Roxanne might see me leave, and I won't get a signature for my forty-hours form.

Maybe I can find a place to sit and read. Behind me, pushed into a corner, is a large cushion: it's gray and has three layers, almost like a cake. I sit down on it, get my book out, and start reading. On my right side is a chest-high case, turned to face the three-layer cake–chair. I can see a set of shelves peeking out from behind a sheet that's attached to the top of the case like a curtain. The corner is pulled aside at the bottom, revealing shirts and underwear, a phalanx of 5-hour energy drinks in tiny red bottles, a pair of slippers, deodorant, shaving cream, and some white underwear. I assume this stuff belongs to RJ's dad. Maybe he sleeps here sometimes.

On the same shelf I can see a bunch of bags of Funyuns. I've never had Funyuns—Mom doesn't let me have junk food.

Suddenly, there's a sharp knock on the door, and it swings open. It's a nurse—not Roxanne but a different one. She has short gray hair and glasses. RJ stops drumming and sticks his arm out obligingly. The nurse sets up some packaged medical stuff on a tray table. RJ ignores her and the nurse ignores RJ as she unwraps a needle.

I hate needles.

I start to feel faint. I want to leave the room, but I'm afraid I'll pass out. I put my head between my knees and start to take deep breaths.

"OW!" says RJ. "Denise! You're trying to find a vein, not dig for treasure!"

The nurse doesn't say anything back. Then RJ starts singing, really loudly:

"You see the rate they come down the escalator!
Now listen to the tube train accelerator!
Then you realize that you got to have a purpose
Or this place is gonna knock you out sooner or later!"

He sings in a loud British accent—*"escalaytah!"* and *"acceleratah"* and *"sooneh o' laytah!"* Then he sings: *"Ner! Ner-ner! Ner! Ner-ner!"* over and over, like he's imitating an electric guitar. Finally, the nurse sweeps up the equipment and leaves the room. My head is still between my knees.

"You all right down there? Drop a contact lens?"

"Needles," I say. "I hate needles."

"How original," says RJ. "Do you also hate spiders, homework, and the word 'moist'?"

"Last summer, I needed about twenty blood tests," I say, ignoring his sarcasm. "The nurse couldn't find the vein, and she kept sticking me with the needle and I actually passed out."

"Ooh, wow. Twenty blood tests," he says. He still sounds unimpressed. "Sounds like an average Tuesday for me. What did you need 'em for?"

I've opened a topic I really do not want to talk about. I'm going to keep my head down and see if he changes the subject.

"What did you need them for?" he asks again, louder.

"I was getting tested to see if I might have any joint diseases," I say, looking up.

He raises his eyebrows.

"And I don't," I say. "But I have aplasia of the mandibular condyles, and micrognathia." As soon as I say it, I wonder why I'm telling him these things. I don't talk about this stuff with anyone.

"I don't know what those things are," he says. "Micro-whatever you said. What is that?"

"It means I need surgery on my jaw," I say. "In December."

"Okay, for what?" He sits up a little straighter.

I really don't like talking about the surgery. It feels different from just *thinking* about it—something about the words coming out of my mouth makes it real, and I don't want it to be any more real.

"I'm waiting!" he says.

"They basically move my jaw forward," I say, and stop, but I feel like I haven't said enough, so I add, "And they take bone out of my hip and put it in my jaw and then wire it shut, and I have to blend up my food so I can eat through a straw for two months."

"Yum!" says RJ. "Like one of those ice cream Blizzards! Vanilla ice cream, Butterfinger, and meatballs!"

I can't believe my ears. This is the scariest, worst thing I can imagine, and he's making fun of it. I'm trying to keep my patience.

"Mint chip with chicken!" he continues. "Ooh, here's a good one: chocolate ice cream with tacos! Compared to the slop they feed me in this place, that actually sounds good."

He grabs his drumsticks and plays—*b'dump-bump*—on his stupid practice pad. It sounds like "b'dack-dack" because the pad is made of rubber and plastic, but I still know what he's doing: he's teasing me.

"I'm not telling you anything else," I say. I pick my book up and angrily page through it.

"You seem like a perfectly normal weirdo seventh grader," he says. "Believe me, I've had my share of Rabbi Harris's dorky Bar Mitzvah kids come through here, and you're all weenies."

I ignore him and continue to page through my book.

"Do they tease you?" he wonders. "The kids at school . . . Do they pick on you?"

I ignore him further, although I realize I'm flipping pages too fast to read anything.

"They call you names?"

I slam my book shut. "Yes, actually, they do!"

"What do they call you?" His eyes are trained on me, and this doesn't feel good at all. He's not asking because he cares; he's asking because he's looking for something new to make fun of. I'm not saying a word, but I've opened my book again, and I'm flipping pages and trying to hide my face, and I'm crying silently.

"They call me Turtle Boy," I say.

My eyes are fixed on my book, so I can't see his reaction, but he's quiet for a minute.

"Turtle Boy," he repeats.

"Yeah."

"So the thing that's making you cry," he says slowly, "sitting right here in front of a kid you don't even know in a hospital, is the fact that kids call you Turtle Boy? What does that even mean?"

I don't lift my head. I look at my shoes. "They say I look like one," I say, wiping my nose with my sleeve. "Something about my face."

I can feel RJ squinting at me for a second.

"Come here," he says. "I can't see for crap because the mito' has wrecked my eyes. Come over here a second."

I don't move.

"Come here," he repeats, not loudly but firmly.

I stand up and take a step closer to him. He's quiet for a minute. "Oh, yeah. I can kind of see that—kind of like a cartoon turtle. Because of how your chin goes— *bloop-bloop.*" He draws a little curve in the air with the tip of his drumstick.

What? That's all he has to say?

He grabs his other drumstick and starts playing a rhythm on his practice pad. He sings, "Tur-tle Boy, Tur-tle Boy; he's a Jew and I'm a goy."

He stops. "Rabbi Harris said I'm never supposed to

say 'goy' because it's a derogatory word," he says. "Sorry about that."

He continues playing the rhythm on his practice pad. I turn and go into his bathroom for some toilet paper to dry my eyes. I never should have come here. This is Rabbi Harris's fault. I come out of the bathroom and, big surprise, RJ's still drumming away: *ticky-ticka-ticky-ticka-ticky-ticka.*

"I have to go," I say quietly. My legs and hands are numb, and my backpack seems weirdly heavy as I lift it by one strap.

"What?" he says. He looks really upset. "Where? Why? It's only—" He looks at a clock on the wall. "You have forty-five minutes left."

I don't respond and avoid his eyes as I cross the room. "Stop!" he says. "Where are you *going*? You just got here!"

His tone changes further as I start to close the door behind me.

"Get lost!" he yells. "Who needs you here, anyway?"

I slip my arms under my backpack straps and hustle toward the hallway restrooms as fast as I can without actually running.

CHAPTER 8

Afterward, I'm in the car with Rabbi Harris, my backpack on my lap.

"So? How was the visit?" he asks.

"It was okay." I don't mention that I spent the final forty-five minutes hiding in a bathroom stall. We pull out of the hospital parking lot into traffic, and Rabbi Harris points to the glove box. "Pop that open, would you?"

I do, and my eyes nearly fall out of my head. The compartment is loaded with all kinds of junk food. The kind you see in gas stations: Moon Pies, Hostess apple and lemon pies, pink Sno Balls.

"Grab me a banana Moon Pie," he says.

I pull out a smushy cream-yellow disk and hand it to him. He grips the steering wheel with one hand, and with the other, he holds the Moon Pie, tearing the wrapper open with his teeth.

"Help yourself," he says. "It's my post-hospital snack stash."

I grab a Hostess lemon pie, rip through the packaging, and bite into the tangy goo at the center. I don't care if flakes of crust scatter everywhere as I eat—I devour half the pie before stopping to breathe.

"So," he goes on. "I'm gathering you had a rough ride in there?"

We're waiting for the car in front of us to move, and Rabbi Harris turns; I can tell he's smiling at me, but I don't look. And I don't care if he sees me eat. My eyes are fixed on the pie in my hands—the glazed crust and almost fluorescent yellow filling. Mom doesn't let me have junk food, so I've always coveted gas-station desserts like this, but now that I'm halfway through one, I think it's kind of gross.

"Reminds me of being a kid," Rabbi Harris says, lifting the Moon Pie wrapper. "So, you want to tell me about what happened that was so bad?"

"He told me he didn't want me to be there," I say, omitting the fact that RJ only yelled this when I got up to leave early.

"That's sort of standard for Ralph," he says. "But I can guarantee, he *definitely did* want you there. And you survived a challenging experience. I truly believe it's good for you."

I scoff and take another bite of my pie. I didn't agree to do this to *survive.* I already have to survive every day at school.

"Here's the thing I want you to know," says Rabbi Harris. "Like anyone sick in the hospital, RJ has a lot of powerful feelings about his situation—he's mad and he's sad and he sometimes feels depressed, and mainly, he's scared."

"That doesn't give him the right to take it out on some kid who's just trying to be friends," I say. I'm not sure why I said that thing about friends. I'm not looking for friends.

Rabbi Harris finishes his Moon Pie, crunches the wrapper, and tosses it onto the floor by my feet. Five or six other wrappers are already down there; I hadn't noticed earlier. "This is how it works," he says. "When someone's really sick . . . they're the bull's-eye in a target." He traces an invisible circle close to the windshield. "And they take out their feelings on the people one circle around them." He draws another circle, wider than the first. "And the people farther out in the bull's-eye, that's us. It's our job to be there for the sick person. And if we're having a hard time, we turn to the people that are farther outside the bull's-eye to help us. If you're having trouble, you can talk to me."

I'm silent for a minute while we pull into my driveway. I feel suddenly self-conscious about the state of our house: the huge cracks in the driveway asphalt, the dent in the garage door from when Mom thought the car was in reverse, the holes in the screen door.

The light is on in the kitchen. That means Mom is home and making dinner. Rabbi Harris is waiting for me to say something before I get out.

I understand what he said about sick people taking out their feelings on the people around them, but I have my own problems. RJ shouldn't take his feelings out on me.

I throw the pie wrapper on the floor, like he did, and I open the door and climb out. Before I slam it shut, I lean down and say "I'm not going back."

CHAPTER 9

FOR THE PAST THREE DAYS, I'VE EATEN LUNCH IN THIS bathroom stall. I don't like it. Actually, I hate it. My nose tricks my mouth into thinking that my PB-and-J sandwich tastes like raspberry-scented urinal cakes. Still, it's better than the cafeteria, where Jake and Spencer start the Turtle Boy chant every time they see me.

The bell rings for fifth period. I open the stall door, taking a huge bite of my sandwich, and who's standing there?

Jake and Spencer.

"Hey, Turtle Boy!" they say. "Long time no see!"

I stand frozen. Should I leave? Lock myself back in the stall? There are three other boys in the bathroom; two are peeing and one is gazing into the mirror, smoothing down his hair. They're ignoring us.

"You gonna be at Dena's Bat Mitzvah party tomorrow?" asks Jake. "I'm sure turtles are allowed."

I gawk at him. Jake is going to Dena's Bat Mitzvah?

"Don't look so surprised," he says. "Dena's on the volleyball team. The whole lacrosse and volleyball team are friends."

Say something! I tell myself. My limbs and tongue are turning to ice. *Say something!*

"You're eating lunch in here?" asks Spencer. "Gross."

I look down and see that I'm still holding the final corner of my PB-and J-sandwich. It's a mangled wreck because of how I chew.

"You got a little something on your chin," says Jake.

Do I have peanut butter on my face? I feel around my chin.

"Oh, my bad," says Jake. "You don't have a chin."

• • •

We're halfway home on the bus when I hear the bus driver yell, "Sit down!"

Shirah is coming down the aisle. She stops next to me.

"Dena's Bat Mitzvah is this weekend," she says. "We'll be up late on Saturday. We should get our science homework out of the way now and do math on Monday morning."

"I'm not going," I say.

"What? Why not?" she asks. She's reacting more strongly than I'd expected. "Why won't you go?"

I can't tell her. I wish I could. If anyone would

understand me, it would be Shirah, but she's on the volleyball team. She's popular. She has so many friends, she doesn't need to hang out with me on weekends or after school anymore. And I know she means well when she says not to let the teasing bother me, but all that does is make me feel worse. Jake and Spencer aren't at the top of the bullying pyramid: they don't pants me in the hallway, and they don't duct-tape my arms behind my back and stuff me into a trash can. But that's exactly why it's so bad: no one else can understand why being called "Turtle Boy" is the worst thing on earth.

"Hey!" calls the bus driver. "If you don't sit down, I'm gonna pull this bus over!"

I turn to Shirah, maybe to apologize. Maybe to explain. But she's already gone.

CHAPTER 10

IT'S SATURDAY, THE MORNING OF DENA'S BAT MITZVAH, and Mom tries to pry me out of bed. I decide to play sick. She sticks a thermometer in my mouth and goes downstairs to boil water for Theraflu, this medicine that tastes like hot lemonade. While she's gone, I reach over and dangle the thermometer around the heating lamp of the box turtle's terrarium, making sure to check it before putting it back into my mouth. Those heat lamps get really hot.

She returns, studies the thermometer, and looks straight at the terrarium. She seems like she's about to speak, but then sighs, like she's too tired to fight.

"That's a pretty bad fever," she says. "I think we need to go to the doctor."

"I don't need the doctor," I say, rasping like a brave, fallen soldier. "I just need rest."

"Fine, Will," she says. "But Shirah's Bat Mitzvah is in one week, and you are not missing it. I don't care if you have a fever of a hundred and nine."

Normally, when I'm ill, Mom makes me chicken soup or Jell-O and endless refills of tea, but this time, she doesn't offer anything but medicine. In fact, a couple hours later, she comes and tells me she's going to do some shopping and get her hair done.

After she drives away, I leap out of bed, get dressed, and check the time to make sure I'll be home before her.

Twenty-five minutes later, I'm at the Back 40.

. . .

Two things catch my eye.

First, next to the chain-link fence, a huge yellow excavator is parked on its giant treads.

Second, Max is here, standing on the roof of the cab, jumping up and down, yelling and waving his arms, like a castaway on an island, flagging down a plane.

"What are you doing here?" I shout.

"What's it look like?" he shouts back. "I've taken control of this claw machine. Climb aboard!"

"No, like—what are you *doing* here?" I ask. "Why aren't you at the Bat Mitzvah?"

"Soooo boring," he says. "My therapist told me I need to move around a lot. I'll go to the party tonight, though—I gotta get my dance on."

He starts dancing, shaking his butt around.

"Hey, maybe that isn't a good idea," I call.

Using his good arm, he climbs up the slant of the enormous digger arm and tiptoes a few feet out. He's about ten feet off the ground. I'm very afraid of heights, and even watching someone else climb that high makes me woozy.

"Watch this!" he says.

I try not to look, but I can't help it; he leaps way up into the air and lands on one foot. I look away in horror. My pulse is speeding up and I'm getting dizzy.

"Max!" I yell, covering my eyes. "Come down! You're going to break your neck!"

"Am not!" he says. "I'm a *track-ee-ur*! Watch this!"

I peek between my fingers. He starts shuffling toward the end of the digger arm, then leaps up and lands on the hinge, the highest point of the excavator.

"Come down and I'll make a parkour video with you," I say.

Max freezes and looks at me.

"For real?" he asks.

"Yes," I say. "If you come down. Now."

"You sure you don't want to come up here?" he asks. He crouches and extends an arm, as if he could reach down and pull me fifteen feet off the ground. "It's an awesome view. I can see all the kick balls that've landed on the school roof."

"You promised you'd come down," I say. "And don't parkour down. Just be careful and come down normally."

"COWABUNGA!" he calls as he jumps from the excavator. He doesn't drop straight down, but rather, he steps off and shoves away from the side of the machine with one foot. He hits the ground and absorbs the impact with his legs, dropping into a crouch with one hand on the ground.

"DID YOU SEE THAT!" he shouts. "WHOO! *L'ART DU DE-PLACE-MENT!*" He's holding up his good arm and marching around in victory until he bumps against the chain-link fence.

He's on the other side.

"Uh-oh," he says. "How are you going to get in?"

"How are you going to get out?" I ask.

. . .

We walk along the length of the fence, and a few minutes later, near some high grasses, the lawn has been dug away—not exactly a tunnel, but deep enough that I can get down on my back and shove myself under inch by inch. I stand up and brush clumps of dirt and grass off my shirt and pants.

I'm not alone in my sanctuary, but at least I'm back in the Back 40.

CHAPTER 11

We walk for a long time, looking for a suitable place for Max to injure himself on camera. First, he considers the old wooden fence that runs along one section of the boundary of the Back 40, but it's full of splinters. Then he suggests we go back and film at the excavator, but that's obviously a terrible idea.

I purposely lead him in the opposite direction, deeper into the Back 40, down a hill and through a wooded area. I don't usually come here because there are so many mosquitoes.

"Come on!" says Max. "I think I see a pond!"

Max plows ahead under the shade of the trees. The branches grab and scratch as we push through them. I hope I can find a trail that will loop back to the parking lot without going past the excavator.

I pass through a cloud of mosquitoes, waving my arms like a windmill to shoo them from my face.

"Max," I say. "We shouldn't be here."

"What are you getting so freaked out about? I thought you were Mr. Back 40!"

Before I can answer, I hear him gasp.

About fifteen feet before us, there's a sign with a skull and crossbones on it.

"Awesome!" he says. "It's a pirate hideout!"

"No, we have to go back. That symbol means there's poison ivy."

"Oh, *whatever*," he says. "It won't hurt us if we don't touch it. Remember the thing from Ms. Kuper's class? 'Leaves of three, let them be.'"

"'Skull and bones, head for home,'" I say, walking back toward the trail.

Then Max lets loose a loud whoop and begins to charge forward through the trees. I follow cautiously, eyes peeled for poison ivy, until we arrive at the edge of a pond. This is nothing like the marshy area, full of cattails and reeds, where I caught my other specimens. Here, the water is deeper, wider, alive—not just with the ripples in the breeze but with a swarm of tadpoles.

I kneel down to look closer. It's hideous, and also sort of beautiful, in a way. For a few minutes, nothing exists except me, the pond, and the tadpoles. No Max. No school. No Turtle Boy. Only this living, underwater cloud.

"Ooh!" says Max, suddenly pointing over my shoulder. "Ooh, ooh, ooh!"

I focus farther out and see it: a small turtle climbs out of the water to bask on a log. It's about four or five feet away from shore.

"Turtle," Max says under his breath. "What kind is it?"

I open my mouth, but I can't speak.

Yellow flecks on the shell and a bright yellow chin: a Blanding's turtle.

They're rare; super-rare. I desperately want it.

"We should catch it," Max says. "Come on!"

He starts taking off his shoes, and I realize what's happening.

"You're going in the water?"

"Well, it's not going to swim to us. Come on!"

He strips down to his underwear, but I don't move. I can't do this. I'm terrified of going in water that isn't a pool, especially water where I can't see the bottom. I'm certain there's leeches in there.

Suddenly, Max leaps forward, arms extended, and he splashes into the pond. At first, I think he's slipped and fallen in too deep, but no, he's standing—or crouching, actually—and he's thrusting his good arm beneath the surface.

Then he rises, waist-deep, holding the turtle with one palm against the crook of his braced arm. He looks as shocked as I am.

It's small, and it rotates its legs, as if swimming through the air.

"Don't drop it," I say. "Give it here."

I take the turtle and lift it up to look at the plastron, the under shell. If it's a female, there will be an indentation.

"It's a male," I say.

"How do you know?" he asks.

I turn and start walking back up the trail toward my bike. Max is calling after me, but I don't answer. My heart is pounding. I've never seen a Blanding's turtle in real life.

And this one's mine.

CHAPTER 12

FOUR TERRARIUMS. FIVE TURTLES.

I was so excited to get my hands on the Blanding's turtle, I forgot to consider where I'd keep it.

My old box turtle and the new Blanding's turtle will need to be roommates. I lower the Blanding's turtle into my box turtle's tank. The two turtles ignore each other. I fetch a housewarming present: some live crickets. As I'm scooping them out of the carrier with a plastic tube, I hear the roiling of water and hurry over to see the smaller Blanding's turtle nipping at the neck of the larger box turtle.

I was afraid this would happen. I drop a few crickets on opposite sides of the tank. The turtles continue to tussle for a few seconds until they freeze, sensing the crickets. The Blanding's turtle drifts off, away from the box turtle, and then each of them bolts after its own cricket. They snap up their treats and float, satisfied, for a few minutes. Maybe they're done fighting.

For the rest of the day, I stay in my room, reading and keeping an eye on the new turtle, and at about four o'clock, Mom comes home. I hear the creak of the stairs and a knock on my door, and now I realize I've made a terrible mistake: I should have intercepted her downstairs. In a moment, she'll be in my room. Last summer, when I brought the box turtle home, she gave me a stern talking-to. *No more terrariums. No more turtles.* If she notices the new turtle, she'll definitely make me let it go.

"Hi, sweetie," she says. "How are you feeling?"

Her tone is much nicer than when she left. Maybe she feels bad for giving me a hard time earlier. Out of the corner of my eye, I can see that the box turtle has climbed up on top of the basking platform, but the Blanding's turtle has crawled into the hiding area. If it stays there, I'm safe.

Then, as if reading my mind, Mom looks directly at the terrarium and gives it an odd look.

"That's not a new turtle, is it?" she asks.

"It *isn't* new," I say truthfully. "That's my *Terrapene carolina*. I've had it forever."

From my spot on the bed, however, I can see the Blanding's turtle starting to rustle around.

I tell it in my head, *Stay there.*

The Blanding's turtle relaxes its limbs. It's looking at me.

Mom shrugs. "I thought I'd heat some chicken soup

for an early dinner," she says. "I've only got the canned kind, but I'll doctor it up."

"Yum!" I say. "I'm starving! When can we eat?"

"Come down in ten minutes," she says, and gives me a strange look before shutting the door.

I flop onto my bed with a loud sigh. I can hear the turtles in their terrariums. And I can hear Mom's feet on the stairs. If I had really good ears, on the other side of town, I'd be able to hear Dena's Bat Mitzvah party. I'd hear the sound of kids dancing and laughing and having fun and not caring whether or not I'm there.

. . .

It's the middle of the night. I awaken to the sound of splashing water. I roll over, flip on a terrarium lamp, and peer through the glass to see the large box turtle's jaw clamped onto the back claw of the Blanding's turtle.

I leap out of bed as the Blanding's turtle thrashes to get free and pull it out of the terrarium. Holding it up to the light, I watch as a bead of blood wells around its claw. The box turtle has bitten one of its toenails off— maybe even the toe. It's bleeding badly.

When a turtle is injured, it needs to be kept warm or it can go into shock and die. Quickly, I gather three lamps from three terrariums and grab my two cricket carriers.

I lift the lids off the carriers and dump several hundred crickets from one into the other. This means I'm mixing adults and maturing crickets, which will screw up the colony a bit, but I can't worry about that now. I steal a dish of water from the musk turtle and position my three heat lamps to concentrate their light down into the cricket carrier. The Blanding's turtle has crawled a few steps across my bed, leaving a few tiny red streaks. I lift it gently and lay it in its new infirmary.

I can't keep it there for more than a day or two. I can't put it back with the box turtle. And now, I can't let it go, not with an injury. Tomorrow, I'll have to come up with an excuse to go to Herb's Herps so I can buy a larger terrarium, one that can house two turtles. Then I'll need to cook up a way to justify another terrarium to Mom. But it's even more complicated than that; large terrariums are expensive, and I only have about twenty dollars.

How did I get myself into this mess?

• • •

The next day, I'm at Herb's Herps, and I push through the curtain of long, transparent plastic strips that keep the warmth and humidity in the live-animal section of the store, even on cold days. The air is musty and it's very quiet. That's what I like about it here. Most herps—like turtles, frogs, and snakes—don't move much. They like to find a nice spot where they won't be bothered. They can sit motionless for ages.

Gwen clumps over in her black boots, wearing her usual green apron over denim overalls. She's the only bad thing about Herb's Herps. She always tries to lecture me about herps when I'm the one who should be working in a place like this. I know at least ten times more than she does, even though she's probably in high school.

"What's the cheapest thirty-gallon terrarium?" I ask.

"Is it for an iguana?" she asks. She's taunting me. She knows I only do turtles.

"It doesn't need to be watertight," I add, ignoring her question.

She points to a small tank on a shelf. The price tag says $120.

"I only have twenty dollars," I say.

"Well, you can't buy *part* of a terrarium," she says. "It's pretty much all or nothing. Better start saving your allowance."

"I have to construct an infirmary right away," I say. "I have a turtle with a major injury."

"What kind of injury?" she asks, getting suddenly serious.

"Territory squabble with another turtle," I say. "It got bit."

She looks up toward the cash register, where Herb

Tsab, the owner of the store, sits with his nose buried in a book on herpetology. He's kind of a big deal among herpetologists—he even has his own Wikipedia page. He came to Wisconsin from a small town near Hanoi about forty years ago. I've read about how he was trying to start a marine conservation program there, but the Viet Nam War ruined it. He moved here with a large group of Hmong refugees. Hmong is an ethnic group that allied with America during the fighting. I had trouble following the details of the war, but it was violent and sad. Now, Herb seems so peaceful, surrounded by dozing herps and the burble of water filters.

"Listen," Gwen says quietly, leaning in closer. "This is your lucky day. My dad just threw a cracked terrarium out by the garbage in the back. It's, like, a fifty-gal. If you want it, it's yours."

Her dad? Herb Tsab is Gwen's dad?

"Well, h-how much is it?" I stammer.

"Shhhh!" she whispers. "I said it's *garbage,* Einstein. It's free. Here, use the service door, go around the corner, walk to the back, and get it!"

She pushes open a door between two sets of shelves and I step into the alley between Herb's Herps and the hardware store. Here's the dumpster. And the terrarium. I can't believe this crazy stroke of luck. I hoist the terrarium up and place the open side over my head, so I'm hugging the whole thing with my arms and supporting the top of it, like a very heavy transparent helmet. I can't see very well, but this is the only way I can carry such a bulky thing alone.

I begin the slow, semi-blind walk, around the building and back toward the front of the store, where Mom is waiting, the driver's-side window rolled down. "What is *that*?" she asks. "I thought you were getting crickets!"

"Free terrarium!" I say, hoping to sound thrifty and practical. "Can you open the trunk?"

"You have four terrariums already, Will. Why do you need a fifth? And don't tell me it's for another turtle. We've already gone over that."

The trunk pops open, and with some difficulty, I lower the terrarium inside.

"It's a backup," I say. "It's always good to have a backup."

CHAPTER 13

THE NEXT MORNING, I CHECK ON THE BLANDING'S TUR-
tle in its new terrarium. The injured toe doesn't look
good at all. It's swollen and probably infected. If an endangered Blanding's turtle died on my watch, I'd never
be able to forgive myself. I need to talk to Ms. Kuper
about this.

Before lunch, I head to the sixth-grade wing, all the
way to the end, where Ms. Kuper's bio lab is the last
classroom. Inside, she's standing at a big metal sink full
of soapy water and gear. I haven't seen her since she announced the bad news about the Back 40 on the first day
of school.

"Will Levine!" she calls brightly. "Long time no see!
How'd your first week of school go? How was your
summer?"

"Fine," I say, laying my backpack on the floor. I don't
want to tell her about my diagnosis or surgery, even
though she'd probably be really nice about it.

"Hey, I have a question," I say. "How do you treat an infection on a turtle's toe?"

"Depends on the type of injury," she says, scrubbing a set of hoses. "Can you be more specific? What kind of turtle is this?"

"Oh, this is hypothetical," I say. I need to be careful or she'll figure out that I have wild turtles at home, which is illegal, or that I've been in the Back 40.

"Okay," she says, playing along. "Can you describe this 'hypothetical' injury?"

"The tip of one of its toes is . . . gone."

"That's usually a result of territorial aggression," she says. "Or mating aggression. You'd normally see that kind of thing in wild turtles, not pets. Did you get a turtle at Herb's Herps?"

"How do I treat it?" I ask, ignoring her question. "The *hypothetical* injury?"

"You *actually* bring it in so we can *actually* treat it, Will!" she says. "It sounds like we're talking about a serious injury, and I'm not going to dispense advice without seeing it for myself. "

Ms. Kuper looks at me for a second.

"There's something you're not telling me, Will," she goes on. "You and I go way back, you know? I'd like to think that we don't tell each other silly lies when the simple truth would be just fine."

I figure I might as well go ahead and explain. At least, *partially* explain.

"I have a great new turtle specimen," I say. "And I put it in too small a terrarium with another turtle, and they fought, but I separated them."

"Two turtles," she says, sounding increasingly concerned. "Or are there more? How many turtles do you have now, Will?"

"Three," I lie.

She peers at me a moment longer through her large glasses.

"Okay, four," I say. "A box turtle, a musk turtle, a snapping turtle, and a painted turtle."

I don't mention the Blanding's turtle.

"Answer me something," she says. "Honestly. How many of those turtles did you catch in the Back 40?"

"Maybe one or two," I say, looking down at my shoes. This is not going in a good direction. "But the other two I found crawling around the school parking lot after a big rain. I basically saved them."

"You of all people should know that's not an excuse," she says. "No matter where you find them, we don't catch wild animals and keep them as pets. Plus, *you know* that catching wild turtles is against the law. You need to release the healthy ones immediately."

"I will," I say.

"And as for the injured one, you're going to dab some iodine on the infected toe once a day, and when it's healed—it
should take a week or two, tops—you're letting it go. I know
it feels like winter is far away, but it'll start getting cold
soon, and then you'll be endangering them. They need to
overwinter, and as soon as it gets cold out, it'll be too late."

"But the Back 40 is off-limits," I say. "You said so on
the first day of school. And there's a fence. I can't get
back there."

I'm not going to tell her I found that spot where I can
shove myself under the fence. And now I won't be able
to ask why the Back 40 is off-limits. She's discovered my
turtle collection, and I have to escape this conversation
as quickly as I can.

"Bring them to me, and we can let them go together,"
she says.

I nod and start to inch toward the door.

"And don't be a stranger," she says. "Even if I'm not
your teacher anymore, you can still come by the bio lab
and say hi. Oh, and take this."

She hands me a small plastic bottle of iodine. I take
the bottle, wave goodbye, and hurry into the hall.

•••

That afternoon, I lift the Blanding's turtle out of its tiny,
temporary tank. It doesn't struggle much. The injured

toe looks puffy and raw, and I dab it with the iodine Ms. Kuper gave me. When I lower the turtle down onto the driftwood platform, it scuttles under it, laying still for a long time.

A while later, I hear Mom come home, and then there's a knock on my door.

"Will, I'd like to talk to you a sec," she says through the door.

I put down my book, and she comes in and sits on my desk chair, near the Blanding's turtle's terrarium.

"I want to talk to you about what happened with the boy you visited in the hospital," she says.

I turn and bury my face in my pillow. I thought I was done with RJ, the obnoxious junk-drummer.

"Will," she says, "Rabbi Harris and I talked this morning. We think you ought to be ready for another visit."

"He didn't like me and I didn't like him," I say.

"You need to do your forty hours of community service."

"Thirty-six," I correct.

"Whatever," she says. "This needs to be dealt with, and it can't wait until next Sunday. You're going back there Wednesday after school. I'll help you figure out the bus route. You're going to give this kid another try."

For Mom, "try" means "yes." For me, "try" means "do once and quit."

CHAPTER 14

WEDNESDAY AFTER SCHOOL I TAKE THE BUS TO THE HOSpital and ride the elevator to RJ's floor. I skip the nurses' station and head straight to his door. I knock. No answer. I knock louder. Still no response. I turn the door handle and step inside. He has headphones on, and he's hammering on his practice pad. He's acting oblivious to my presence, but he definitely sees me. I don't care.

I sit on the gray cake-chair and pull out my paperback on herps and terrariums. I don't want RJ to know that I love turtles. He'd probably think my stupid nickname, Turtle Boy, is hilariously appropriate. Fortunately, I have my math workbook with me. I tuck the book on terrariums inside it and read about advanced filtration systems. I read for a while, feeling like this visit is going way better than the first one. I could do this seventeen more times and be done with my hours, and done with this kid forever.

...

I'm getting bored, and the sound of the drumming is driving me crazy. Maybe I'll wander around the halls and eat up some time. I stand and head to the door.

The second my hand touches the door handle, the drumming stops and RJ speaks, startling me.

"Wait," he says. "Where are you going?"

"Bathroom," I say.

He points to the only other door in the room: his bathroom.

"Actually, I'm taking a walk," I say. "Stretch my legs."

"Perfect," he says. "I have a task for you. Get me three bags of Funyuns from the vending machines."

I remember the Funyuns I saw on the shelf last time. From where I'm standing, I can see that they're gone. I'm surprised that RJ can have junk food.

"Are you allowed to eat that stuff?" I ask. I don't want to get in trouble for making him sick.

"No, I'm not allowed," he says. "But (A) that's none of your business, and (B) they aren't for me; they're for Mrs. Barnes. She's down the hall a bit on the left side. I bet you have a couple bucks on you."

It's true, I do have a few dollars. Mom gives me five dollars a week as allowance for easy chores: refilling the beans, rice, and pasta in the bulk food bins. But I don't want to spend my money on Funyuns for some random lady down the hall. I can feel myself getting angry. I don't move and I don't say anything.

"Look," says RJ. "You need your hours so you can get Rabbi Harris off your back. And I need three bags of Funyuns. So do the math."

I'm doing the math. What do I hate more: being in the room with RJ . . . or the fact that he's manipulating me? The calculation doesn't take very long.

"Where's the vending machine?" I ask.

. . .

Out in the hall, I walk slowly. Extra, extra slowly. The trip to the elevator takes at least ten minutes, and once I'm in front of the vending machines, I lose myself, admiring all the snacks. I take my time inserting the bills, pushing the buttons, collecting change. On the walk back to RJ's room, I take twice as long. In total, I'm gone at least twenty minutes.

Back at RJ's door, I knock quietly. Much softer than Roxanne did when she first accompanied me. I knock a little louder, and then just a little louder, until the mean nurse, the one with the needle—Denise—looks up from her computer.

"He can't hear you," she says impatiently. "Just go in."

RJ has fallen asleep. His headphones are on, and the sticks have fallen out of his hands. The music continues to blare out of his headphones.

Now that he's lying still, I can see how thin he is, how pale his skin is. I tuck the three bags of Funyuns on the shelf, out of sight. As I'm packing my books into my backpack, I glance at the wall behind the bed. Up near RJ's head is a lone picture. A woman with straight black hair and a little boy squint into the camera, both dressed in swimsuits. They're on some sort of tropical beach. The endless blue ocean stretches out behind them.

Next to the photo hangs a piece of notebook paper. At the top, in big letters, it says BUCKET LIST. Under that, in smaller writing, there are a couple of words per line. Next to each line is an empty box, like a checklist. I lean in closer to read the list, but RJ's hand flies up, startling me, snatching the paper away.

"That's not for you," he says quietly. He folds it in half and holds it close to his chest.

"I didn't know it was private," I say.

"I didn't know you were so nosey," he says.

Then he notices that I'm standing with my backpack.

"Whoa, whoa," he says. "Where are you going?"

"I'm leaving."

"Why? It's only—" He looks at the clock. "We have ten minutes left!"

"I got here at one-fifty-seven," I say. "It's two-forty-seven now, and it takes ten minutes to get downstairs. That's an hour."

Without waiting for him to respond, I step into the hall and I'm free.

CHAPTER 15

"WILL!"

I hear my Mom's voice, but I don't move.

"I've been calling you for twenty minutes! You have to get up. Now! We *cannot* be late for Shirah's Bat Mitzvah!"

I roll over and curl up, facing the wall.

"Will!" My mom's voice is loud and intense.

"I don't feel good," I say.

"There's nothing wrong with you," she says. "Get up and get dressed; we're going to be late."

She stomps out of the room. I get dressed in slow, clunky movements: my dumb black pants and black sneakers and white shirt.

"Your hair's a mess," Mom says as I come into the kitchen.

I turn on my heel and head to the bathroom. I don't look at my reflection in the mirror. I don't like what I see.

I never like what I see. I run water on my hands, smooth down my hair, and return to the kitchen.

Mom hands me my *kippah.* "Now, that's a handsome boy," she says.

We drive together, mostly silent. The synagogue is packed, so we sit way in the back. Shirah has a lot of family. And friends. She's up on the *bimah,* running the service, even the sections that kids don't need to lead. Rabbi Harris is off to the side with his own prayer book, as if he's just one of the congregation.

When Shirah leads songs, everyone sings and claps and sways to the music. She doesn't have the fake voice of someone who's practiced too many times. She sounds like herself: strong and confident.

Her mom and dad sit on the *bimah* in the large chairs against the back wall of the sanctuary. I watch them as they watch Shirah, looks of joy on their faces. Shirah's mom looks just like her: big, curly hair and freckles. Her dad looks like her, too: heavy eyebrows and big shoulders. She probably got her strong volleyball arms from him.

I think about what I got from Mom. To start with, my love of reading. She always has three or four books open on her bedside table at any given time. And she prefers real books to ebooks, just like me. Now I've learned what I got from Dad: my chin. Looking at the photos of him with his beard, I couldn't really tell. It's hard to get my head around the idea that he passed me the genes that have made me into what I am. I really don't like that idea. It feels just as weird to think that if I have the surgery, I'll be erasing something that I inherited from him.

He gave me so little else.

And even if my chin is my dad's fault, I *still* wish he could be here so I could blame him without feeling guilty. I'm also starting to wish I could go home. Obviously, I'm happy for Shirah. But being here in this synagogue is reminding me of everything I don't have: Family. Lots of friends. A dad.

It's time for the Torah reading. The congregation sings while Rabbi Harris opens the Ark, leans in, grabs the Torah scroll, and carefully hands it to Shirah. As she walks down the aisles, people gather to kiss the scroll or touch it with their prayer books, an old tradition to show respect. Max stands up and she pauses in front of him. He kisses the Torah, looking thrilled.

Eventually, Shirah makes it to the back of the room where Mom and I are sitting. When she sees me, her eyebrows pop and she waves. I can feel my face grow hot: she actually broke her concentration to wave at me.

Once Shirah is back up on the *bimah,* she unrolls the Torah scroll, and after chanting the opening blessing, she begins to read. Her expression strikes me. Surrounded by all these people and all this Jewish stuff, she's calm. At peace. She's at home.

The only time I feel at home is when I'm alone, whether in my room or in the Back 40.

I wish I could always feel the way she looks right now.

CHAPTER 16

IT'S DARK IN THE SYNAGOGUE REC HALL. THERE'S A disco ball and some laser lights. Shirah is wearing a really nice dress—black with white polka dots—and her hair is in a fancy do. She looks different from this morning. More grown up, surrounded by a bunch of other girls: everyone from Hebrew school and also her volleyball team. They're all wearing fancy dresses. I stand near a clump of kids until Shirah sees me. She waves again, and I wave back, but with all those kids around her, I don't want to get any closer. I don't want to dance or have a good time or do what other kids do at parties. I just want to be invisible.

Suddenly I feel fingers drilling into my sides. I whip around. It's Max.

"Max!" I say. "What the *heck*?"

"This party is awesome," he says. "Did you see the Belgian waffle bar?"

"Yes," I say, annoyed.

"Let's go get one!" He pulls me with him, and we load up plates with waffles and ice cream. We stand and eat until the music gets louder and a bunch of girls and guys move toward the dance floor.

"I'm gonna go dance!" says Max.

Now I'm standing by myself. I look at my watch. It's nine o'clock. I watch the kids shaking around under the flashing lights. If I can stomach this for another hour, I can leave.

The song ends and Shirah heads toward the DJ. I try to catch up to her, but I'm intercepted by two boys.

Jake and Spencer.

"Hey! What's going on, Turtle Boy?" Jake asks brightly.

I freeze. Maybe I should run . . . disappear into the crowd. I hear Shirah's voice: "Haven't I told you to stop calling him that?!" Then she says: "Hey, Will! Having a good time?"

I nod.

"I'm so glad I'm done!" Shirah says, making her way toward me, smiling, eyes wide. "Bat Mitzvah . . . OVER! Big relief!"

I know she's trying to make conversation, but my brain is soaking in the fact that Jake and Spencer are at Shirah's party. I can't believe she would do this to me.

"I'm going to get another drink," Jake says. He and Spencer walk off, leaving me with Shirah.

"What is wrong with you?" she asks. "Why are you being so weird?"

"What are those guys doing at your party?" I demand.

"I'm friends with them!" she says. "What's it to you, anyhow?"

"They call me Turtle Boy!" I say, forcing myself to say the name. It sounds so ugly. "But apparently, that's just fine by you."

"Obviously not," she says. "Didn't you hear me tell them to knock it off?"

I watch the crowd for a while, and then I find myself turning and moving away from Shirah.

"Where are you going?" she asks. "Will! WILL!"

Everything feels like it's in slow motion, as if I were swimming—swimming through the crowd and swimming past Max, who's devouring another Belgian waffle, holding it up to his face and trying not to let a mountain of whipped cream slide off.

I sit on a bench outside. I can hear the music. No one cares that I've left the party. No one even notices.

It's amazing how in the synagogue service this morning, one hour felt like a million years.

But sitting alone, waiting for Mom to pick me up, an hour flies by in a snap.

CHAPTER 17

As I get on the bus, I have a bad feeling. Shirah's backpack is on the seat next to her. Her face is turned to the window. I stand there for a minute, wondering if I'm supposed to move the backpack. We have math and science first and second periods, so we should be sharing our homework right away.

I put my hand out, but she grabs the bag, her fingers tight, like a claw. I stand there awkwardly for a moment before retreating halfway down the aisle, trying to escape the cloud of anger that seems to hover around her. A minute later, Max gets on and he looks at the bag next to Shirah. He seems to register that I'm not sitting with her. He lifts his gaze and spots me. He thinks I'm saving him a seat.

I pull my backpack from my feet and plop it on the seat next to me, just like Shirah did. I look out the window. I can feel Max standing there, looking at the backpack. Then he continues slowly toward the back of the bus.

If I'm not going to sit with Shirah, I don't want to sit with anyone.

. . .

In Hebrew school, Rabbi Harris compliments Shirah on her excellent Bat Mitzvah.

"And how was your party?" he asks in front of the class.

"It was great," she says. "Really fun."

The other students add their congratulations on the ceremony and the party, but I lower my eyes—just in case she's looking at me.

Then we move on to learning the Hebrew vocabulary for a hypothetical trip to a grocery market: "Eat." "Shop." "Food."

"And how do you say 'eat' if you're a girl?" asks Rabbi Harris. *"O-chel . . ."*

"O-chelet," says Shirah. I can never remember the right masculine and feminine suffixes, but for Shirah, it's no problem. She can actually speak a lot of Hebrew. I only know about twenty words.

"Yofi, Shirah," Rabbi Harris says. "Now let's get into teams to improvise skits."

"Shirah and Will and me!" shouts Max. Normally, the three of us make a decent team, but Shirah isn't talking to me, so I'm not sure how this is going to work.

"Shmarya, Mordechai, and Shirah." Rabbi Harris writes on the board, using Max's and my Hebrew names. "Your skit," he says, pausing to think, "is . . . to go into the market and buy ingredients to make a Shabbat dinner."

He separates the rest of the class into teams and gives us all a minute to prepare. As usual, Shirah takes charge. Max is going to be the shopkeeper, and Shirah and I are customers. Shirah is loud and sort of curt. It's not clear if she's mad at me, exactly, but she doesn't seem happy, either.

Standing in front of the class, I start to get nervous. I wipe my palms on my pants.

"And . . . action!" shouts Rabbi Harris, trying to move us along.

I walk into the store.

"Ding-a-ling," I say. I have no idea what noise a door makes in Hebrew.

"Shalom," says Max. *"Mah atah rotzeh?"*

I become aware of the eyes in the room. Everyone is staring at us with amused expressions.

"Ani rotzeh," I say, meaning, "I want." It's by far the most common phrase in our Hebrew class. "What's the word for 'fruit'?"

"Perot," says Shirah.

"That's right," says Rabbi Harris. *"Perot!* You know, like *borei pri hagafen*?" He's referring to the prayer we say before drinking wine—or actually, the sweet grape juice they hand out at the end of synagogue services. *"Pri"* is "fruit," and *"hagafen"* is "of the vine." We've all said it a million times.

"Ani rotzeh perot?" I ask.

"Mordechai, you're the grocer, right? What do you say back?"

"Ayn perot," he says. There is no fruit.

"Ani rozeh," I say, preparing my counterattack. "How do you say 'bread'?"

"Lechem," mumbles Shirah. She's avoiding my eyes.

"Like *hamotzei lechem min ha artetz,"* Rabbi Harris says encouragingly. He's referring to the only other prayer I know: the prayer over challah.

"Ayn lechem," says Max. There is no bread.

"This is seriously the last one," I say, growing tired of this exercise. *"Ani rozeh dahg."*

We'd all learned that in Hebrew; *dahg* is "fish."

"Ayn dahg," says Max.

Rabbi Harris must be getting sick of Max's routine as well, because he jumps in: "Mordechai," he interrupts, *"Lamah* . . . Everyone remembers *lamah*? *Lamah* means 'why.' Mordechai, *Lamah ayn perot, ayn lechem, v' ayn dahg?"*

I followed that. *Why isn't there any fruit or bread or wine in the store?* Wow, after three years of Hebrew, I understood a whole sentence!

Max says that there's no more food in the grocery

store because "Shirah blah, blah, blah." I don't under-stand most of it. Either his pronunciation is terrible or my vocabulary is too limited. He holds his arms out to the sides—his one good arm and the arm in its brace. He's imitating someone fat. There is a huge round of laughter, mostly from the boys. Shirah stands frozen for a second, and then her eyes dart to me.

Only now do I realize that Max has made a joke about Shirah. I don't think of Shirah as fat. Am I supposed to say that she isn't fat? I don't know how to say it in He-brew. Or should I just tell Max to shut up in English? Or pretend I didn't hear it? My mind goes blank. I jam my hands into my pockets and don't say anything.

Shirah storms out of the room and leaves me standing at the front of the room with Max.

"Max," says Rabbi Harris, exasperated. "Wait outside. In the hall." He points to the door. His voice is calm, but his face is red. In three years of Hebrew, I've seen Rabbi Harris be stern plenty of times, but I've never seen him look that angry.

Max turns and leaves the room and Rabbi Harris fol-lows him.

The rest of the class bursts into chatter the instant the rabbi steps out the door.

"Rabbi Harris is pissed."

"Can't Shirah take a joke?"

"Boys are jerks."

I don't say a word.

...

Mom picks up Shirah, Max, and me after Hebrew school, and on the drive home, no one speaks. My mom seems to figure out that something isn't right and turns on the radio. Ten awkward minutes later, after dropping off Max, we pull into Shirah's driveway. Shirah grabs her backpack and opens the car door. I get out of the car to take Shirah's place in the front. She surprises me by speaking as we pass each other: "If that had been the other way around," she says, "I would have stuck up for you."

She leaves me standing by the open car door and heads up to her house.

"What was that?" Mom asks as we drive away. "Is everything okay?"

"Yep," I say, even though it's not. Nothing is.

CHAPTER 18

I DON'T BOTHER KNOCKING, AND RJ DOESN'T LOOK UP when I go into the room. Like last time, he continues to drum while I read, but this time, I catch him looking at me a few times.

After the third or fourth glance, I've had enough: "What's your *problem*?" I nearly shout. I've had a very short temper the past few days, ever since Shirah's and my friendship went kablooey for the second time.

RJ stops playing and gives me an angry look. "My problem? You're the one with the problem."

"You're staring at me."

"I'm not staring at you, Turtle Boy," he says. "I'm looking at the clock."

I feel a surge of anger when he calls me by that name, and I don't believe him—I'm certain he was staring at me—but I turn and look, and yes, there is a clock on the wall. It's big, made from an old record, with the hands at the center. Instead of numbers, words are painted: THE CLASH—LONDON CALLING.

"That say three-thirty?" he asks.

I nod: then, remembering that he might not be able to see me because of his illness, I nod bigger.

"Okay, it's time," he says. "I have a task for you. I need you to deliver those bags of Funyuns you got last time to Mrs. Barnes in room eleven thirty-two."

"I'm not your servant," I say.

"My *servant*?" he says, laughing. "Ha-ha! That's awesome! Thanks so much for clarifying."

He has another laugh, and then he gets serious.

"Okay, kid," he says. "I need these Funyuns to get to Mrs. Barnes, right now. Go do it. Two bags."

He points to his shelves, the front partially covered with a piece of cloth, fastened in place with a neat row of nails. "Room eleven thirty-two," he says. And before I leave the room, he adds, "Don't let anyone see you. Hide the goods under your sweatshirt."

I lift up my sweatshirt, shove the Funyuns underneath, and head into the hall.

• • •

I'm standing outside 1132. I knock once, lightly, and a voice calls: "It's about time!"

Inside, an old lady lies in bed. On the TV is a wrestling match, the kind with skintight outfits and masks and a screaming, hysterical audience.

"Why don't you open up a couple of bags and sit down," she says, pointing to a three-layer chair like RJ has in his room. She takes a bag and we munch Funyuns and watch the match. She smiles.

On the screen, one wrestler wears shiny green shorts and a lizard mask. The other guy has long, stringy hair. He's all in black. There are punches and dives and body slams, and in a confusing reversal, the lizard-man gets his arms pinned behind his back.

"Go, Manzilla!" yells Mrs. Barnes. "You can do it!"

Manzilla breaks out of the hold, but the guy in black knocks him to the mat and jumps on him. The referee slaps the mat three times, and it's over. Mrs. Barnes grabs a remote control and turns off the TV.

"Well, I'll be," she says. "Manzilla's always been my favorite, even if he loses pretty much every time."

"Why do you like him, then?" I ask.

"His mask!" she says. "Don't you think it's dandy? I have one just like it."

She points to a shelf, where a gleaming green mask complete with frills leans on the windowsill.

"Well, thanks for the company, young man," she says. "And tell RJ I'll be ready for action at three-forty-five!"

I leave the room slowly. I wish I could stay. Now, *this* is community service I can do! On the walk back to RJ's, I decide I'll tell Rabbi Harris that I want to trade: I don't want to visit RJ anymore. Instead, I'll spend a few hours every Sunday watching TV with Mrs. Barnes.

• • •

I return to RJ's door with a lighter step, now that I have a plan. I knock and walk in, but RJ isn't drumming. His head is back on the pillow, and he's staring at the ceiling. It startles me to see him like that, but it doesn't last long; he snaps his head up and looks around.

"Who's there?" he asks, anxious. "What time is it?"

I look at the clock: "Three-forty."

"Oh, it's you. Okay, five minutes till the show starts. Prop the door open. I need to be able to hear anyone coming."

I don't like the sound of this.

"Here," says RJ. "Catch."

He tosses something to me. I flinch, and whatever he flung at me hits the ground. It's a small, sealed cup of orange juice. Fortunately, it doesn't explode or leak.

"What, your old man never taught you how to catch?"

"Old man?" I ask, leaning down to pick up the juice. "What old man?"

"Your dad," he says impatiently. "It's an expression."

"No, my 'old man' didn't teach me how to catch," I say with a fierce edge I hardly recognize. "He died when I was four."

RJ raises his eyebrows and looks at me. "Sorry, I didn't know." He's quiet for a minute. "My mom died when I was in first grade. That's her and me." He points to the photo taped to the wall, next to his bed: the woman with straight, dark hair, tied back in a ponytail, and the kid, both dressed in swimsuits, on a tropical beach. In the child's thick brows and squinty eyes, I can see RJ.

"Is that Florida?" I ask.

"No, dude," he says. "It's Hawaii. I grew up there."

"You grew up in Hawaii?" I ask. I know a few kids from Illinois and Minnesota, and a couple from the East Coast, but I've never met anyone from Hawaii. I know that Hawaii is home to three species of turtle. Giant green sea turtles, *Chelonia mydas,* can swim more than thirty-five miles an hour, can stay underwater for five hours, and can grow to weigh over eight hundred pounds. I would give anything to see one, but that'll never happen. I'd have to go all the way to Hawaii, and worse, I'd have to swim in the ocean. I hate swimming unless I can see the bottom of the pool. I always stay in the shallow end.

I look back at the picture, this time captivated by the similarity between RJ and his mother.

"Can I ask a weird question?"

"Everything about you is weird, so do I have a choice?"

"Do you remember her?" I ask.

"My mom?" I can see I caught him off guard.

I nod. I can feel blood pouring into my cheeks—they tingle and burn.

"Well . . . yeah, sort of. I don't have too many actual memories—mostly I remember a feeling. Not something I can describe. Just a . . . sense."

He's quiet for a minute.

"Sometimes," he adds softly, like he's not sure he wants to go on, "sometimes I get that feeling. Out of nowhere it'll come over me, and I'll be like, *Oh. She's with me now. She's here with me.*"

I don't know what to say. I just peel open my orange juice and take a sip. It's half frozen.

"See, it's like a slushie," he says, opening his own cup of OJ. "I have all sorts of tricks for making this place less horrible.

"What about you? You remember your dad?"

"Not really," I say. "I mean, I know what my dad looked like—we have a few pictures around the house. And I know the basics about him, but I don't remember him. Definitely not the feeling of being with him."

"That sucks," says RJ, crunching thoughtfully on some ice chunks.

Does it? I wonder. Suddenly, I understand why Rabbi Harris wanted me to meet RJ. We both lost a parent. Maybe this is supposed to help me in some way.

I can't think about it more because the weirdest sound comes from down the hall. It sounds like a ghost—a ghoul—howling in pain.

"Nurse! Nurse!" comes a high-pitched shriek. "I've spilled my soup! It's burning me alive!"

I jump up in alarm, but RJ only waves at the door. "That's Mrs. Barnes," he says. "Right on time. Quick, grab the door! Shut it!"

I close the door, and RJ whips a blanket off a mound next to him—a pile of junk, probably scavenged from around the hospital. Soon he's got an assortment of stainless-steel surgical trays and washing bowls, a caf-eteria tray, some heavy plastic pipes, and a bunch of metal bins spread out on the bed in front of him.

Before I know what's happening, the room explodes in noise—noise so loud, I have to hold my hands over my ears. With his drumsticks, he bangs and clangs on every surface—with just as much intensity as on the practice pad—but *loud*! His arms fly, sticks trilling the metal, and every so often, a hand flies out to smack the metal bin—*CLANG!* It sounds like an entire fleet of trucks fall-ing down the stairs of the Empire State Building, all 102 floors, and the grand finale is when they all get to the bottom. Arms fly, sticks fly, every conceivable noise flies, faster and faster, and finally, *Ba-CLANG! Ba-CLANG! Ba-CLANG!*

RJ stops and cocks his ear. Suddenly, as fast as it started, he's throwing the junk back into the pile next to his bed. Tosses the gray hospital blanket over it just as the door opens.

It's the mean nurse from last time, the one with the needle.

"What was all that racket, Ralph?" she demands.

"What racket, Denise?" says RJ. He's concealing the fact that he's short of breath, exhausted from the physical effort. "Hey, kid—you hear any racket?"

I shake my head obediently.

The nurse gives us an irritated look and shuts the door. RJ and I are quiet, and when I venture a look at him, we both laugh, just for a second.

"Did you see her face?" he asks. "Priceless."

"That drum set is *awesome*," I say. "And you're so *good*."

"I haven't played my real set in two years—I have a vintage Slingerland set at home. I *dream* about playing it. Maybe I'll get to show it to you someday."

"Is Mrs. Barnes okay?" I ask.

"Yes, brainiac!" he says. "That's what I pay her for. She distracts the nurses just long enough for me to get a good drum solo out of my system. You wanna try? We'll use the practice pad."

He holds out a pair of sticks and points them at me. I take a step back.

"Just take them and stop being such a baby," he says, exasperated.

My first instinct is to stay away, but I feel a flush of adrenaline and take the sticks. They're heavier than I imagined, and the wood is pitted so deeply around the tips it looks like a hamster has been gnawing on them. RJ must go through a dozen pairs of sticks a week.

"Stop, you're holding them like a zombie," he says. "Just relax; relax your grip a little."

I do, or I try to, anyway. "Okay," he says, "Now repeat after me: *Boom. Pack! Boom-boom pack!*"

I don't say anything, and he leans toward me with wide eyes.

"Boom. Pack. Boom-boom pack," he says, a little louder.

"Boom. Pack. Boom-boom pack," I say begrudgingly.

"Weak," he says. "Do it better. *Boom. Pack! Boom-boom pack!* Say it."

I say it again.

"Bravo," he says. "Now, the middle of the pad is the '*boom.*' The ridge of the pad is '*Pack!*' So it's like this. . . ."

He bounces the tips of the sticks off the plastic pad, and then he smacks them against the ridge, one on each side. He repeats this, and all the while, he chants out loud: *"Boom. Pack! Boom-boom pack! Boom. Pack. Boom-boom pack!"*

I reach over with my sticks and play the rhythm, fast as I can, hoping to get it over with.

"No," he says. "You're rushing and you're not saying it. You can't play it if you can't say it. *Boom. Pack! Boom-boom pack.*"

Okay, I think. Don't embarrass yourself. Show him that you can do it. I play it and say it: "Boom. Pack! Boom-boom pack! Boom. Pack! Boom-boom pack!"

He gestures with his hands, making little circles—*Keep going, keep going*—so I keep going. I'm playing it over and over and over. Then I stop and look at him.

"That's good," he says. "But you're still rushing."

I start to play the rhythm again, and he grabs the tips of the sticks.

"You're rushing!" he repeats, looking me in the eye.

"It's boring," I say. "What else is there?"

"Nothing," he says. "There is nothing else; nothing more than *Boom-boom pack!* If you're playing *Boom-boom pack!* then that's it. That's the entire world."

Weirdly, I know what he's talking about. When I'm alone with my turtles, I look in their little terrariums, and they're so happy. They're not worried about what else they could be eating, or where they could be swimming. Maybe that's why they take my mind off everything else. I turn my attention to the practice pad and adjust my grip on the sticks.

I start to play: *Boom. Pack! Boom-boom pack! Boom.*

Pack! Boom-boom pack! My mind goes to the same place it does when my turtles are swimming in their terrariums. Just floating. There are no walls. There is no ceiling. For a minute, there are no sticks and no bed and no RJ—just *Boom-boom pack!*

"Okay," says a voice. I stop and realize RJ has spoken. "Denise is going to be here soon to help me shower, and I'd rather you not be around for that."

I look at the clock. It's 3:10. I just played *Boom-boom pack!* for ten minutes. Rabbi Harris is waiting in the atrium!

"I need to go—I'm late!" I say, grabbing my backpack.

"Wait," says RJ. "I wanna give you an extra pair of my sticks so you can practice at home. And this."

He holds up the practice pad.

"But if I take that, what will you play?" I ask.

"Dude," he says. "I can play anything. Don't worry about me."

I take the pad from his hands. I put it in my backpack, along with a pair of drumsticks RJ had tucked next to his bed.

Standing there, I want to tell RJ I'm sorry for everything that happened last time; for leaving early and for being nosey, for trying to read his bucket list. I notice it's no longer hanging on the wall. He's hiding it from me.

Instead, I pull my forty-hours form from my pocket.

I need Roxanne to sign it before I leave. I go to the door but stop and wave back at RJ before opening it.

RJ points at me with a drumstick, a kind of *You go!* gesture, and returns to his drumming, now on a white hospital pillow.

CHAPTER 19

I BEGIN TO FEEL BETTER AND BETTER ABOUT RJ. HE'S funny, and he seems smart, even though he doesn't have any books in his room.

It's Saturday, and I have the whole day to myself. Tonight, Mom and I are going to La Crosse to have Rosh Hashanah dinner with Aunt Mo and her friends. Aunt Mo's really different from Mom—she's loud and laughs a lot. I wish we saw her more often.

I get up, and before even getting dressed, I get the drumsticks and practice pad out from under my bed.

I play *Boom. Pack! Boom-boom pack!* over and over and over until I can't stand it anymore. *Two minutes have passed? That's all?*

I drop the sticks, throw on some clothes, and head downstairs. Mom has left a note: *Gone to farmers market to get flowers/fruit for Aunt Mo.*

I didn't realize that I was alone in the house. I eat some cereal and head back to my room. I watch my turtles for a while and try to read, but the house is so quiet, it makes my mind drift. I start thinking about Shirah and what happened last week at Hebrew school.

Why didn't I tell Max to shut up? Or follow Shirah out of the room to make sure she was okay? I could see she was upset, so why didn't I do or say anything to try to make her feel better?

I had a chance to defend Shirah. I did nothing. And since then, Shirah won't talk to Max. Max seems clueless about how to deal with the fallout. And I've been standing by, silent. Stuck.

I decide to go to the Back 40, the one place I can go and be free of my thoughts, free of myself.

. . .

I lie on my back and shove myself under the fence. On the other side, I pick myself up and jump to dislodge the clumps of dirt from my back. I noticed that it was easier to squeeze under the fence this time. Every time I use the tunnel, it wears away at the dirt and the opening gets wider. Soon I'll be able to shove underneath without any trouble at all.

I begin to walk down the path through the patches of milkweed and goldenrod. I can hear the chirring of katydids and crickets, and my mood begins to improve.

The path winds around a hill before it descends to

the pond. A sudden movement from the corner of my eye jolts me, and I jump about a foot off the ground.

Ms. Kuper?

"Will!" she says, putting a hand over her heart. "You scared me! You're not supposed to be here."

"Do I have to leave?" I ask.

"Unfortunately, yes," she says. "How did you get in?"

"I found a spot where I can scoot under the fence," I say.

"Oh, right," she says. She seems to know what I'm talking about. Maybe she dug the tunnel herself?

"How about I walk you out?" she asks. As we walk, she asks me how life is. I wish I could tell her about what's really going on. Instead, I tell her I wish she were my science teacher again.

"Mr. Firenze and I are very different teachers," she says. "But give him a chance. He has a lot to offer."

We move on to talking about the flowers in bloom in the Back 40, pointing out purple swamp asters, the sunny goldenrod. I love talking with Ms. Kuper. I didn't come out here hoping to find her, but now that we're together, I don't want to leave.

"Before you go," she says as we arrive at the tunnel, "I want to remind you—you were supposed to bring the turtles to me at least a week ago."

"I was going to," I say quickly, not making eye contact. I add brightly, "The injured one is much better!"

This is the one topic I've been hoping she wouldn't bring up. She looks a little angry, and I'm hit by a wave of shame. I said I would do something, and then I didn't.

"You weren't really planning on letting the turtles go, were you," Ms. Kuper says, more a statement than a question.

I shrug, my throat closing up.

"Well, then let's do it today," she says. "Right now. Go get them. I'll be waiting."

CHAPTER 20

I'M IN MY ROOM WITH THE DOOR CLOSED, GAZING AT THE box turtle, the snapper, the musk turtle, the other box turtle, and the Blanding's turtle.

They know me. When they see me coming, they wag their heads for treats. I couldn't possibly let them go. But if I refuse, Ms. Kuper might call Mom. If I cooperate, I can always catch new turtles later on—once this all blows over.

I grab my musk turtle and box turtle and place them into the first carrier, one on either side. I do the same with my snapping turtle and painted turtle. I lower both carriers into my backpack and cushion them so they won't jostle around.

Lastly, I look down at the Blanding's turtle, with the gold speckles on its shell, and its yellow chin.

"You too," I say. I don't have another cricket carrier to put it in, so I go to the kitchen and get a small cereal box. I empty the contents into a ziplock bag, and turning the box sideways, I put the Blanding's turtle in it. I place the box in my backpack, up toward the top.

. . .

I've returned to the Back 40, where I'm crouched at the edge of the pond. Ms. Kuper is standing about ten paces back.

"Can you give me a minute with them?" I ask.

"Of course," she says, walking farther away from the pond. "I know this is hard for you, but it's the right thing to do. Go on, four turtles in the water."

I begin with the musk and the snapping turtles.

"Hey, guys," I say, too quiet for Ms. Kuper to hear. "Remember when I saved you from the parking lot? I hope you have good lives."

I put them down at the edge of the water, and they both take a few steps until they're partially submerged. They wriggle their limbs, and soon they're invisible— just a ripple beneath the surface.

"Two turtles gone!" I shout.

"Good job, Will," Ms. Kuper yells. "Keep going. Two more."

Then it's the box turtle.

"Three turtles gone!"

I follow it with the painted turtle. They both swim off, their snouts above the water for a moment, then disappear.

"Four turtles gone," I call.

Now I'm sitting here with the Blanding's turtle in my hands.

It begins to move its limbs. It sees the water. It knows its freedom is nearby, and I'm about to release it when suddenly, I remember Max, leaping into the water to catch it in the pond, murky and deep. If I let it go, I'll never have the courage to swim out and find another.

I peek over my shoulder, and Ms. Kuper is pacing around, scanning the ground for something. She doesn't even know I have a fifth turtle. She doesn't know it's in my hands.

My hands trembling, I return the Blanding's turtle to the cereal box.

"Okay?" says Ms. Kuper. "Finished? I think we learned our lesson."

"We sure did," I say, zipping my backpack shut.

CHAPTER 21

I'M SITTING ON THE FLOOR, PRACTICING *BOOM-BOOM PACK!*
I can only play it for fifteen minutes before I get so
bored, I want to throw the sticks across the room. I'm
going to need to learn some more beats. The Blanding's
turtle is crawling on the floor somewhere. I used to let
all my turtles roam around. I'd leave a few crickets in
the corners and let them hunt. I already miss my other
turtles, but as long as I have my Blanding's turtle, I'm
happy.

There's a knock on the door.

"I'm busy," I yell.

The door opens, and my mom is standing there. She
looks angry. *Beyond* angry. Pissed. She *never* looks this mad.

"Wild animals?" she says. "You had wild animals
in the house, Will? I thought you got those at that pet
store!"

"No, I never said that," I say, forcing a calm tone. I
peek out of the corner of my eye to see that the Blanding's

turtle has crawled under the bed. I can see its beady eyes in the shadows. I shift to face my mom, blocking the bed with my butt.

"I just got off the phone with Ms. Kuper," she says flatly.

Ms. Kuper called? Why did Ms. Kuper call Mom? On a Saturday?

"What did she say?"

"She told me that she made you let your turtles go," says Mom. I can see her glancing in the now-empty terrariums. "And that you knew you weren't supposed to have them."

Busted.

"I promise I won't catch any more wild turtles," I say, choosing my words carefully.

This is when she drops the bomb. "You already had more animals in the house than I was comfortable with, but I trusted you. How am I supposed to let you have turtles now?"

"Let me"? Suddenly I need permission to have turtles?

"Besides," Mom continues, "I think it's time for you to take a break from turtles. At least until your Bar Mitzvah."

At that moment, I feel motion against my hand, near the edge of the bed. Something brushing past it.

"Yah!" I shout in surprise.

"What's the matter?" asks Mom.

"Yah," I repeat, recovering from my outburst. "Yes—there will be no more turtles."

Now it's scratching at my hand. I can't let it past, though. If Mom sees it, she'll make me let it go.

"No!" I shout as the turtle bites my thumb. Not hard, but a turtle can take out a chunk of flesh if it's provoked. "No *problem*," I add.

"You are acting so odd, Will," says Mom. She stares at me a moment and says, "Get dressed. We're leaving for Aunt Mo's in thirty minutes. And put on something nice—you can't wear that awful sweatshirt to Rosh Hashanah dinner." She closes the door behind her. I pull my hand away and look down in time to see the Blanding's turtle crawl out from under the bed.

"We're going to need a better place for you to hide," I say.

CHAPTER 22

RJ's HEAD IS ON THE PILLOW. HE LOOKS GROGGY.

"Turtle Boy," he says, looking at me. "How's it going?"

"Pretty good," I say, choosing to ignore the nickname. "Sorry I couldn't come on Sunday. Rosh Hashanah. Jewish holiday."

"I know," he says. "Rabbi Harris said you'd be here today. Jewish kids are so lucky. Eight days of presents for Hanukkah and extra holidays with no school."

I'm a little surprised he's referring to school since he hasn't been there in two years.

"How's the *boom-boom pack!* going?" he asks.

I get out the practice pad and sticks, lay the pad on the stand next to his bed, and play *boom-boom pack!* eight times—four measures.

I stop and look at him.

"Cool," he says. "You've been practicing. You ready for the next step? *Boom-boom pack!* is just the beginning. Now it's *Boom-boom pack, chacka-lacka.*"

I compute this for a minute.

"You have a problem?" he asks.

"That rhythm," I say. "It doesn't make sense."

"You think way too much," he says, annoyed. "Just play the rhythm already. Do the *chacka-lacka*s on this clipboard."

He pulls a clipboard from under the blanket that covers his junk drum set.

I grab the sticks. I'm going to prove my point. I play it: *Boom-boom pack, chacka-lacka.*

"See," I say. "It's weird."

Impatiently, RJ grabs the sticks out of my hand and begins playing, the sticks rapping on the clipboard and bouncing on the practice pad. The rhythm isn't the sound of marching feet. It's the rhythm of a kid on a swing, flying to and fro, the chains squeaking and groaning. It doesn't end—there's no start and no finish; the rhythm just flows together, on and on.

Then he stops and looks at me.

"Oh," he says, mocking me. *"But it doesn't work. It doesn't make sense.* You quit before you even tried it," he adds. "You think music needs to go one, two, three, four. Well, *this* rhythm goes ONE-two-three, FOUR-five. ONE-two-three, FOUR-five." He emphasizes the "one" and the "four" with a nod of his head.

That explains it. I was using the wrong formula. I didn't even know there was such a thing as a time signature that counts to five.

"Can you teach me how to play it the way you do?" I ask.

"No," he says. "Because you're a stubborn little seventh grader who doesn't want to learn."

He goes back to playing the sweeping, rocking, flowing rhythm, but this time, he's showing off with fancy twists and turns, and sometimes he extends the rolling up over the wave a beat too long, only to rush back the other way, making up the time. It reminds me of chasing waves on the shores of Lake Michigan and charging toward the water line as a wave recedes, then running twice as fast to escape.

On and on he plays, a cycle of running and returning, and in the midst of this perfection, the door opens and a nurse comes in. It's Denise, the mean one. RJ continues to play, oblivious, while I back away and sit down in the cake-chair.

"Hey!" Denise calls down at RJ, standing with her white sneaker tapping on the ground. "Ralph!"

He plays for another moment, then stops, the music vanishing into the air. He opens his eyes, and I notice how quickly his expression changes from concentrated intensity to resigned annoyance.

He sticks his arm out.

The nurse unwraps something and hunches over RJ. Here comes my nausea. I swallow hard and try to clear my mind, but my vision begins to go blotchy. The whole universe is squeezed into my stomach, my bile, the sweat beading on my forehead—it's all throbbing together. I put my head down between my knees.

"Hey, kid," RJ says loudly. "What are you into? Do you have any hobbies?"

I look up at RJ. What's he talking about? Why is he asking about my hobbies now—he's getting stuck with a needle!

"Will!" he says, almost urgently. "What are you into?"

"Turtles," I say, or sort of moan. My cheeks feel cold and weird against the corduroy of my pants.

"Turtles?" he says, and laughs. I'm too dizzy to care that he's laughed at me. "Your nickname is Turtle Boy and your hobby is also turtles?"

"Turtles are my favorite," I say. "But I like herps in general."

"*Herpes?*" he asks with a snicker. "Like the disease?"

"*What?* No!" I say, and give a big, annoyed sigh. "*Herps.* Like 'herpetology.' It's Greek. Reptiles and amphibians. You know, turtles and frogs and lizards and stuff."

"Well, it *sounds* like 'herpes,'" says RJ. "So I wouldn't go around telling people how much you love herps."

The nurse holds a hypodermic up to the light and flicks its tip, then leans over a tube in RJ's wrist. This is the moment of truth. The needle is about to go in.

"Do you, like, *own* any turtles?" he asks.

"I had four specimens at home—all different species," I say. "But I had to let them go."

"That's quite a herpes collection," he says.

A moment later, the nurse gathers the supplies and swishes out of the room without saying a thing. The second the door closes, RJ bursts into laughter.

"We're sitting here talking about herpes and turtles, and she did not bat one eyelash. I think she's a robot," he says.

I'm less impressed by the nurse's lack of reaction to our conversation than by the fact that I didn't pass out or puke. Most of all, I can't believe I told someone about my love of turtles and nothing bad happened. He didn't make fun of me.

"But you're serious about the turtle thing? You love turtles?"

I look down at my bag, take a deep breath, and pull out the largest book. On the cover is a close-up of a box turtle floating in a terrarium. For a moment, I'm afraid RJ will say that the turtle looks like me.

"No kidding," he says. "So you have actual turtles at home. As pets?"

"They're not pets," I say. "They're cold-blooded—they live in a different world than we do."

"What did you keep them in?" he asks. "Fish tanks?"

"Terrariums," I say. "They need water areas to swim and hunt, and places to bask under a heat lamp, and they like something to hide under too. I've built a whole bunch of designer terrariums."

"What do they eat?" he asks.

"Crickets," I say. "They'll eat frozen crickets, but they love fresh crickets. They stalk them and snap them up. Turtles aren't actually slow at all. They're quick when they need to be. You can coat live crickets with vitamin dust, which keeps turtles from getting nutrient deficiencies."

I talk for a few more minutes about turtles: where each type is from in North America, how they breed and hatch, how they survive in the wild, and that myth about their rings—that you can tell how old a turtle is by how many rings are on the scutes of the shells. Not true. The rings can tell you if a turtle is old, sure, but not *how* old.

RJ seemed really interested, so I'm disappointed to look back at him and discover that he's tipped his head back. He's staring at the ceiling. Great, I've bored him. I didn't mean to. I need to learn to shut up.

Then he speaks. "I really want a pet," he says. "I don't even care what it is. I've never had a pet, not even once."

"Really?" I ask. "Never?"

"My dad is allergic to dogs and cats and anything with fur. And there's some dumb policy here about not having pets. Trust me, I've asked *you know who*."

RJ points his thumb toward the door. The nurse. Probably the one with the needles, Denise.

"But here's the thing: if I had a small, quiet pet—something that didn't make noise or run on a wheel or smell like pee or need me to change its wood shavings—no one would notice."

"What did you have in mind?" I ask. "A goldfish?

"Duh, no!" he says impatiently. "A *turtle*!"

I stare at him. I *just* explained that turtles aren't pets.

"Yeah!" he goes on. "It'd be so cool to watch it swim and feed it crickets."

I don't say anything, mainly because I can't believe I'm hearing this. A minute ago, when he was staring at the ceiling, he was actually *daydreaming* about having a turtle?

"You'd have to smuggle it in here," he says, eyes wide, "but it would be so cool! We could make some space down on my dad's shelf."

The shelf is just large enough for the cracked terrarium I got for free. RJ's face has brightened in a way I've never ever seen it. He looks less like a sixteen-year-old and more like a little boy, thrilled about a birthday present.

And I happen to have a secret turtle who needs a home.

"We have to do it right away," I say. "Saturday. But how are we supposed to get all the gear into your room? The nurses are going to see me carrying a big pail and a terrarium. We'll get caught." The moment the words leave my mouth, I start to get anxious.

"Be at the hospital at one-thirty," he says. "Call me from the atrium. I'll make sure the nurses are occupied in someone else's room."

I promise, and for the next half hour, we continue playing drums—this weird, new beat, this impossible, never-ending rhythm I couldn't understand until I heard RJ play it, easily, effortlessly.

Once it's time to go, I bring my form to Roxanne to sign, and while I ride the elevator, I silently tap the beat, a rhythm I never want to forget: *Boom-boom pack, chacka-lacka. Boom-boom pack, chacka-lacka. Boom-boom pack, chacka-lacka . . .*

CHAPTER 23

IT'S SATURDAY AFTERNOON. IN THE TRUNK OF THE CAR, I've loaded the terrarium, packed inside a large cardboard box. The turtle pellets and the filtration gear are in the small pocket of my backpack, while a cricket carrier stuffed halfway into the main section holds the turtle.

On the drive to the hospital, Mom says, "I think it's really great what you're doing. Helping this kid be less lonely, sharing your books with him? You're a really super guy, Will, you know that?"

I can feel my face burn with shame. I told her the giant box in the trunk is full of books.

Once we pull up to the hospital, I open the door to get out, and Mom says, "You're sure you don't want help carrying everything up to his room?"

I ignore the offer and close the door, and through the open window, she calls, "Beep!"

"Beep," I answer, and begin dragging the box to the hospital doors.

I decide that's the last time we're doing the "beep" thing.

···

I call RJ from the atrium, using Mom's cell phone. She lent it to me so she can call me before she leaves home.

"It's me," I say. "I have the goods."

"Be up here in exactly *five minutes,*" he whispers, and hangs up.

My heart starts pounding. I look at my watch and calculate how long it takes to ride the elevator up: about a minute and a half, plus maybe a minute to get down the hall. I ditch the cardboard box near a trash can, press the elevator button, and wait.

When the elevator arrives, there are people inside: a lady and a little kid three or four years old, who's staring at me while he picks his nose. There are also two guys in white uniforms with name tags and carts full of meal trays. I have to be really careful.

I enter the elevator and try to keep my backpack facing the door so no one can see the cricket carrier with the turtle sticking out. I set the terrarium down near my feet, hoping no one will notice, and the elevator door closes.

"That's a fish tank," the little kid says loudly.

I ignore him.

"I have fishes at home," he says. "I have better fishes than you do."

"Joseph, that isn't nice," says the mother.

"We're visiting my daddy," Joseph says. "I had an accident with him and a hockey stick."

The woman sighs and goes back to looking at the floor numbers.

We arrive at RJ's floor, and I hoist up my terrarium, but one of the men in uniform says, "Pardon me."

He starts to push the cart toward the elevator door, but Joseph grabs his mom's hand and yanks her out first. The men with the carts follow. I head in the other direction to the end of the hall, terrarium over my head, and station myself behind a bin full of linens. No one is around. Once I come out of hiding, I'll be exposed. Now that I'm in RJ's wing, if a nurse comes out of a room, especially Denise, I'm busted.

It looks like the coast is clear. I shuffle toward RJ's door as quickly as I can, and as I approach, it opens. I scoot through and RJ shuts the door behind me.

"We did it," he says. "Nice job."

I pull out the cricket carrier with the Blanding's turtle inside. Then I inspect RJ's dad's milk-crate shelves.

The middle shelf is mainly empty, and it has holes for air. I lift the top crate, set the terrarium on it, and transfer the gravel, driftwood, and herp hotel. Then I lay the other milk crate on top. Unless you went over to the shelves and looked down at them, you wouldn't see anything. It could be weeks before anyone notices. Maybe months.

"You wanna see it?" I bring the cricket carrier over to RJ and lift the lid. Sensing the sudden motion, the Blanding's turtle scrabbles at the plastic with its claws.

"WOW!" says RJ. He isn't concealing his excitement anymore. It's as if there were a tiny dragon in the carrier.

"Glad you like it," I say.

"What's its name?"

"Turtles aren't like dogs; they're not pets. They don't need names."

"He looks like pictures I've seen of my grandpa," says RJ. "How about 'Grampy'?" His voice gets really sweet. "Hi, Grampy!" He taps on the carrier.

I spend a few minutes explaining how to feed it, how many pellets, where to put the water, and the rules of handling. RJ listens closely, but when I ask him if he wants to pick it up—I show him how to hold it so it won't bite and it won't fall—he draws away.

"It's not going to hurt you," I say. "What are you afraid of?"

"I'm not afraid, you weenie," he says. "I don't want to drop it."

"Hold it like this, right over the blankets." I hold it just a few inches over RJ's lap, but he recoils. He loves the turtle, but he's at least a little afraid of it. Then he looks at the turtle more closely, and his eyes widen, and I see them for the first time. They're deep blue—blue like the color of Lake Michigan when it's sunny out. I've never seen the ocean, but I imagine it to be like Lake Michigan, but even more blue. I glance at the pictures around RJ's bed, and in the pictures, the ocean is all different colors. Blue. Slate gray. Green.

He looks up at me. "Thanks, dude," he says. "You did me a solid."

"A solid what?"

"Oh, come on, dude—you've never heard of doing someone a solid? It's like a favor. I've always wanted a pet."

"Oh," I say, suddenly shy.

"I've had having a pet on my list for a long time," he adds.

The list? The bucket list?

I'm shocked that he even mentioned it. Back when it was hanging on the wall, he snatched the paper away so aggressively, I figured it was a secret. I have a dozen questions, but I'm not sure if I'm allowed to ask them. At the same time, I feel like he's holding the door open. He wants me to ask.

"So," I say casually. "What's the deal with this list?"

"What about it?" he says. He looks at me, and I hold my silence. "I started it way before I got here, spring of eighth grade. I had a few dumb things on it, stuff I wanted to do in my life. You know—all the clichés. 'Make a billion dollars. Buy a Lamborghini.' But I've had a lot of time to lie here and think. Too much time. I'm not a kid anymore, but who knows if I'm going to make it to being an adult. Now it's all about the really big priorities. I've narrowed down my list to a few essentials."

"Can I see it?"

"I told you the first time you were snooping," he says sharply. "It's not for you to look at. But since you're so nosey, I can tell you the next thing on it."

I lean forward.

"You remember how I grew up in Hawaii until my dad had more work in Wisconsin and I moved to this hellhole when my mom died? I haven't been back to Hawaii, or any ocean, since. I really, really want to swim in the ocean again."

I'm sitting still, waiting for him to go on.

"So, that's it," he says. "Go swimming in the ocean."

"Will they let you out of here to go swimming?" I ask.

"Is the pope Jewish?" he says. "No, dude. You're going to do it, and you'll tell me all about it. Details. I want details."

"The ocean?" I ask. "How am I supposed to get to the ocean? We're in the middle of Wisconsin."

"Okay, so what's the closest body of water that's *like* the ocean?"

"Lake Michigan," I say. "But that's three hours away. I'm not going to Lake Michigan."

"Work with me," he says. He sounds annoyed. "Where do you go swimming?"

"The Horicon public pool," I say.

"That's not going to cut it," he says, sounding irritated. "Let's agree it needs to be a natural body of water. What's the nearest natural body of water you can get to?"

"The pond in the Back 40," I say.

"Behind Prairie Marsh?" he says. "Not exactly what I had in mind, but whatever. Go for it."

"That pond is full of leeches," I say. "I can't swim there. What's the next thing on the list? I'll do something else."

"No, no, no," says RJ, suddenly angry. "That is not how this works. You don't get to pick and choose. This is *my list*."

I did not see this coming. We were having such a good time, and suddenly, it's all falling apart.

"You know what your problem is?" asks RJ.

As soon as he says this, a wave of fear passes over me. I'm not good with criticism. I brace myself, but as RJ opens his mouth, there's a buzz in my pocket. Mom's phone.

I pull the cell phone out.

"Will?" says Mom. "Where are you? I'm at the front desk! I've been calling you for twenty minutes!"

"I didn't notice," I say. I look up at RJ and tell him I have to go, my mom's waiting.

I grab my backpack and hurry to the door with the phone to my ear. I babble something about getting my forty-hours form signed. I keep talking, but only so I won't have to face RJ as I escape the room.

CHAPTER 24

"Okay, Will," says Rabbi Harris. "Have a look here at the Hebrew."

He arranges the packets on his desk and separates the pages of Hebrew from their translations. Above and below the Hebrew letters are tiny marks. One looks like a horseshoe, others look like Tetris pieces, and some look like wizard symbols from a comic book—lightning bolts and zigzags.

"Each has a different melody," he says. "None of them are very complicated. We're going to start with this symbol and this symbol." He points them out. "The first one that looks like a little hook is called a *mercha*. And this one that looks like a backward comma is a *tipcha*. They sound like this. . . ."

He sings, *"Mercha, tip-cha-a-ah."* He's very precise with his "ch" sound, making a noise like he's dislodging a popcorn kernel from the back of his throat.

"Try it with me now," he says.

It's a chirpy melody. Repeated over and over, it would sound like the red-winged blackbirds in the Back 40.

"Now we add this one," he says. "See how it looks like a backward *mercha*? But it's called a *munach,* and it goes like this: *mu-na-ach . . .*"

This melody sinks lower. It almost sounds disappointed.

We repeat these trope marks over and over, which is a breeze, until we start applying the melody to the Hebrew phrases in my Torah portion. As soon as I think I know how to predict the end of the phrase, a new trope mark comes along and surprises me. The melody doesn't resolve neatly the way normal music does; each phrase wanders aimlessly, unable to find a harmonic home. I'm becoming disoriented and grope for the next note.

"Couldn't I bring this sheet up with me at my Bar Mitzvah?" I ask. "To remind me if I get lost?"

"I'll be there if you get lost," Rabbi Harris says. "It happens all the time. I'll sing the next few words to you, and you'll find your way."

"Why can't I bring the photocopy?"

"When you read from the Torah, it needs to be from the Torah. No copies. No cheat sheets."

"But why not?"

Rabbi Harris looks me in the eye. "In life," he says, "we have moments of truth, where everything is on the line. And when these moments happen, we never have cheat sheets. We only have our instincts and the skills we've developed over the years."

I can feel myself starting to sweat.

"Trust me, you're gonna be fine," says Rabbi Harris, a bit lighter in his tone. "Plus, it's a great Torah portion and it'll give you all sorts of material for your speech."

Speech.

The second he says that, I stand up instinctively, as if to run from the room. I've somehow been blocking out the fact that at my Bar Mitzvah, I'm going to need to talk in front of a room full of people.

"Going somewhere?" asks Rabbi Harris. "We have ten minutes left."

"Public speaking," I say. "Not good."

"Everybody gets scared," says Rabbi Harris. "But like everybody, you'll be fine."

I ignore his encouragement and begin to gather my papers.

"Before you go, Shmarya," he says, "I wanted to talk with you about your time with Ralph." He stands up. "Maybe we'll go outside and get some sun? We've been cooped up in here."

I follow him out of his office and down the temple's back staircase. Once we're outside, I can hear the shouting of children near the synagogue's Sunday camp. We walk closer and sit down on a bench near the playground. In front of us, little kids are running around playing some version of tag.

"Tell me all about it," he says. "How're you finding your visits with Ralph?"

"They're good," I say. "He's showing me how to play drums. We just hang out."

"I'm glad you changed your mind about him," says Rabbi Harris. "For years we've been hoping and praying that he improves, or at least stabilizes. For a while, signs were good. But lately, not so much."

We both sit in silence for a minute. Then he takes off his glasses and looks me straight in the eye, making me cringe.

"Shmarya," he says. "I have to tell you some hard news. This is a truth we both must accept: RJ is dying. I know you knew that already, but we're no longer talking about someday. I want to be optimistic, but if you're going to be able to support your friend, you need to know what he's up against."

A cold river flows from my chest and to my arms and legs. Rabbi Harris goes on. "We're talking about pretty serious organ failure—mainly his kidneys and his liver. It's also affecting his sight and his muscles. It's going to affect his breathing and his heart, and soon things are going to get really rough for him. This is where the real *mitzvah* comes in," says Rabbi Harris. "His father drives a truck long distances and can only see him a few nights a week. He doesn't have other family, and he doesn't have other young people to be with. I need you to know the truth, going forward. It's not clear how long he has. Could be a year. Could be six months. We just don't know. But we do know he's dying, and we need to face that reality."

I don't say a word. What is there to say? But this reminds me of RJ's bucket list: whatever's on it needs to be completed, right away.

I feel a wave of guilt. What if I'm never able to swim in the pond? How would I ever make that up to him? Suddenly, RJ's annoying qualities don't seem so bad. The mean things he said about me, his impatience, his rudeness—none of it matters. And even more overwhelming is the idea that of all the people on Earth, he might be spending the last months of his life hanging out with me.

"Which leads me to a different topic," Rabbi Harris says, his voice softening a little more. "You've already been through the death of a loved one."

"Who?" I ask.

"Your father?" Rabbi Harris says, eyebrows raised, and leans toward me. "And sometimes, when we experience difficult things, it can bring back old memories. Old feelings."

"There's nothing to remember," I say. "So it doesn't affect me."

"Well, memory is funny like that," says Rabbi Harris. "It can be like a dream. You know how sometimes you wake up and you think, 'I didn't dream at all.' And then you're brushing your teeth, and suddenly, you remember: last night, you dreamed you were flying."

"That never happens to me," I answer.

"The point is, we forget what we remember and we remember what we forget. You may find yourself remembering things, remembering your father in new ways. Can I ask you . . . how would you feel if memories started bubbling up? Some of those memories might be nice. Some maybe not so nice."

I sit for a moment.

"I'm okay with it," I say, though in reality, it sounds sort of scary. What could I remember about Dad that wouldn't be nice?

"Once you have your Bar Mitzvah," Rabbi Harris continues, "you'll start saying Mourner's Kaddish on your father's *Yahrzeit,* the anniversary of his passing. You will stand up at the end of services and chant the prayer along with all the other mourners—anyone who's recently lost a loved one, plus anyone observing the yearly *Yahrzeit.*"

Rabbi Harris stands up, a sign for me to join him for the walk back to the building.

"What do you think, Will?" he asks. "Are you ready to remember?"

"Sure," I say, though as I say it, I have the feeling that I'm inviting something into my life, something big, something I won't be able to control.

PART TWO

CHAPTER 25

IT'S A COOL DAY; NOT A GOOD DAY FOR SWIMMING IN A pond, but what Rabbi Harris told me this morning has been haunting me. RJ's bucket list isn't just a list of hopes for "someday." He has a really limited amount of time to accomplish them. He needs them done *now*.

As soon as I get home from my lesson, I pack my back-pack with a towel, my swim trunks, and goggles from when I took swimming lessons in third grade, which didn't end well. I managed to doggy-paddle around, but I refused to put my face in the water, and to this day, when I go swimming, I try to keep my face dry.

Once I'm at the pond in the Back 40, I look around to see if I'm alone. Of course I am. I pull off my shirt. The wind bites my back and neck. I take a few steps closer to the water, near where Max leaped in to catch the Blanding's turtle. A thin layer of duckweed bobs across the surface like a green carpet. I grab a stick and poke it through, the tip disappearing, swallowed up. I don't know what's on the other side. It gives me chills to imagine it.

I move along the edge of the pond, about fifteen feet, where the water is a bit clearer. I spot my reflection—ripply and distorted, swampy green. I tell myself I only need to get in the water for a second—RJ didn't say I needed to swim across the pond, or even that I need to submerge my head. I can get in, get out, dry off, and be done.

But then I'm starting to tell myself stories. I don't have to do this. I don't swim in ponds—there are leeches in the water. I can't do it.

I'll tell RJ that I swam, though. I can exaggerate a little. He won't know the truth.

While I'm considering this choice, my body has already begun to move, getting dressed—first pants, then shirt. Before I've even made up my mind, I'm on my bike, riding home as fast as I can.

CHAPTER 26

I'M IN MY ROOM. I'M NOT IN THE MOOD TO STUDY MY Torah portion. I set up the practice pad on my bed, sit cross-legged in front of it, and begin playing: *Boom-boom pack! Chaka-laka. Boom-boom pack!*

My sticks don't flow, and the rhythm turns into a train wreck. Why does it look so easy when RJ does it? I try it a few more times, but I can't get it.

I drop the sticks and pick up the Bar Mitzvah sheets Rabbi Harris made for me, my Torah portion in Hebrew and English. I lay them out on my bed and start singing the trope. I make it through a verse without a single mistake. I feel pretty good about it until I skim the rest of the pages—I've only learned one verse out of a hundred.

"*Will!* Come get the phone."

Normally, it would be Max, wanting help on his homework. But Max and I aren't talking to each other, so why would he be calling?

"Dude, dude—we have a major problem." The voice is hushed but urgent.

"Max?"

"No, it's RJ. Something's wrong with Grampy."

"What's the matter?"

"His eyes are swollen shut and he won't eat. All he does is hide in the Herp Hotel."

I consider what might cause a turtle's eyes to swell shut and make it stop eating. It could be a serious infection. That would require a trip to a specialist vet.

"What sort of water are you using in his tank?" I ask. "Are you using distilled water, like I told you?"

"Well, my dad couldn't come for a few days," RJ explains. "He's been on a long trip, so I used water from the bathroom."

"Problem solved," I say. "We'll switch to distilled water as soon as we can."

"But he's not eating!" says RJ. "I think he's dying, Will!"

"Turtles don't like change," I explain. "If they get moved from one terrarium to another, they sometimes refuse to move or eat for a few days. Try feeding it something really tempting. Like . . . if they serve you meat for meals, you can give it a little piece."

"We just had ham for dinner. Is he allowed to eat ham? Isn't he a Jewish turtle?"

"It's okay," I say. "He's Reform. It's his choice."

RJ is quiet for a minute, as if considering this.

"Yes!" says RJ, startling me. "YES! It's eating the ham!"

"Don't give it too much," I say. "It can't live on people food. Tomorrow I can bring some extra gut-loaded crickets, and medicine drops for its eyes."

After we hang up, I get ready for bed, and Rabbi Harris's words strike me as I climb under the blankets—words that burned the first time I heard them: *Ralph is dying. . . . We're no longer talking about "someday." . . . If you're going to be able to support Ralph, you need to know what he's up against.*

I hear those words again and again. I lie in bed, tucking my limbs under the blankets, as if the feelings can't find me here. But they do, and I groan. I need to chase these feelings away.

I switch on my lamp and grab the drumsticks and practice pad. I hold one stick in each hand, the way RJ showed me. Their balance feels good. I bounce the tip of the right stick off the pad, then the left stick, and it works, the rhythm comes to me: *Boom-boom pack! Chaka-laka. Boom-boom pack! Chaka-laka.* I play for a long, long time, the rhythm of endless ocean waves chasing one another up the beach. I won't say it's making me feel better, but it is making me sleepy.

CHAPTER 27

At Herb's Herps, Gwen is showing an iguana to a guy in a puffy blue coat. The guy reaches out to stroke the iguana's back.

"Look who's here," Gwen says, suddenly seeing me. She jiggles the iguana as she talks, as if it's a puppet. "Fellow iguanas! Make way for the Turtle King of Horicon!"

I don't like how she's holding the iguana, and I'm not in the mood for her games.

"I need some anti-chlorine drops," I say.

"Let me know if you need anything else, sir," she says to the customer, putting the iguana back in its terrarium.

"Anti-chlorine?" she says. "Are you not using distilled water?"

"Duh!" I say, incredulous. "I use *gourmet* distilled water. This isn't for me; it's for a friend. He lives in a hospital, and he doesn't have distilled water lying around. He's new at all this, so it's not his fault."

I'm surprised at how defensive I am of RJ. I don't want anyone thinking he's done something bad.

"Anti-chlorine drops are over by the tropical fish," Gwen says.

"And I need a bottle of Medi-Eye," I add.

"Medi-Eye?" asks Gwen, handing me a box off the shelf. "It has an eye infection? Are you not filtering the water?"

"Of course I'm filtering the water! I'm using a Repo 5000!"

"Not a strong enough filter," she says. "You'll accumulate substrata. Repo 5000s are for little fish tanks."

"It's fine," I say. "I tested it myself. I used it at home for three weeks."

"If it's fine, then what do you need Medi-Eye for?" She crosses her arms. "Uh-huh," she says. "Obviously, your terrarium isn't clean."

Gwen walks off and returns with a paper bag. Inside is a brand-new Repo 7000 filter.

These things are more than fifty dollars. It would take me weeks to earn enough allowance to buy it.

"The company sends us free stuff as a promo," she says before I can turn it down. "My dad lets me keep most of it. It's yours. On the house."

"Free?" I ask.

"Yes, genius," she says. " 'On the house' means 'free.' "

CHAPTER 28

RJ IS ASLEEP. HE'S ON HIS BACK, AND HIS MOUTH IS OPEN. I don't like seeing him like this. I want to lock the door, but there's no lock. I'll have to be speedy. If Denise comes in while I'm working on the terrarium, we're busted.

I pull the curtain away from the shelf, and there's the Blanding's turtle, basking under its heat lamp. I tear open the package of Medi-Eye, remove the cap, grab the turtle, and put drops in its eyes. It struggles a little. Once RJ wakes up, I'll show him the chapter on simple medical care, how to put drops in, tell him when to change the water.

The room is quiet now—just the sound of RJ's snoring and the gentle trickle of water through the terrarium filter. I sit down to read, hoping RJ will wake up before I leave, and a few minutes later, his gravelly breathing ends with a loud snort, and he turns and looks at me with wide eyes.

"What's happening?" he asks, a look of terror on his face.

"It's me, Will," I say. "I brought some medicine for the turtle. I think it's going to be all right."

He shifts and sits up a little.

"And I brought you a book," I say. I lay it on his tray. "This is the book that taught me pretty much everything I know. You should read the sections on keeping a terrarium clean."

He looks at me a second, takes a breath, and says, "Thanks, but *not gonna happen*."

"What?" I say. "Why not? It's super-helpful information."

"I'm not blind," he explains, "but my sight's gotten worse. I can't really read. I can't see anything beyond a few feet. Like, I can see you're there, but if you kept your big mouth shut, I might not know who you are."

I remember when we first met, when I told him my nickname. He made me come over and stand right by the bed.

"Secret's out; might as well put these on," he says. He reaches behind the pile of drums and pulls out a pair of glasses with the thickest lenses I've ever seen. He puts them on and shrugs.

"I look like a total dork," he says. "And they barely help, so I don't usually wear them."

They do make his eyes look enormous, but I don't think he looks like a dork. I don't think anything could make RJ look like a dork.

He switches the subject fast, grabbing his drumsticks. "How's the playing going?" he asks, handing me the sticks. "Let's hear *boom-boom pack! Chaka-laka.*"

He pulls out a clipboard, and I position myself to play. I begin the rhythm and settle into an easy swing. RJ watches and wags his head from side to side, as if watching the beats flow out.

"Okay, you're ready for the next step," he says. "Try this."

He pulls a plastic bowl from his junk pile, turns it upside down, takes my sticks, and bounces the right drumstick off the bottom of the bowl twice, followed by the left stick, back and forth: *Botta batta botta batta botta batta,* on and on.

I take the sticks back and try it, but he grabs a tip.

"That's good," he says. "But you're *hitting* the bowl. Don't *hit* the bowl. Let the stick bounce."

I try to repeat it: *Botta batta botta batta,* and each time I screw up, I curse under my breath, but I keep trying.

"Okay, that's it for today," RJ interrupts, lying back against his pillows. "I'm really tired."

"That's okay," I say. "I need to go home and get ready for synagogue. It's Yom Kippur tonight."

I wonder if RJ will ask questions about it, but it seems like he's dozing.

"Did you go swimming already?" he asks suddenly, startling me.

"Not yet," I say. "I mean, I will. I'm going to."

"You said you'd do it," he says. "It's really important."

"I will. I promise."

He raises his eyebrows. "Fine," he says, but I can tell he's disappointed. "If you're serious about helping me, here's the next thing on my list, because it can't wait. It so happens that one of my favorite bands is playing an all-ages show in Madison on October fifth. That's a week from Saturday. I really, really wish I could go, but obviously, I can't."

I look at him.

"I want you to go to the show and get a pair of the drummer's drumsticks."

I stare at him and he raises his eyebrows.

"What?" I say, breaking the silence. "You want me to steal drumsticks from some band?"

"No, dummy," he says. "Go to see the show! They're called Dog Complex. They're a punk band, so it's gonna be intense. After the show, tell the drummer, Brett Canto, you want some drumsticks for a sick kid in the hospital. Tell him I'm his *biggest* fan."

CHAPTER 29

THE TEMPLE IS PACKED. EVEN THE OVERFLOW SEATS ARE full. Jewish holidays start at sundown, but Mom and I don't usually go to nighttime services. *Kol Nidre* is the exception. She always drags me to *Kol Nidre*.

I told Mom that the room would be so full, Rabbi Harris wouldn't notice whether I was there or not.

"We're not going for Rabbi Harris," said Mom.

"Well, I don't want to go, either," I said.

"We're not going for you," said Mom. I could hear her voice getting more and more tense.

"Then why are we going?" I asked. "It's so crowded, and it's so boring."

"We're going for *me*, Will!" she snapped. "Please stop thinking about yourself—for once, okay? Do something for someone else. Go get your shoes on and let's go, or we're gonna miss *Kol Nidre*!"

That really stung. Was there truth to that? Did I only think about myself? I couldn't get it out of my head during the whole ride to temple. Once we got settled and the service began, Mom rubbed the back of my shoulder and leaned over. "I'm sorry I yelled at you," she said.

I nodded, but I didn't respond.

...

The synagogue service goes on and on, and mainly, I distract myself by thinking about RJ's most recent task. How am I going to get to Madison? How am I going to get tickets to a punk rock show? How am I going to get drumsticks? It all seems impossible. But I can't stop thinking about it. If nothing else, it helps pass the time.

The congregation is singing the final song, the *aleinu*. Mom and I will have to come back tomorrow morning for the even longer daytime service. Midsong, I stand up to leave, and Mom instantly presses down on my shoulder. She shows me a stern index finger. Surprised, I lower myself back to my seat. Then she and approximately twenty other people rise to their feet and begin to chant a prayer out loud. It's the same prayer that's already been recited a bunch of times throughout the service, the Kaddish. I can see the page of her open prayer book: it says *Mourner's Kaddish*.

The words flow together, rhythmic. In fact, I can imagine how it would sound, played on drums:

Yitgadal v'yitkadash sh'mei raba. Amen.

Bappa dum, b'dada-bum, boom-boom-boom. Amen.

I tap out the rhythm on my knees with the palms of my hands and then comes the line the entire congregation says together: *"Y'hei sh'mei raba m'vorach."*

B'dum, bum, ba-da, da'bum-bum!

It's almost thunderous, from so many hundreds of people saying it. The rhythm is loud. So loud, I can feel it down in my chest.

I continue listening to the hypnotic rhythm of the words:

Ba-ba-dum, b'dada-bum, b'dada-bum, b'dada-bum.

Ba-ba-dum, b'dada-bum, b'dada-bum, b'dada-bum.

It goes on, word after word in Hebrew. My mind finally grasps the obvious: she's saying the Mourner's Kaddish. For Dad. This is the prayer Rabbi Harris was talking about.

If Mom is a mourner, does that make me a mourner? The problem is, no memories of Dad equals nothing to feel.

What would it feel like to have him in my mind, to see his face, to hear his voice? Instead of two plates at the dinner table every night, there'd be three—Mom, me, and the memory of Dad. And on the day of my Bar Mitzvah, up on the *bimah* with me, there'd be a chair for Dad.

This loosens something in my mind, maybe a memory.

Dad is on my right, Mom on my left. We're here in temple. Dad stands up and I stand up too. Mom gently presses on my shoulder. I sit back down. Dad chants the

Hebrew, along with a pocket of other people scattered around the room:

Bappa dum, b'dappa dum, boom-boom-boom. Amen.

Dad is so tall, standing beside me, and his tallit—his prayer shawl—over his head. But I can see his face, his eyes closed, and then I see that his cheeks are wet.

Is he crying? Does Dad cry?

The whole congregation chants together; a hushed chorus of *"Y'hei sh'mei raba m'vorach l'olam ul'almei almaya."*

The mourners chant on and on until Mom takes three tiny steps back, bowing slightly to the left, the right, the middle, and the memory recedes. I close my eyes, wishing I could keep on dreaming, but Dad's face fades, and soon, it's gone.

• • •

We're driving home from synagogue, headlights on, windows up, air-conditioning blasting. It's hot and muggy out, as it is every Yom Kippur, a sure sign that winter is lurking around the corner.

"How long have you been saying the Mourner's Kaddish?" I ask.

"Since your Dad died," Mom says. She turns and glances at me. "Three times a year. Rosh Hashanah, Yom Kippur, and Dad's *Yahrzeit*."

She doesn't say more, and when the light changes she

drives on. Mom often doesn't want to talk about Dad, but this time, I want to tell her about my memory. I want to know if it was real.

"I remembered something in temple today," I say. "About Dad. Or I think I did."

"Really?" says Mom.

"He was saying Kaddish," I explain. "And I tried to stand up next to him, but you didn't let me."

"A child doesn't stand for Kaddish until after their Bar Mitzvah," she says, as if that's the end of the conversation.

"I know that," I say slowly, annoyed. "But did that actually happen? My memory?"

"I can't imagine how *you'd* remember such a thing," she says. "You must have been three or four."

This is not what I want to hear. Maybe it isn't a real memory. Maybe it's something I made up, something I *wish* I remembered.

Mom pulls the car up to the garage and we get out. It's dark here by the garage. The overhead light doesn't work, so we keep a flashlight on a hook. I grab it and we make our way up the brick path to the door.

"Go up and change out of your nice clothes," she says once we're in the house.

"Who was Dad mourning?" I ask, turning off the flashlight. "Why was he saying Kaddish?"

Mom looks up for a second. "He was probably mourning

his father. Your grandpa Wilbur, the one you're named after. He died before you were born."

"It's weird to think of Dad mourning," I say.

"Why's it weird?"

"Well, you say Kaddish for him, but a few years before he died, he was saying it for Grandpa Wilbur. It's like . . . everyone's saying Kaddish for someone who came before them."

I read a myth once about the universe being a giant tower, turtle on top of turtle, all the way down. Maybe that's what the myth is really about—each of us takes our place, loving someone, grieving, then one day being grieved. It's heavy stuff, but I'd feel better if I could talk about it.

"You know what," Mom says. "You want some ice cream? I won't tell anyone."

The look on her face says she expects me to say yes. Maybe last year, I would have.

"No thanks. I'm fasting."

"Who is this kid, *fasting* on Yom Kippur?" she remarks. "I was all ready to bust out the Ben and Jerry's!"

The next thing I know, she's sped up the stairs and I'm alone in the kitchen.

CHAPTER 30

WE'VE ALREADY BEEN IN YOM KIPPUR MORNING SER-vices for an excruciating hour when I decide to kill some time in the men's room. I sit in the stall and practice drumming on my thighs with my open palms: *botta-batta-botta-batta-botta-batta*. It's getting easier as my muscles learn to be relaxed and engaged at the same time. Eventually, I decide to head back to the sanctuary. I open the men's room door, and there is Shirah, about to go into the women's room.

"Oh, hi," I say.

She stops and looks at me impatiently.

"How's it going?" I ask. Shirah and I haven't spoken in so long, I don't remember how to talk to her.

"Will, what do you want?"

"You gonna be at the break-fast?" I ask. After services, everyone breaks the fast on bagels and lox and onions and tomatoes and these little green things called capers, which taste a little like olives.

"My mom and I are going to Madison to break the fast with my aunt and uncle," says Shirah.

Madison.

"How long does it take to get there?" I ask.

"About an hour," she says. "Why do you care?"

"That kid I visit in the hospital," I say. "He wants me to go to Madison, this weekend, to see a punk band and get him drumsticks."

She laughs and I feel really silly.

"I cannot picture you going to a punk concert," she says.

"He asks me to do all this crazy stuff," I say. "I've smuggled Funyuns for him, and I set up a secret turtle terrarium in his room, and now he wants me to go to this concert and get him a pair of drumsticks."

"So go do it!" she says. "You're making it sound like it's impossible."

"How am I supposed to get to Madison?" I ask. "Plus, you know me—I hate crowds."

"Will," she says, "if this kid is so sick that he needs a random Bar Mitzvah kid to visit him in the hospital, then you *have* to do this! You *have* to go! There's even a bus. I take it all the time."

I don't say anything.

"Because if you're *able* to go to a punk concert," she says, "and you could get this kid some drumsticks and you won't do it just because you don't like buses or crowds or whatever, then you're so selfish, I'm glad we're not friends anymore."

I'm stunned. I feel my pulse quicken.

"I mean it," she says.

"I think you're hungry," I say. "Obviously, not eating is making you say dumb things."

"Okay, so now I need to eat?" she asks bitterly. "Is this the setup for another fat joke?"

I'm shocked. I cannot believe she brought that up. Here. In synagogue. On Yom Kippur. I don't believe in any of this Yom Kippur forgiveness, but still, I would never, ever bring up things *she's* done wrong, right here, today. Is she trying to get me struck by lightning?

Someone calls from the doorway of the sanctuary. "Shirah, you're up. Time to open the Ark."

Shirah slips into the sanctuary and scampers up the three small steps to the wooden Ark; the Torah scrolls are placed inside.

Then, just at the second she's about to close the doors, she looks up and our eyes meet. She looks really angry. She closes the wooden doors on cue, but hard. There's a *bang* of wood slamming shut and it zaps the room—anyone who was dozing is shocked awake. Even people who saw it happen are startled. And I feel her judgment rattle through me, shaking every bone.

CHAPTER 31

THE NEXT DAY, I CLIMB ONTO THE BUS, AND AS USUAL, Shirah's bag is on the seat next to her. Her face is turned to the window.

"Shirah," I say.

She doesn't budge.

"Hey, kid," says the bus driver, looking over her shoulder. "Sit down."

"Shirah, can we talk?"

"So talk," Shirah says.

"Hey, *kid*," says the bus driver, louder. "I can't operate the bus while you're standing!"

Shirah grabs her bag and pulls it closer to her, creating a tiny ledge at the end of her seat. I squeeze in next to her.

"Okay, listen," I say. "I'm going to get those drumsticks for RJ. But . . . I don't think I can do it by myself. Would you be willing to go with me? You don't have to talk to me. You can ignore me the whole time. But I can't do it alone."

Shirah continues to look at the seat in front of her.

"If I say yes," she says, "it's only because I want to help that kid in the hospital. You don't deserve any favors."

"Fine," I say. "Don't do it for me. Do it for him."

"What time is the concert?"

"Eight," I say. "We can get the tickets there."

She appears to be counting in her head.

"Okay, on Saturday, we'll catch the four-thirty bus downtown. You know where the park-and-ride is?"

"I'll figure it out," I say.

"Don't be late," she says.

We sit for a minute in silence until she turns to me.

"Are we *done*?" she asks.

I nod.

She makes a shoving motion toward me. I go sit with the sixth graders in the back of the bus.

CHAPTER 32

I HAVE A PROBLEM.

Mom is not going to let me get on a bus and go to Madison, even if Shirah's mom lets her. And she's not going to let me go to a punk concert, even if it's an all-ages show.

"Tomorrow after school, don't take the bus home," Mom says as I set the table for dinner. "You have an appointment with the orthodontist."

"What? No! That's not for two more weeks!"

"A slot opened up," she explains. "He's doing molds and fittings in one visit."

And so it begins. Stage one: braces. Stage two: surgery. Stage three: whatever shreds of dignity I have left are pulverized when I have to eat my lunch at school through a straw. And that's assuming I survive surgery.

I put the plates down, nearly dropping them on the table. My head swims, and I rub my temples.

"It's gonna be okay, Will," she says. "It really is. Also,

this weekend, we're going to La Crosse to help Aunt Mo move into her new condo. It'll take most of the day."

The concert! La Crosse is almost three hours to the west. I need to get forty-five minutes south. That's the wrong direction! I'm going to blow another task on RJ's list!

. . .

I'm in the orthodontist's chair. Near my head, he's using a metal spatula to smear pinkish putty into a pair of U-shaped trays.

"Open big," he says.

I think the tray is going to fit around my teeth, like sliding a shoe onto a foot, but it's nothing like that. It feels like *my entire head* is being crammed into a shoe. He's mashing the tray up against my jaw and working it around.

I feel like I'm drowning in cement. I start to gag and thrash around.

He sits down next to me, ignoring my waving hands: "Twenty seconds, buddy. Try panting like a dog."

I try it, but it makes me gag again. My stomach convulses and my head is spinning and tears are flowing out of my eyes and the orthodontist starts counting down.

"Ten . . . nine . . . eight . . ."

I wave my hands more violently, clipping his glasses. They fly off his head and clatter onto the floor.

"Whatever, good enough," he says. He yanks the tray out of my mouth. Giant ropes of drool flow from the tray and land on the green paper bib on my chest. I'm panting now, for real.

"Fantastic job, buddy," he says flatly, putting his glasses back on. He's obviously annoyed, but it's not my fault. I didn't ask for any of this. "The good news is we got a good impression."

I'm too wobbly to refuse the bad news.

"The bad news," he continues anyhow, "is we still have to do the lower jaw."

• • •

After two hours of pain and pulling and pushing and stretching, along with cold bursts of air and water, the orthodontist sits back and pulls off his blue latex gloves.

"Okay, go have a look. They look really cool," he says brightly.

"No thanks," I say. I don't want to see. He follows me out to the waiting room, where Mom is sitting. I hope she doesn't ask me to smile.

"How's it feel, Will?" she asks.

"Awful," I say. It feels like my mouth is being folded in half in the wrong direction.

"He can take something for the pain," says the ortho-dontist. "No hard foods for a few days. Soup, applesauce, that sort of stuff. By the weekend, he should be fine. And, Will, if you get any hot spots from the metal rubbing on the insides of your cheek, you can stick some of this on the brackets."

He gives me a bag full of strips of white wax and a pamphlet with all the dos and don'ts of braces.

He turns to Mom. "In about a month, you'll want to pay a visit to Dr. Haffetz and see if Will's ready to go forward with the surgery."

Silently, I count the weeks remaining until that very real terror comes to my life: ten.

That's seventy days.

CHAPTER 33

EVER SINCE MY APPOINTMENT WITH DR. HAFFETZ THIS
past summer, I've tried to keep the surgery pushed far,
far out of my mind. But now it's here. All the things he
told me, the things they're going to do to me—they're all
back from deep freeze.

Break jaw hinge.

Move jaw forward.

Transplant bone from hip.

Wire teeth shut.

Eat through a straw.

"You're quiet," says Mom. "You okay?"

"Remember this summer," I say, "when the doctor
said that the surgery is risky?"

"That's not what he said," she says. "He was just explaining that with any surgery requiring anesthesia,
there's always a teeny risk. But you don't need to worry
about it. Thousands of people all over the world have
surgery all the time."

I take a deep breath. "But sometimes . . ."

We both know where I'm going with this. The one person in thousands who died was Dad. His hernia operation wasn't supposed to be a big deal, but something went wrong during the surgery, and he never came home. If it could happen to him . . .

"You're going to be fine," says Mom, her voice becoming tense. "What happened to your father has nothing to do with you."

We ride for a while longer without talking. We didn't talk about Dad, but we sort of did, and now, it's in the car with us.

"I feel sick," I say.

"This happens when you're anxious," she says. "Open the window to get some fresh air and think about something else."

It's probably the right advice, but I don't follow it. I think about Dad dying. I count ten weeks until my surgery, over and over, all the way home.

At dinner, my face hurts too much to eat. Mom makes me a smoothie and doesn't even try to sneak kale into it. It's mainly yogurt and frozen berries. It would taste good if I weren't so miserable.

Now I'm lying in bed, my mouth full of pain. It hurts when I open my mouth. It hurts when I close my mouth. It hurts when I'm just lying here, thinking about how much it hurts.

How am I supposed to go to school tomorrow in this condition? I start wondering if I could leverage this to stay home. Maybe for a day. Maybe even two?

And suddenly, an idea flows into my head, almost from my mouth itself.

· · ·

It's Friday, and we're eating soup for the second night in a row. My teeth still hurt too much to chew. I don't talk much because I'm planning my next move.

"Aunt Mo called," says Mom. "She found other people to help her move, but she wants to have a party to celebrate her new place, and I think maybe she still needs my help. I wonder how you'd feel about staying at home alone tomorrow."

I literally cannot believe my ears. She solved my problem for me!

"You're going to a party?" I ask, shifting the topic away from my plan. "Like, with people?"

"You're always saying I need to get out and do things," she explains.

That's not exactly true. I only said that one time. But now that she's doing it, oddly enough, I forget completely about RJ, the drumsticks, my plan to get to Madison, the surgery, the braces, my chin—all of it. I just want to stay home and have Mom take care of me and make everything better.

But that's little me. Kid me. Real me has real responsibilities. To RJ and to myself.

"Go," I say. I manage to sound confident but not quite eager. "I got this."

Mom is quiet for a minute. She looks pained.

"What's the matter?" I ask.

"I feel guilty, leaving you like this," she says. "Maybe it isn't right."

I shake my head vigorously, feeling the motion in my teeth and gums. "No, Mom, you *have* to go. I'm completely fine staying home."

"I could leave you my phone," she says, more to comfort herself than me. "And if you needed to reach me, you could just text Aunt Mo. She won't mind if I hang on to her phone for the day."

"I'm just going to eat soup and watch movies all day," I say.

"That sounds awesome," she says.

It does, I think. It does sound awesome.

But that's not what I'll be doing tomorrow.

• • •

The seats on a Marten's Express aren't like school bus seats or city bus seats. They're more like airplane chairs. Two on the left of the aisle and two on the right.

Shirah is sitting about ten rows back. Her backpack is on the seat next to her. At first, I think she's going to make me sit alone, but when she sees me, she makes space. The bus lurches forward. My stomach drops like we're on a roller coaster.

"You okay?" asks Shirah.

"Totally," I say.

I text Mom: Watching movies. Teeth sore but ok. How are you doing? Almost party time!

Ha ha! Fun! she texts back, followed by way too many emojis, some of them seemingly random faces. Is she hiding in the kitchen, pretending to help so she doesn't have to talk to anyone? She's with Aunt Mo, who will take care of her. She'll be fine. I shift around, anxious, until I bump elbows with Shirah. Now, I'm very aware of her body: where her knee is next to mine, where her arm is. She pulls out her headphones and is about to put them on when she suddenly says, "Oh, here," and pulls out a small cellophane package. Inside are two small squishy yellow cylinders.

"Earplugs," she says. "To protect our hearing at the show. I've been streaming their music for days, and it's definitely gonna be loud. But I have to say, their stuff's really good. I'm excited. And I think it's really cool that you're doing this."

A smile escapes my lips.

"Wait, look at me," she orders. "You got braces?"

I nod.

"How much does it suck?" she asks, and then slips her headphones over her ears.

Shirah has had braces for a while, and I sort of enjoy the fact that we have something in common. But she doesn't need surgery. I'm tempted to tell her about it. I used to think of her as my best friend, sometimes even my only friend, and it makes me sad that she doesn't know this major thing about me.

I catch a glimpse of her, headphones on, and I realize that there are a million things I don't know about her too.

CHAPTER 34

IT'S DARK IN HERE. THERE'S A PRETTY BIG CROWD, MAINLY clustered near the stage. Most of the people look like they're in high school—maybe RJ's age. Shirah's taller than I am, and she looks older than I do, so she probably feels like she fits right in. Then again, with everyone completely fixated on the stage, I could be wearing a gorilla costume and no one would notice.

Two guys with flannel shirts and long hair come out onstage, and at first I think that's the band, but the crowd barely responds. One of the guys picks up a guitar and plays a few chords, and the other guy bangs on the drum, over and over.

"What are they doing?" I yell to Shirah.

"Testing the volumes!" she yells back. "They're roadies."

She gets out her phone and sets an alarm. "When this goes off," she says, "we have to leave and get to the bus stop or we'll miss our ride home. Got it?"

I nod.

Eventually, the already-dim room goes pitch-black, and a voice comes booming out of the speakers and says, *"Hey, Madison! Mad Town! Mad City! Please make some noise for Dog Complex!"*

A swell of yelling washes over the room, and bass noise explodes in my chest. It's so loud, it feels like my ears are going to bleed. I stick a finger in each ear and feel a bump from the side that almost knocks me off balance. It's Shirah—she holds up her packet of earplugs, reminding me. We roll the foam into skinny tubes and ease them into our ears. The noise in the room goes *shoooop* as the plugs expand. It's like I'm underwater. I can feel the crashing of guitars and the bass in my chest, and also in my teeth and jaw, which throbs to the pulse of the music. I hold my palms up to my cheeks and massage them, wondering how I'm going to make it through the show.

And then I see what's onstage and I forget the pain.

The band moves like a single unit, all thrashing and playing their instruments with their whole bodies. The singer throttles the mic stand like he's trying to strangle it, and the guitar player is hammering on the strings. There's a guy playing another instrument that looks like an electric guitar, but it's got a really long neck. He's kind of boring—he doesn't move much. But the drummer—I've never watched a real drummer at a drum set—looks like he's dancing while sitting down, and then a rage seems to overcome him and he goes berserk, smashing the drums, sticks flying, head pounding.

Hundreds of heads bob rhythmically, and then, when the sound and lights erupt, the crowd bursts into constant motion. Bodies jump and bump and collide, and sometimes a kid climbs onstage and dives into the audience.

Shirah yanks me along, closer to the crowd, closer to the band. The drummer's limbs look like they each have a mind of their own. His feet bounce up and down on pedals—one for the big drum and one that raises a cymbal up and down—and with my eyes locked on him, I'm entranced; time melts away, until I turn and discover that Shirah isn't next to me anymore.

I'm alone, and the crowd is getting wilder, pushing and shoving, and I get knocked hard from the side. I see Shirah; she's deep in the thick of the crowd—thrashing and wild and part of it. I don't even realize that I'm doing it, but I lower my head and charge into the wall of bodies, a scream escaping my lips, a scream no one can hear. I'm buffeted from side to side, and it feels like I'm falling down the side of a mountain—I hit the floor hard and close my eyes and cover the back of my head with my hands. The thought flashes through my mind:

This is how I die. I'm going to be trampled to death. Then: Hands under my arms. Someone lifts me to my feet. Not Shirah—she's in front of me. I look around at the dancing bodies. It could've been anyone.

...

Abruptly, the final song ends, and the room is flooded with darkness. The band leaves the stage and the overhead lights come on. I gotta get the drumsticks and get out of here. I look at my watch. We're running out of time. We have to catch the last bus to Horricon in less than half an hour, and the station is five blocks away. The audience screams and whoops, and suddenly, the band returns to the stage.

Now frantic, I nudge Shirah and shove my watch in her face. She pushes it away and shrugs.

"It's an encore!" she yells. "One or two more songs!"

I know there's nothing she can do about it, but if the band plays much longer, or if they don't come out for autographs, then the whole trip to Madison was for nothing. I'll have to go back and tell RJ that I blew the mission.

The shame of such a failure fills me with dread, but what happens next takes me by surprise.

Ner! Ner-ner! Ner! Ner-ner! The chords blast, over and over, until the singer grabs the mic:

> *"You see the rate they come down the escalator!*
> *Now listen to the tube train accelerator!*
> *Then you realize that you got to have a purpose*
> *Or this place is gonna knock you out sooner or*
>   *later!"*

I know this song! It's the song that RJ was singing while Denise took his blood on my first visit! It sounds much better with real electric guitars and drums, and soon, I find myself banging my head, harder and harder, until I'm bouncing along with the crowd, with Shirah, with the band, with the drums. Everything is pulsing like a single slamming heart.

The song ends with a supernova of sound: electric guitar squealing, cymbals and the thump-bump of drums. The crowd claps and hollers, and the band waves, drops their instruments, and leaves the stage.

It's over.

Shirah's phone suddenly lights up. It's her alarm.

"We have to leave right now," she says.

"But . . . the drumsticks," I say.

The band is nowhere to be seen. I turn in circles, trying to spot the musicians. They've turned up by some tables where there are T-shirts for sale. A long line of teenagers has already formed and we're at the other end.

Shirah grabs me and plows me through the crowd. I feel shoulders and elbows. The next thing I know, I'm standing in front of the drummer, who's sitting at a table with some Dog Complex patches and bandannas.

"Hey, what's up!" he yells. It's still incredibly loud in here.

This is no time to choke on my words, but the harder I try to speak, the more my mind blanks. Why am I here? What am I asking for?

I'm standing here at the front of this line. I feel the presence of a hundred teenagers waiting to talk to these people.

"Drumsticks," I say. I'm sure he can't hear. I take a deep breath, and with every ounce of strength I yell, "I need your drumsticks!"

The drummer gives me an odd look, does a little shrug, gets up, and walks away from the table. *Where'd he go?* I hear someone say, as if I scared him off, but he returns with a pair of sticks. They are gnarled and pitted like my pencils when I chew on them, and one of the sticks is shorter because the tip split off.

"What's your name?" he yells.

"Will!" I scream, and before I can stop him, he's grabbed a black marker and he's writing something. He hands the sticks to me, and the next person in line shoves me aside. I float to the door, gripping these sticks, and once Shirah and I are out into the cool evening air, it hits me: I have achieved the impossible. I'm floating on a cloud of my own victory.

Until I realize that I have ruined everything. On the sticks is written *ROCK ON, WILL!*

CHAPTER 35

At school on Monday, there are signs and banners everywhere: ALL LACROSSE THE DANCE FLOOR.

I don't know if they were there before or if I'm just paying more attention. It's like when you first notice a mosquito bite, and then it starts itching like crazy. Did it itch *before* you noticed it?

All day long, I can hear kids talking about the dance. I hear people talking about who is "going" with who. Is "going" like . . . carpooling together? I'm really not in the mood for any of this—I've ruined RJ's drumsticks, and I'm panicking about how he'll react. I skipped my visit with him yesterday—like a total coward, I left a message with Roxanne saying that I wouldn't be visiting him.

I'm sitting at my desk before second period, trying to come up with a solution for the sticks, when Spencer turns around from the far corner of the class. "Hey," he says. "Turtle Boy, I hear you were on a hot date this weekend."

I ignore him and return my attention to my conundrum. Maybe I could try to shave off the marker with a knife and write RJ's name instead?

"Yup," says Spencer. "A concert! My brother is friends with someone who's into that kind of music, and he says he was there! With a girl. He recognized you from your Jewish church."

"Yeah, Turtle Boy!" says Jake. "So who's the lucky lady?"

"It was *not* a date," I say, my face flushing with heat. "Shirah and I are just friends."

"You were on a date with Shirah?" says Jake. I can't tell if he's making fun of me, which is bad enough, or of Shirah, which is even worse. "Wow! Go, Turtle Boy!"

He and Spencer start the *Tur-tle Boy! Tur-tle Boy!* chant. I keep my head down and wait for it to pass.

Between classes, a few other kids also comment on my "hot date." Word must have spread; I hear them talking to one another. "I bet they kissed," I hear one kid say. It's humiliating and makes the blood pound in my ears. I hear a couple of other kids laughing hysterically, and I can't help it—I look, and one of them is imitating me, imitating the way my lip hangs down, and he's kissing the side of his fist.

"Oh, Shiwah!" he yells into his fist, "My bwaces! My bwaces are shtuck to yo bwaces!"

The first kid laughs so hard he falls out of his chair. The teacher scowls. "Mr. Andersen! Get back into your seat!"

He and his friend continue to laugh. I stick my face so close to my workbook, I can't read the print.

•••

Since Jake and Spencer figured out that I was eating in the restroom, I stopped going there for lunch. Even though Max and I aren't talking, I'll be safer at his table in the cafeteria. He's sitting with a weird mix of sixth graders and an eighth grader named Kyle, who should be over at Horicon High but flunked sixth grade.

I sit down, but the moment I do, Kyle says, "Your girlfriend's sitting over there. Why don't you go sit with her?"

"Knock it off," I say. Sitting here was obviously a terrible idea, and at this point, I'm starting to regret going to the concert. If I had known it was going to draw so much attention, I wouldn't have gone.

"Look, he's turning red," says Max. As usual, he says whatever he's thinking, pointing out the obvious, uncomfortable thing.

"Max," I say, "maybe you could learn to keep your big mouth shut."

"At least I can shut my mouth," he says, and there's a pause. At first, I don't know what he means, and then I do: he just made a joke about my face. Everyone goes: "Whoooaaa! SHOTS FIRED!"

I can't believe it. In front of all these people? He just

made fun of me? He doesn't exactly look pleased for having said it, but he doesn't apologize, either. He's waiting for me to make the next move.

"At least I don't see a shrink," I say, expecting another *"Whoooaaaa!"*

Instead, total silence. Everyone turns and looks at me, eyes wide.

"Hey," says Kyle, the eighth grader. "That's none of your business if he sees a therapist."

"I do not see a shrink," Max says, suddenly serious. I catch a glimpse of his eyes. I've never seen Max look truly hurt before, but I recognize the flash of betrayal. I wish I could turn back time and erase it, but it's been said. Max doesn't get a chance to respond because Shirah walks up to the table, her backpack over her shoulder.

"Hey, guys," she says, swerving a little closer to Max and me. "My mom has a presentation tomorrow and can't bring us to Hebrew school."

The mood at the table is so tense, no one turns or looks at Shirah. No one says anything.

Then Kyle speaks. "Hey, Will, if you wanna go to the dance with Shirah, you should ask her now."

"I don't think turtles are allowed," Max interjects.

"But if you're with a girl," says Kyle, "maybe they'll let you in. What a pair! *Turtle Boy* and *Big Butt*!"

The minute he finishes the sentence, two things

happen: Shirah storms away from the table, and a flood of words pours out of my mouth.

"Kyle, you're a moron!" I shout. "You flunked sixth grade, and you probably can't even read! And you"— I point at Max—"you can't control your mouth! You should try your stupid dive roll again, and this time, you can break your arm *and* your face!"

The whole table bursts into laughter, everyone except Kyle and Max. I get up and stomp away—away from Max, away from the table, away from the laughter. I've grabbed the remnants of my lunch in both hands, and I pick up speed as I push through the cafeteria double doors, finally peeling down the hallway.

I can't go to the library. I can't stay in the hall. I need to be alone. I run down to the bottom floor, which is mainly empty during lunch. Down here, there's a closed, empty art room and the band-orchestra room where a few kids are tooting on their instruments. I feel horrible. Ashamed and guilty. But then I see the big marching drums stacked against the back wall, and that gives me a great idea.

CHAPTER 36

In the hall outside RJ's room, I knock.

No answer.

I feel weird about barging in, especially on a day he isn't expecting me to visit, so I knock again, louder. Finally, I crack open the door. RJ's head is back on the pillow, eyes shut, and I'm startled by how fragile he looks, sicker than I remember—maybe because he's not awake to fight his illness.

I lay the sticks I stole from the band-orchestra room on his table tray and carefully arrange them side by side. This is perfect—he'll find them when he wakes up. That's better than giving him counterfeit Dog Complex drumsticks in person.

I decide to have a look at the Blanding's turtle before I go. I pull the blanket on the shelf back. The filter is humming and the light is on, and the turtle is basking, but something is wrong. There's a bad smell, like old food. I reach in and pick up the turtle. It has a couple of softish spots on its shell. I hope it isn't shell rot. Shell rot can be deadly. Despite the light and the filter, the water probably needs to be changed more often. RJ must not be getting out of bed much.

"How's Grampy?" RJ asks. It startles me.

"He looks great," I say. "Happy turtle."

He smiles. He hasn't noticed the sticks yet.

"How've you been?" he asks. "It's been a while. I missed you last week."

"I got your drumsticks," I say.

"Drumsticks?" he says. Then a surge of energy washes over his face, and his eyes brighten. "From Dog Complex? You went to the show?"

I point to the bedside table. He squints but doesn't see the sticks. I grab them and hold them under his eyes.

"No way!" he says, taking them in his hands. *'Rock on, RJ . . . ,'"* he reads, peering down at the black letters. *" 'Get well soon.' "*

He lays the sticks down on the stand and crosses his hands on his stomach. The sudden motion tugs on his IV, which runs from the stand next to his bed into his arm.

"What's the matter?" I ask. He does not look happy.

"So Brett Canto, drummer for Dog Complex, left the concert hall, went all the way to Prairie Marsh Middle

School, and got himself a fresh pair of Prairie Marsh drum corps sticks, just for you?"

I freeze.

"Dude," he says, "I thought we were done with telling stupid lies in here."

I grab the sticks. They're marked with the name of my school. How did I not see that?

"What the heck, Will," he says. "Did you even go to the concert? Are you going to do any of the things on my list, or are you going to lie your way through the rest of 'em?"

"No!" I shout. "I went all the way to Madison, and I spent all my allowance on a ticket, and I got bashed around a mosh pit, and I waited in a long line and fought my way to the front and got your stupid sticks!"

I grab my backpack and pull out the real sticks—the pitted, dented sticks—one splintered, one with the wrong name. I toss them on the bed.

"Here," I say.

"What's this?" he says, lifting one. Then he reads: *"Rock on, Will!"*

I'm prepared to grab my backpack and leave the hospital in shame and defeat, but RJ doesn't yell at me. He gets quiet. He looks at them more closely, inspecting each one. "Who wrote this?" he asks. "Who wrote *'Rock on, Will!'*?"

"The drummer," I say. "Brett whatever-his-name-is. He asked for my name, and I told him and—I tried to stop him, but the next person pushed in front of me, and it was too late to get him to do it right."

"So *you* wrote on the other ones," he says. "To replace the ones you thought you ruined."

I nod.

"But Brett wrote this," he says quietly, almost like he can't believe it. "You waited in line and got to the front, and Brett was like, 'What's your name, kid?' and you were like 'Will.' "

I nod. That's pretty much how it happened.

He laughs and looks at the sticks even closer, and I realize he hasn't been inspecting the sticks or the writing: he's *admiring* the sticks. He looks kind of ecstatic.

"This is the best. Thing. Ever."

I cannot believe I am hearing this. He looks at me and shakes his head. "Dude, in the future, please, please, please don't lie to me! You can tell me if you freaked out and messed up, but anyhow, it's not the autograph I wanted! Who cares what he wrote! It's not even really about the sticks."

"It's not?" I ask.

"No! I couldn't go to the show, but the sticks have the show *in* them. These are the sticks that made that concert happen! His hands were *right here*! And there's probably like, sweat from his hands all soaked in. This is a pair of sticks that will never exist again! They're mine!"

"So," I say. "You like them?"

"Dude, you did me such a solid," he says. "Now let's do some drums."

. . .

We set up the bed drum set, and he explains that a rhythm is made up of two parts: the "ride," which is the repeated sound, keeping the tempo and holding it together, and the accents, which add flavor and depth. He shows me a couple of rock rhythms. I pick them up fairly easily.

"What I recommend," he says, "is putting on head-phones and, whatever music you listen to, just play along."

I look at him blankly.

"What do you listen to?" he asks. "Besides, obviously, Dog Complex."

I shrug.

"*Nothing?*" he says. "Will, you need to listen to music. You can't *not* listen to music. I'm giving you homework. Ten groups to listen to. You may like them; you may hate them. Find *one* you like and play your rhythms along with the music."

He starts rummaging for a piece of paper and a pen.

"I haven't been doing much schoolwork," he explains. "You got something to write on? Gimme that stupid chart you always get signed when you come here."

I pull my forty-hours form out of my pocket and unfold it.

"Oh, look," he says, peering at it. "You've done seven hours. Thirty-three more and you're done with me."

I look at him in shock. Is *that* what he thinks? That I'm just doing this for the hours? He studies my expression for a long moment.

"I'm just messing with you," he says, breaking the tension. "You got a pen?"

He scribbles on the back, writing furiously, sometimes stopping and thinking. He hands it over and I glance at it. I've seen some of the bands' names before, mostly on his T-shirts. I tuck the page into my backpack.

"Okay," I say. "Two things on the bucket list done. What's next?"

"Did you go swimming yet?"

"Not yet," I say. "I'm going to."

"Come on, dude!" he says. "It's gonna be winter soon. When's it going to happen?"

"It will," I say.

He shakes his head, sighs, and reaches under the blanket that covers his junk-drums. Then he pulls out a crumpled piece of paper: the bucket list. He holds it up to his eyes.

"I have a feeling you aren't going to like this one," he says, shaking his head a bit.

I wait for him to go on, but instead, he says, "Hey, let's take a walk."

He pushes the nurse call button, and a few moments later, Roxanne appears in the doorway. I step back to allow her to go over to the bed, and she fiddles with RJ's IV, checking the drip bag on the tall, rolling stand.

"Ready to go," she says. "Not too long, okay?"

RJ swings his feet off the bed, and Roxanne stands nearby, holding his IV stand in place as he grips the chrome with one hand and rises to his feet. He takes a few tentative steps, then nods to her, and we all head out into the hallway. Seeing how difficult it is for RJ to walk makes me understand how challenging it is for him to do anything: go to the bathroom on his own, see the turtle. Cleaning the tank must be out of the question.

He's sicker than I realized. His disease isn't in any one place. It's in his arms, his legs, his organs.

"I can't see for crap," he says, "especially in the hallways, so you'll lead, okay?"

He holds my arm in one hand and the IV stand in the other. Walking down the hall, we pass open doors, and anyone who sees us calls out, "Hey, RJ!"

He waves or says, "Hey, Mrs. Barnes," or "Evening, Mr. Peterson!" I'm happy so many people know him, but it's also a sign of how long he's been in the hospital. And that makes me sad.

•••

RJ and I fill paper cups with hot water from a big machine, and RJ grabs two packets of Swiss Miss: regular for me, sugar-free for him. We sit down, and for the first time, he and I are face to face. Usually, I'm standing near him or sitting near the side of his bed, but it's different this way. I can see how thin his cheeks are, how gray his skin, the dark rings around his eyes. And yet those eyes are full of that deep ocean blue.

We sip our hot chocolate, and he says, "So, the next task on my bucket list." He runs his hand through his hair and takes a sip of hot chocolate. He's staring down at the table. He's embarrassed. This is a new RJ—I've never seen him like this.

"Prairie Marsh is having a dance this weekend," he says. "All *Lacrosse* the Dance Floor. I want you to go."

He was right. I don't like that task at all.

"All right, what's the problem?" he says impatiently, seeing my reaction. "You should be a pro. Haven't you already been to a bunch of Bar Mitzvah parties?"

"Hardly any," I say. I don't tell him that a dance is a totally hostile environment to begin with. Add to that the fact that I basically torpedoed my friendship with Shirah by leaving her Bat Mitzvah party halfway through. Then there was that thing that happened in the cafeteria today: *Turtle Boy and Big Butt.*

"How do you know even know about the dance?" I ask, changing the subject.

"Because," he says slowly, and with a touch of annoyance in his voice, "when my dad and I left Horicon in sixth grade, it was exactly this time of year, and everyone was amped up about All *Lacrosse* the Dance Floor, and I didn't get to go. We moved to Baraboo, but their dances sucked—nobody went, myself included, and then in high school, I got sick and ended up back here. So *you* can go and tell me everything about it. Like, every little detail. That way, I can know what I've been missing."

"Isn't there something I could just *get* for you?" I ask. "I'm going to have a bunch of Bar Mitzvah money coming. I could get you anything you want."

Then it hits me that RJ might not live until June.

"Okay," I say. "I'll go."

"Yes!" says RJ. He looks truly happy, and that makes me happy. At the same time, I realize that I'm not just agreeing to the dance. I'm agreeing to the whole thing. There is no halfway in this.

RJ's bucket list is now my bucket list.

CHAPTER 37

THE DANCE FLOOR IS LOCATED IN ONE SECTION OF THE gym. Purple and black streamers are taped to the walls, and in every corner, there lurks a giant cluster of balloons. At the center of the room is our giant papier-mâché mascot, Martin the Prairie Marten. A marten is woodlands predator, like a weasel. This marten's eyes are painted so poorly, it looks drunk. The lacrosse team poses for pictures in front of it, sticks in hands. They seem like the happiest people in the gym. I envy them. They're unified around something—lacrosse—even if it's something I think is totally stupid. They fight for one another. I wish I had that.

Along the edges of the gym are bleachers and a couple of tables with punch and snacks. From where I stand in line, I can see Shirah in a clump of friends. I recognize her from behind, green and red lights playing off her wild tangle of curls. I scan the bleachers for Max, but he's nowhere to be seen.

I sip my punch and stand in line for snacks behind a few big eighth graders who are blocking the way. They grab handfuls of chips and head off in opposite directions, revealing the last two people I want to see: Jake and Spencer.

"It's Turtle Boy!" says Jake.

"Gross, there's something in his cup," says Spencer.

I peer down to see what they're talking about. With a flick of his arm, Spencer gives my wrist a powerful pop, which splashes the contents of the cup all over my shirt, face, and glasses.

My instinct is to take a big step back. Fast. Which I do, bumping into someone behind me: one of the big eighth graders.

"Watch it, shrimp," the guy yells, and shoves me toward Spencer. I collide straight into him, soaking him with his own punch.

I turn and bolt through the crowd to the double doors into the hallway. A parent volunteer is ensuring that no one goes past her checkpoint.

"What happened to you?" she chirps, pointing at my shirt. "Little accident?"

"I need to wash this off," I say.

"How about you use the bathroom right here?" she says, pointing to the boys' room.

Before she can say another word, I'm halfway down the hall, nearly running. I need to get away. I need to make a plan—possibly to hide in the sixth-grade wing until the end of the dance. Then I can meet Mom and escape without Spencer stuffing me into a garbage can.

I round the corner and head down the hall, where I use a water fountain to wash my glasses. I dry the lenses on a punch-free section of my shirt and spend another twenty minutes haunting the semidark, deserted hallways. An adult I don't know approaches from the opposite direction: a hall monitor, maybe sent to find me. This forces me back around the corner, closer to the dance.

Up ahead, I see my science teacher, Mr. Firenze, talking with Ms. Kuper. They're just past the boundary that the parent volunteers have set for kids, so they must have come here for a private conversation.

I can hear Mr. Firenze's voice. "This is the absolute worst-case scenario," he says. "When did you find out?"

"Yesterday, end of the day," says Ms. Kuper. "I'm sorry I didn't tell you earlier. I wanted to do it in person."

"Well," he says, "it breaks my heart. The school won't be the same without it."

"Without it?" says Ms. Kuper. "This isn't the end! We have to fight."

"It's pointless to fight," says Mr. Firenze. "Maybe we could negotiate. In exchange for the Back 40, a sum of money for the school. We'd be able to afford all sorts of special programs."

"You're being naive, Mike," Ms. Kuper says. "The school

wouldn't see one cent from that. The county would use the money to buy new parking meters."

They stand there for a moment, looking at each other.

It's obvious that something *bad* has been happening in the Back 40, but from Ms. Kuper's words and tone, it sounds much worse than the temporary inconvenience of a fence.

"Well, you can quit if you want," says Ms. Kuper. "I'm not done fighting."

Suddenly, Jake comes barreling down the hallway, holding a lacrosse stick aloft like an Olympic javelin. Spencer streaks after him.

"Gimme my stick, Jake!" he yells. "Jake! Give it!"

"Or what?" says Jake.

"Or I'll . . ." Spencer suddenly notices Ms. Kuper and Mr. Firenze. "Or I'll walk quickly and apologetically back into the gym."

They turn and start to walk back, but Ms. Kuper calls after them. "Gentlemen, may I speak with you!" She follows them down the hall. Mr. Firenze goes too. I give them a few minutes, to make sure they're not returning, then come out of hiding and return to the dance.

I need to talk to Ms. Kuper.

. . .

More kids have arrived, and the dancing crowd has swelled into a giant, moving herd. It's impossible to see who's here and who isn't. I stand against the wall, feeling alone and upset. And yet, I can't leave, not without knowing more about what Ms. Kuper and Mr. Firenze were talking about.

I finally find Ms. Kuper serving Italian sodas at one of the refreshment tables, along with Mr. Firenze. I won't be able to ask her about the Back 40, not with a long line of kids waiting for their drinks. The person in front of me turns around, cup in hand.

It's Shirah.

"Well, look who's here," she says. I can't tell whether she's happy to see me.

What should I say? Should I apologize for what happened in the cafeteria earlier in the week? Should I ask her if she's having a good time? Should I ask her what's she's drinking?

Idiot, idiot, idiot. I stare down at my shoes.

"Well, I'm not going to stand here while you ignore me," she says, and turns to walk away.

"Wait," I say. "Shirah!"

She turns and glares at me.

"About what happened in the cafeteria . . . ," I say. Instantly, my hands and feet go numb, and my heart begins to pound so hard, it feels like my head is going to explode off my neck.

At that moment, the music changes—from something peppy to a slow song. All around us, the dance floor starts to clear, and couples are forming.

I see this happening. And Shirah sees this happening. I can tell because her eyes widen and she looks from left to right, as if she were crossing a busy street.

I need to get off the dance floor before someone sees me. I start to back away, and Shirah's face flashes with fierce anger.

"Where are you going!" she says, stepping toward me. "It's a slow dance."

"I don't know how," I say.

She puts her cup on the nearest table, steps closer to me, and says, "You are *not* leaving me alone on a slow dance."

She takes my hands and places them on her sides. She puts her hands on my shoulders.

We're dancing.

This is weird.

This is so weird.

She's about six inches taller than I am, and my feet feel like they're cement blocks. My face is burning so hot, it could illuminate the whole gym. What was I so upset about before? I can't remember. I can't remember. I can't think about anything as we sway side to side.

The minute the song ends, there's an awkward moment when Shirah and I are standing much closer than we would normally stand. Kids who were hovering around the edge of the dance floor are returning, filling the space around us. Shirah's volleyball friends and some of the lacrosse players are closing in. I need to get out of here, now, before Jake and Spencer spot me.

Shirah grabs my arm as I walk off. "Where are you going?"

"I'm done dancing," I say. I pull away from her and hurry to the side of the gym. My hands are shaking. I need to sit down. There's an open section of bleachers, and I climb up to the top row. From here, maybe I can keep an eye on Ms. Kuper; catch her when she takes a break.

I notice that the bleachers are vibrating, and the vibrations turn into pounding. Lower down, a few kids look around frantically, get up, and scramble to the floor.

I'm about to follow them when I catch a glimpse of something moving in the shadows underneath the bleachers. Between the steps, I can see it: a face.

"Max?" I say, crouching down. "What are you doing in there?"

"Nothing," he says. "Go away."

The back of his shirt is snagged on a section of the bleacher frame. There's a long drop below him.

"I'm going to get help," I say.

"No!" he says. "I'll be suspended." He wiggles a little

and adds, "No pun intended." He snickers to himself in the darkness.

"You're being ridiculous," I say. "Why would you be suspended?"

"I got in trouble last week for climbing the flagpole. I got my arm brace off, and I was so excited I couldn't help it. Dr. Monk made me sign a 'personal contract' not to climb more stuff."

"Well, let me at least help get your shirt uncaught. It's stuck on that metal thing."

"Get away from me!" he barks.

"Max," I say, "this isn't the time for your parkour-pride crap. Let me help you."

"I don't want your help," he says. "I don't want anything to do with you."

I leave him where he is, cross the gym, and head to the checkpoint with the parent chaperones.

"There's an idiot kid caught underneath the bleachers," I inform them, pointing. "But don't tell him I told you."

CHAPTER 38

RABBI HARRIS AND I ARE ON THE WAY TO THE HOSPITAL from the synagogue. My mood is truly mixed. On the one hand, I've been tormented by what I overheard at the dance—Ms. Kuper made it sound like the Back 40 is in terrible danger. Plus, by the time I found someone to help Max, Ms. Kuper was gone. First thing tomorrow, I need to ask her about it. On the other hand, Rabbi Harris just gave me my first compliment on my Torah chanting. It probably helped that I actually practiced before our lesson. Not because I wanted to, but because I can't stand the face Rabbi Harris makes when he's disappointed.

On top of that, I'm excited to tell RJ about the dance—especially about finding Max caught under the bleachers after the slow dance. He'll think that's hilarious.

"I need to tell you something," Rabbi Harris says abruptly, his tone darkening. "About RJ."

We pull out of the synagogue parking lot and merge with traffic. I swallow hard.

"Shmarya, I always want you to be informed," he says, "about RJ and what's happening with him. Your mom and I have spoken about this several times, and she agrees."

I don't say anything. I nod.

"RJ has an infection in his renal system," Rabbi Harris goes on. "His kidneys. It's something that can happen when people have a suppressed immune system. You're not in any danger, visiting him. But the nurses will give you a gown, mask, gloves, and special booties to keep you from bringing germs into the room."

I nod.

"Also, he's on lots of medications for pain and he might be a little out of sorts."

I nod.

"We should be hopeful that this will clear up, but there is no guarantee."

I nod.

"The infection could spread. It could get much worse. And if it gets worse, the doctors will have to do surgery, and that can lead to complications. We have to be prepared for anything."

I nod.

"Would you like me to go with you?" Rabbi Harris says. "Up to his room?"

I shake my head.

"Okay," he says. "You'll tell me if you change your mind. Hand me an apple pie, would you?"

I open the glove box and pull out the pie. The red and white wrapper crackles loudly as Rabbi Harris splits it open and takes a bite. Not knowing what else to do, I grab a pie and do the same.

...

Roxanne smiles when she sees me and comes around the desk with a paper gown, gloves, and booties. She slips the elastic over my shoes and helps me tie the back of my gown. Lastly, I slide a hair cover, like a shower cap, over my head.

"You can go in," says Roxanne. "He might be sleeping, but I know he's expecting you."

I walk in and RJ is lying back on his pillow. His glasses are off and his eyes are closed. The TV is on. RJ never watches TV.

I sit down on the cake-chair. For the first time in weeks, my phobia about hospitals is returning. For a while, I stopped thinking of this as a hospital. It's just where RJ lives. But with all this sterile equipment and with RJ asleep in front of me, I know exactly where I am. And I remember all the bad things that happen in hospitals.

A few minutes later, RJ stirs. I'm quiet, and he sleeps a while longer. Then he jerks his head up with a start, as if he's heard a loud noise.

"Who's there?" he asks. He sounds scared.

"It's me," I say.

"Will?" he says. "Grab my glasses, would you?"

I stand up and hand him the glasses that sit on the side table. He squints at me in my white gown and puffy hair cover.

"Cool outfit," he says. "You look like a super-nerdy cloud."

I circle over to the shelves, pull the curtain aside, and peer down at the turtle. It seems fine. I reach in, pick it up with a thumb on its shell and my fingers underneath, and look at its eyes. They seem clear. The Medi-Eye is working. The soft spots on its shell, however, are still there.

"His eyes look good," I say.

The turtle starts struggling, so I lay it back in the terrarium.

"So listen, I went to the dance," I say, pulling the curtain back over the shelf.

RJ's face brightens, and I tell him about the layout of the gym: the lights, the balloons, the papier-mâché mascot, the loud music. "Oh, and I slow danced with a girl," I say. I'd considered omitting that part of the story because I wasn't sure if dancing with Shirah even counted.

"Whoa-ho!" says RJ. He sits up a little higher in bed. "Tell me! What was it like? How was it?"

He's gritting his teeth a little. He looks excited to hear

more, but also nervous, as if this were his own moment of truth.

I describe the way it felt to have my hands on Shirah's sides, the unnerving closeness, the strange lack of talking. As I tell him, though, the memory itself feels weird. Like it didn't happen, like it couldn't happen. But it did. It's also weird to have RJ asking so many questions. I can see that he doesn't have a clue about slow dances. But now, somehow, I do. I'll never be someone who's never had a slow dance again. It makes RJ seem a little smaller, and it makes me feel like I don't even know who I am.

"Kind of scary," I say. I need to change the subject. "But now it's over. So what's next on the list?"

I'm hoping for an easy task: maybe a trip to a museum. I could bring him maps and pictures and something from the gift shop.

"You ever been on a roller coaster?" he asks.

I'm afraid of heights. I'm afraid of speed. I don't even like to *look* at roller coasters, but at this point, I know I can't say that to RJ. I take a deep breath and try to calm myself.

"Not yet," I say.

"The scariest one you can find," he commands with a wicked smile. "And I want you to bring me a video of the ride, okay? Make me a roller-coaster movie!"

• • •

We hang out and listen to music for a while, and then RJ wants to see how I'm doing with my drumming. I set up the practice pad, laying it on the seat of the only other chair in the room. I've been excited to show him my progress: the ride, the backbeat, the accents. I've been working on little *r-r-uffs* to make it sound fuller: *dip, dip, dap, b-r-r-uf dip-dap! B'dip, dip, dap, b-r-r-uf dip dap!*

I break into the rock rhythm I've been working on, something I copied from one of the bands he made me listen to. It comes out naturally, and I embellish with *b'dips* and *b'daps* here and there. I speed up and my head bobs, and I'm really flowing with it, and when I look at RJ, hoping to catch an approving eye, I stop.

He's asleep.

His head is on the pillow, and his eyes are closed.

I'm not sad he missed it. But I'm sad he's tired. I'm sad he's sick.

CHAPTER 39

THE NEXT MORNING, I GET ON THE BUS. I NEED TO TALK to Shirah. I'm dying to tell her the news I overheard at the dance about the Back 40, how it's going to be sold. She'll know what to do. Also, I'm terrified to ride a roller coaster alone at the Dane County Fair. Mom said she'll take me this weekend, but she hates roller coasters. These two things together are so overwhelming, they make me want to lock myself in my room for a month, but I know that's not an option. I need Shirah's help again. Unfortunately, she's staring down at her homework, headphones on. Her backpack takes up the rest of the seat. Clearly, she's ignoring me.

"Hey, kid," says the bus driver. "People are trying to get on the bus. Move it!"

Begrudgingly, Shirah pulls her bag closer, just enough that I can squeeze onto the end, but my butt is sort of half on, half off. Kids shove past me to get to their seats.

"Can I ask you for a favor?" I'm about to tell her the

news I learned from Ms. Kuper, but I'm clonked on the head with a passing backpack.

"Ow!" I yell angrily.

"You've got some nerve, coming and asking for favors!" she interjects. "You've been such a jerk lately, Will!"

My hands clamp instinctively around the straps of my own backpack.

"You want me to be your friend when you want something, and then you ditch me when it's convenient. You acted like a child at my Bat Mitzvah, just because there were kids there you didn't like. You haven't stuck up for me, what—*twice* now? At Hebrew school and then with Max and his stupid friends in the cafeteria."

She doesn't know that I did stick up for her. I stuck up for her too much! I told everyone about Max's therapist, and I called Kyle a moron. I'm about to say this, to defend myself, when another backpack knocks me in the head.

"Ow!" I yell again.

"And then at the dance," Shirah continues, "you were *so rude*!"

This catches me by surprise.

"Rude?" I say. "What did I do? How was I rude?"

"Um, you don't remember? After we danced, you just ran off! It was so embarrassing, Will. It looked like you couldn't wait to get away from me!"

"I didn't run off! *You* ran off! You had to go be with

your dumb volleyball friends and those lacrosse butt-heads. Why do you even *like* those guys?"

Shirah takes a deep breath and glares at me. "Do not tell me who I can be friends with."

Bang! I'm knocked in the head by another kid squeezing past.

"Hey!" I yell after him. "Watch it!"

Shirah goes back to her homework. I get up to move toward the rear of the bus. I don't like sitting back there, but I'm not going to sit here and take this abuse. A few rows down, I see Max. His sweatshirt hood is pulled low over his eyes.

I sit alone on the other side of the aisle.

. . .

During my free period, I run to the sixth-grade wing, to Ms. Kuper's bio lab, and find her putting a bunch of tools into a large cardboard box. I'm so glad she's here. I've been aching to talk to her since Saturday night.

"Is the Back 40 being destroyed?" I blurt out. "Is that why it's been fenced off?"

"What?" she says. "Where did you hear that?"

"At the dance," I say. "I heard you and Mr. Firenze talking in the hall."

Ms. Kuper is silent, and then she takes a big breath.

She pulls a chair next to her trademark upholstered stool and offers me my choice of seats. I perch on the edge of the stool.

"There is some concerning news," says Ms. Kuper, looking me in the eye. "The county is in the process of selling the Back 40 to a developer."

She stops. I don't know what she means.

"What do they develop?" I ask.

"Houses," she says.

"Someone wants to build a house in the Back 40?" I ask. I'm picturing the marsh, the pond, the woods, and the meadow interrupted by a house with a white picket fence.

"No, Will," she says. "If they sell the land, the developer would clear the entire Back 40. To put up a whole neighborhood."

"Clear it? Like destroy it!?" I nearly shout. "They can't do that! The Back 40 is ours!"

"Unfortunately, we don't own the Back 40," she says. "You know that."

"But we're *Prairie Marsh* Middle School!" I protest. "Not Houses in the Backyard Middle School. The Back 40 is a major part of the school. That's why our science classes are so great."

"And that's exactly why I'm trying to get the board of supervisors to meet with me," she says. "That's the

211

county government. My goal is to convince them that they shouldn't sell the land because it's essential for our science program."

"Of course it's essential!" I shout.

Ms. Kuper looks at me, arms crossed.

"Will it work?" I ask, trying harder to control myself.

"There's only one way to find out."

CHAPTER 40

ON SATURDAY AFTERNOON, MOM AND I DRIVE THROUGH a large, dusty field, where two teenagers in orange safety vests wave us into a parking space. As we approach the front gate of the fair, the smell of fried food wafts toward us. I wish I could skip the roller coaster and spend my fifteen dollars on a mountain of fried Twinkies and Oreos, pretzels, and my favorite, funnel cake. It might help me forget about the Back 40. Then I turn toward the monstrous white scaffolding just beyond the food stands, where I see roller-coaster cars inching up a track. As they reach the peak, time stops, hands are raised, and then it's all screams as the cars flood down and up and fly into loop-de-loops that leave me dizzy just watching.

"You want to meet back here at four?" Mom asks. "I'm going to get a cream puff."

"Okay," I say, and start to walk away, in the opposite direction of the roller coaster.

"Will!" she calls after me. "Beep?"

I don't answer.

• • •

I put off going on the roller coaster by wandering around the food stands. Maybe I should tell RJ that I rode the roller coaster without actually going on it. Then I remember: the movie. He wants me to take a movie while I'm on the ride. And *that* reminds me I forgot to borrow Mom's phone to take the video.

Idiot, idiot, idiot.

I could search and search and never find Mom in this crowd. I buy fifteen dollars' worth of tickets, and I'm heading for the funnel cake when I hear someone shouting my name.

I turn, and it's Max's mother, Lucy, and his little brother, Mikey, wearing a GoPro camera on his forehead.

"Hi, Will!" Lucy says. "How are you?"

"I'm fine," I say. "I was about to get a funnel cake."

"I hate funnel cake," says Mikey. "You should go on the roller coaster with us."

At that moment, Max walks up to us. "I failed at the rope ladder!" he says to no one in particular. "What kind of *track-ee-ur* am I?"

"Those games are rigged, honey," says Lucy. "No one ever gets to the top."

That's when he notices that I'm standing there with his family.

"Will is going to ride the roller coaster with us," says Mikey.

"Oh, isn't that fun?" says Lucy. "We're all going to ride together! This is going to be Mikey's first ride on a roller coaster, isn't it, Mikey?"

"I'm a member of ACE!" Mikey says. "You heard of them? American Coaster Enthusiasts. I even have a card!" He pulls out a Spider-Man wallet, rips open the Velcro, pulls out a laminated card, and shoves it in my face.

"See! Novice rider! I've never been on a coaster, but I designed a track with a four-point-nine-star rating on the ACE website, and it's been ridden about maybe five hundred times!"

"No one cares, Mikey," says Max.

"Max," scolds his mother.

"This coaster here doesn't even figure on ACE's database," Mikey goes on. "It's way too puny."

Maybe, but when the cars crest the first big hill and zoom down, the passengers' screams are very real, and the way the cars twist along the main track makes me queasy.

There's no point in going on the roller coaster if I don't have a camera. Of course, it occurs to me—*Max has a phone*. He could make a video of the ride. The fact that he refuses to talk to me makes this a problem.

We stand and wait for a long, long time. Finally, we're close enough to the ride that we're being corralled like cows through a series of ropes.

"Oh no!" says Mikey. We all turn to see what he's looking at.

It's a painted cutout of a pirate, and it's holding a cutlass, on which is written in red letters: *Ye must be this tall to ride, matey.*

Mikey runs and stands under the cutlass—there's at least a handsbreadth gap between the top of his head and the sword. He arches his back and cranes his neck, but it's hopeless. He's way too short.

"But the website said eight years old!" he wails.

"Eight years and at least that tall!" says Max. "I *told* you!"

"How am I going to level up on the ACE website if I don't post a video?" He looks like he's going to cry. "Evil county fair! I'm gonna sue you!"

"I have an idea," Lucy says in a voice so chipper it hurts my ears. "I'm going to take Mikey to get a cream puff. Mikey, give Max your GoPro. He'll make your video. We'll all meet up in half an hour."

Lucy pulls Mikey, who's still whining, away, leaving Max and me standing in line in awkward silence, the camera perched on Max's forehead. But if Max won't talk to me, he certainly won't share the video with me.

"You ratted me out at the dance!" he finally mutters. "Do you know how much trouble I got in?"

That makes me fume with anger. I only ratted him out so he wouldn't hurt himself falling from the bleachers. I should have left him there. One day the janitor would've found nothing but his bones.

It's a long line, and Max is clearly agitated, shifting from side to side and flapping his arms, something he does when he's upset. Meanwhile, I'm getting more and more nervous as we get closer and closer to the front of the line. Soon it's our turn. I climb into the car, next to Max. We lower a safety bar onto our laps, and I'm thinking, *I can't do this. Maybe it's not too late to escape.*

A guy with long hair runs down the train of cars and checks our safety bars, and then before I know it, Max starts screaming, "HEY, I HAVE TO GET OUT! LEMME OUT!"

The guy with long hair turns around and comes back to the car.

"What's the matter?" he asks.

"I'd like to get out," Max says. "I need to get out."

There's a click, and the safety bars rise. I put my arm in front of Max to block him.

"Don't go, Max," I say, gripping the safety bar and pulling it back down. If Max leaves, he takes the GoPro with him. No camera, no video, no bucket list.

"Let go," Max says. "Will, let go!"

"Come *on,* you two!" shouts the long-haired guy. "People are waiting!"

Max's eyes are rimmed with white. He looks terrified. I tug gently on his arm, and he sits down.

The tracks under us clang a few times, and the cars move forward with a lurch. Max and I both jerk from the motion and from our hair-trigger nerves. We can hear everyone chattering excitedly.

"I thought you did this all the time," I say through clenched teeth as we climb higher and higher.

"Mikey thinks I do," he says. "I tried once with Mom, but I got scared, and we got off before the ride started."

Now my heart is pounding hard—really hard—and I'm feeling dizzy.

"Don't look down," he says, and instantly I do. The ground is not only a million miles away, but also it's bouncing around as if my eyeballs are yo-yos.

"Oh God," I say. "Oh God. Oh God."

Max is silent, frozen.

"Will," he says through gritted teeth. "I'm sorry; I'm really sorry about how I've been lately."

"What?" I say.

"That joke I made in Hebrew school," he says, almost in tears. "About Shirah, that joke I told. And making fun of you in the cafeteria. My therapist said I should talk to you about it."

"I don't think he meant on a roller coaster," I say. "Maybe we could talk about this later?"

"If we make it through this, I want to be friends again," he says. "You're my best friend."

"Okay," I say. "Fine. I forgive you. And I'm sorry too. Now can you leave me alone so I can panic in peace?"

We're near the top of the hill and I can see the track starting to level out.

"It's cool about you and Shirah," Max says. "Going out or whatever." Despite his own warning, he looks down, over the edge of the car. "Oh my God, we're high up."

"What are you even talking about?" I ask. "Shirah and I aren't going out."

"You're not?" he asks. "You went to that concert together! And I *saw* you slow dance!"

"It didn't mean anything," I say. "Why do you even care?"

"Well," says Max. "The thing is . . ."

For a moment, everyone in the cars gets quiet. The wind is blowing, whistling through my ears. My heart pounds, and everything is huge and bright. Then the cars tip forward, we're picking up speed, and as we're hurtling through space, Max screams one last thing: *"I like Shiraaaaaaaah!"*

We're falling, we're flying, we're tumbling—all my organs plunge into my feet, and my lungs are being crushed, and the world is rocking and shaking, and I'm clenching my jaw and holding my breath. We zoom over a bump, which rocks us off our seat, and then we hit a twist so sharp, we're thrown to the left and then the right. Max and I squish against each other, like wet clothes spinning in a dryer.

There's a series of curves, and I think maybe I'm getting the hang of this, maybe I'm not going to die, but then we rocket up, float, and plunge down a spiral, as if we're going down a drain and falling through the center of the earth.

Suddenly, we're on a straightaway, slowing past a bunch of people and parked roller-coaster cars, and like *that,* it's over. We crawl to a stop.

It's so weird how something so big and so scary and so overwhelming can just end. And how everything goes back to normal.

There's a buzzer, and the safety bar flies up.

I turn to Max. "We did it!" I yell. "We did it! We didn't die."

That's when I realize that Max isn't okay; he's holding really still, and there are tears and snot all over his face. I help him out of the car. He's shaking and his color is weird, almost green, and as we walk past the line, we pass a trash can, and he turns away from me, leans over it, and pukes.

While Max heaves, I review the events of the last minutes in my mind: the flying, the falling, the floating. I'm so relieved it's over. It was horrible, and I never want to do it again, but it doesn't matter because I did it. I can cross it off my list. Well, RJ's list. Which is now my list.

Once he's done, Max stands up, still wobbling. He's a mess. Totally gross.

"Wait here," I say. I run to a lemonade stand. A bunch of people are lined up, but I cut straight to the front, where a man with a trucker cap and a giant belly is about to order.

"My friend just barfed," I say urgently to the teenager behind the counter. "Can I please have a small lemonade and some napkins?"

"On the house," he says as I try to give him my tickets. He hands me a cup of lemonade and points to the napkin dispenser. I take five or six and run back to Max.

"Sip this," I say. "Rinse your mouth."

He takes a sip, spits into the trash can, repeats this a few times, and follows me obediently to a bench where we sit.

"You still dizzy?" I ask. "Put your head between your knees."

He does so, and he's saying something. I can't hear him, though.

I put my head between my own knees so I can hear him.

"What?" I ask. "Max, what are you saying?"

"That was awesome," he whispers.

"*What?*" I say again, certain I misheard.

"That was AWESOME," he repeats, louder. "AWE-SOME!"

I can't believe I'm hearing this. If I'd just puked in a trash can, I'd be feeling sorry for myself. Max has this ridiculous ability to bounce back from anything. He jumps to his feet and points back at the roller coaster.

"Why'd I wait so long to try that?" he says. "I can't wait to show Mikey the video!"

Then I remember what Max called out at the top of the hill.

"Max," I say. "Up there, did you say . . . you like Shirah? As in *like her* like her?"

"Oh my God," he says. He grabs both of my wrists. "I said that out loud? Will, you can't tell anyone!"

"Okay, let go of me," I say, prying one hand loose. "Let go."

"PLEASE," he says, taking a step away, then covering his mouth with his palms. He's hysterical.

"Calm down. I'm not telling anyone," I say.

Suddenly, it's so obvious, I can't believe I didn't put it together.

"How did you know about the slow dance, anyway?" I ask him. "Is that why you were hiding in the bleachers?"

Max covers his face with his hands.

"Max, that's creepy," I say.

"For your information, I wasn't spying," he says. "I

was going to ask her to dance, but then you did first, and I climbed into the bleachers to get away."

That same strange feeling I had after dancing with Shirah is back. I've known her for a long time, and Max for a year now, and yet I don't know who either of them is. Or maybe I do know them . . . maybe I don't know who *I* am.

"Why don't you tell her how you feel?" I ask.

"Because she hates me," he repeats.

"You did humiliate her in front of the whole Hebrew class and wouldn't apologize," I say.

"It was just a joke," he says, looking down at his shoes. "Sometimes I say stuff without thinking. I can't help it."

"Well, learn to help it," I say. "Apologize to her and hope for the best. Now let's hurry and get a funnel cake. I've been waiting all day for one."

I'm supposed to meet Mom in ten minutes. I'm hurrying and looking at my watch, and as I arrive at the delicious-smelling booth, I see that Max isn't with me any longer. He's in front of a game where people are climbing up wobbly spinning rope ladders. He's pulling tickets out of his pocket and shoving them into the game operator's hands.

"He's back!" says the operator into his microphone. "A crowd favorite has returned to test his skill!"

"Look at how he climbs," says one kid, watching Max creep up the ladder, his body low like a lizard. "What a goof."

I flush and tremble with rage. It feels like my body isn't under control. My hands rise, ready to shove the kid, but then I freeze—I hear Max yelling, wailing. He's spun on his ladder. He hangs for a moment before dropping down to the bouncy cushion.

"I'm out of tickets," he says, walking between me and the kid. "Let's go."

I feel myself return to my senses. On the one hand, I don't really think Shirah wants a giant panda from Max. On the other hand, I can see that Max is incredibly disappointed in himself, and I feel bad for him.

"Here," I say, pulling out my tickets.

"But those are for your funnel cake," he says.

"Take them," I say. "Go win the panda."

He goes back to the game operator, hands over my tickets, and begins the climb—inch by inch, left hand, right foot, slithering up the ladder. Unlike last time, he never stops the slow and steady motion upward.

"Go, Max!" I yell.

There's a loud bell, and a voice booms over the loudspeaker: "We have a winner!"

Max is standing on the platform, waving at me with both hands.

"Go, Max!" I call, waving back. "Whoo-hoooooo!"

CHAPTER 41

It's Sunday, and Rabbi Harris and I are on our way to the hospital. As we drive along, I chant my Torah portion.

"Good," he says, somewhat absently.

To see if he's listening, I purposely mess up a word, and his hand flies up, stopping me.

"*Re'ach ni-cho-ach,*" he sings, correcting me. He gives me an odd little half smile.

Between my feet, inside my backpack, is a digital projector. It was Max's idea. I asked him to send me the video he made on the roller coaster, and once I told him who it was for and why, he was adamant: *showing a movie of a roller coaster on a laptop won't cut it.* He begged his mom to lend me her projector, and he brought it over himself.

I say goodbye to Rabbi Harris in the hospital atrium, and when I get to the nurses' station on RJ's floor, Roxanne greets me and helps me into my sterile gown, booties, and head cover.

I enter RJ's room. He's lying on his back with his glasses off and his eyes closed. He lifts his head and looks in my direction, but I can see that his eyes aren't focusing on me.

"Who's there?" he asks.

"Hey, RJ," I say. "It's Will."

"Oh, hey," he says. He shifts a little, trying to sit up. "Can you raise the bed?" He nods toward the remote.

I grab it and press the rocker switch up. "How's it going?" I ask.

He shrugs. He doesn't know that we're about to cross something exciting off his bucket list.

"I have a surprise for you," I say. "You're about to go on a roller coaster."

He watches as I stand on the cake-chair and hang a sheet from the ceiling with a few long pieces of duct tape, then drape it down by the foot of the bed, securing it with more tape. Then I set the projector on the shelf above RJ's head, carefully moving the cord over the photos taped to the wall, and I close the blinds.

"Are you ready?" I ask.

I hit play, and there they are: the roller-coaster tracks. They're big. The camera pans to the right, to the people standing in line, and then to me.

My huge head.

My turtle face.

"We're going on a roller coaster!" says RJ. "We're going on a roller coaster! Who's holding the camera?"

"My friend Max," I say.

There's a loud buzzer, and the car starts moving.

RJ leans toward the screen. His mouth is open, and he looks a little bit excited, a little bit afraid.

I can hear tinny voices chattering through RJ's headphones. The car is climbing the first big hill, and I can see RJ is gripping the blanket with his bony hands. His wrists are even thinner than I remember, and the IV tube bobs against his arm as he squeezes. I notice that the bracelets—his knotted string bracelets—on that wrist are gone; maybe to keep the IV from getting tangled. He's still got some on his other wrist, though, and he's still wearing his shell necklace.

On the sheet, I can see the beautiful blue sky, and the clouds, and for a moment, the camera turns and picks up a view of the whole county fair: crowds of people, big buildings where the prize cows are, the carnival games—everything. And then it's back to the tracks as the car inches forward, begins its descent, and starts to zoom.

RJ lets out a little yelp as we plummet down the first hill, and then, as the car veers left, he leans right; when the car veers right, he leans left. He's completely transfixed, *in* the car, riding the roller coaster. His teeth are clenched. As the car dives into a tight curve, he even squints against imaginary g-forces. He rumbles along the straightaway, his head bobbing. And when the car slows and comes to its end, he jerks forward, as if anticipating the sudden stop.

The video ends, and we get a blank screen with a re-play arrow.

He flips off his headphones.

"That was incredible," he says. His voice is hoarse and quiet. "I rode a roller coaster!"

"You liked it?" I ask.

"I loved it!"

"Did I do you a solid?"

"Yes!" he says. He has a huge, beautiful grin. "You did me a solid."

"Oh, good," I say. I'm playing it cool, but inside, I'm whirling; I'm dancing, I'm so happy.

"Want to see it again?" I ask.

We spend the rest of the hour watching it over and over and over, screaming and leaning into the turns. It's insanely fun, but eventually, it's time for me to go.

"Will, I have something I want to give you," he says, pointing across the room.

On the shelf there's a metal thing with a felt mallet sticking out of it. The metal is stamped with a big, bold logo: *Slingerland*.

"My drum pedal," says RJ. "From my vintage set. I want you to add it to your rhythm. When you play *boom-boom, pack!* you strike it on the *boom-boom*. You're better than you think you are. You'll figure it out."

I look at it closely. Scratched into the metal, near the logo, are the letters: *RJ*. Is he giving me his drum pedal?

"No, no," I say. "I can't take this."

"Yes, you can," he says. "You gave me a turtle; I'm giving you a bass drum pedal. Now we're even. But you can't let it gather dust under your bed. You need to play with it. Learn how to use it."

I put it in my backpack. I wish it were not coming home with me. I wish it was staying with RJ. I wish he could play his own drum set. I wish things weren't the way they are.

But if he needs to give it away, I'm glad I can give it a good home.

"What's next on the bucket list?" I ask.

"Uh . . . what's the date?" he asks. "I'm so out of it."

I look at my watch and tell him.

"Okay, so it's not quite time for the next task," he says with a sly smile. "For now, use your practice pad. A lot."

CHAPTER 42

After school, I'm heading for the bus when Max comes running after me, his arms gyrating like propellers.

"Wait!" he says. "Stop! We have an emergency!"

I can't imagine what Max's idea of an emergency consists of.

"I'm in Spanish class with Dena and Shirah," he explains, panting. "Last period. They were talking about tonight's volleyball game. Shirah said she isn't going to have anyone there to root her on because her little sister's in the school play and the game's in Waupun."

"So what's the emergency?" I ask.

"Duh," says Max. "Shirah won't have any fans there! What do we do?"

"You want to go?" I ask. I've never been to a volleyball game, but I guess we could go. I wonder: Would Shirah even want us there?

"How do we get to Waupun?" asks Max.

"You take the Martens Express. I've gone through Waupun on the way to Madison."

"So, we could just . . . take the bus?" he asks.

A month ago, that would have seemed like an impossible ordeal. Now, I know it's just a bunch of steps from Horicon to Waupun. You only have to take them one at a time.

• • •

The game is already in play. It's crowded and noisy in the bleachers.

"I thought there weren't going to be any fans here," I remark.

"These are the other team's fans," Max says. "Our side is over there."

We go and sit among a handful of parents and a few siblings wearing purple and black: Prairie Marsh's school colors.

"How's Shirah playing?" asks Max.

"Sucky," says a girl about nine years old. "She's shanking all her serves."

"We're only down by seven points," I say, noticing that the scoreboard says it's 9 to 16.

"We've already lost a game," explains the girl. "And it's best out of five games, so we're probably toast."

The gym is loud, but it's mainly due to the cries of

the other team's fans: the Waupun Wildcats. Waupun Middle School is much bigger than Prairie Marsh. Even if you didn't know that, you'd know from looking at their volleyball team. Every girl on the team is built like a giraffe. On top of that, they're really good. The girl next to me explains what's going on. I watch how the Wildcats play together as a unit. Each time the ball is on their side, the players bump and set it into place for someone in the front row to spike over the net.

This goes on for a while, the other team racking up points. It looks like we don't have the defense to keep the ball off the ground.

Finally, it's Shirah's turn to serve. She dribbles the ball twice, lofts it, raises a fist, and slams it straight into the net. Shirah's teammates give her a low five, and play continues as if nothing bad has happened. If that had been me, I would have walked off the court, humiliated.

The other team returns to their fantastic teamwork, and soon the game is over. If the Martens don't win the next match, they lose the whole set.

Unfortunately, it begins like the last one ended: the Waupun Wildcats shoot way ahead. Their players seem to read one another's minds, lofting the ball into the sweet spot to let the next player drive it back over the net.

Now it's 8 to 3, and the Martens are falling further and further behind.

"Dude," says Max, panicking. "If they're going to get killed, maybe we shouldn't be here. Maybe Shirah wouldn't want us to see her team lose. Maybe we should go."

If I played badly in a game, I wouldn't want anyone I know to see. Then again, I don't want anyone to see me do anything. Maybe Shirah's different. Something tells me leaving now is a bad idea. I have a bad history with leaving things early.

"I think we need to stick it out," I say to Max.

The Wildcats climb nearly ten points before it's the Martens' turn to serve, and the other team blocks it with ease. Meanwhile, there's a player on the other side, the tallest on the entire court, and when she spikes the ball, she smashes it with such force, no one can stop it. They score again and again with this play.

The whistle blows. The Wildcats huddle up on the other side of the net, and the Martens gather around their coach.

I see Shirah nod, then nod again. She seems to be remembering something important. Then the team breaks with all hands in the center and a cry of "Go Purple Martens!"

Shirah is in the front row now, and the Wildcats' tallest player is facing her. They look each other in the eye, neither one looking away, a blank expression on their faces. It makes me wince to see it; I don't like confrontations, but Shirah holds the other girl's gaze until the loud pop of the serve moves all the players into action.

The ball flies over the net, and the Wildcats bump it up, setting it in place. The tall girl opposite Shirah charges for the spike, and then I see something I never expected: Shirah jumps and pushes the ball, stuffing it straight into the other player's face. The ball hits the ground on the Wildcats side, and the whistle blows.

This goes on for a while, the Martens catching up point by point, though the next time the tall girl and Shirah face off, Shirah can't stop the spike and we lose the rally.

The other team earns another few points, and now it's Shirah's turn to serve.

This time, instead of bouncing the ball and immediately serving, I see her close her eyes for a second. She quickly kisses her fist, lofts the ball, and slams it. It rockets to the other side, the Wildcats miss the return, and the Martens earn a point.

The small Martens cheering section makes a lot of noise, but we get silent when Shirah serves again. This time she's unstoppable. Serve after serve either hits the floor or, when a player digs for it, careens crazily out of bounds. Shirah racks up more than ten points this way, and though her rally doesn't last forever, it turns the tide. The game ends with a win for the Martens.

The fourth game starts, and it begins with the Martens out in front, but the Wildcats catch up. Then the same thing happens. Shirah is in the front row; she and the tall girl face off, but Shirah is an impenetrable wall.

I feel something crushing my arm, and I look down to see it's Max.

"Dude," I say. "Relax. Let go."

"Did you know she could play like that?" he says quietly, as if enchanted. "I had no idea she was so good."

"I've never seen her play," I say. The second I say those words, it sounds absurd. How is it that in all the years Shirah has been playing volleyball, I've never once come to a match?

Soon it's Shirah's turn to serve again. Shirah closes her eyes, kisses her fist, bounces the ball, lofts it into the air, and raises her arm back as if she were going to chop a tree—the ball rockets to the other side, and the Wildcats miss the return. Another point.

"Oh my God," says Max. "That's incredible. Go, Shirah!"

She sends five more of these unstoppable serves over the line, but the sixth goes out of bounds. We've caught up to the Wildcats and stopped their momentum. This game goes much more slowly, each side inching closer and closer to twenty-five. A few more rallies go by before it's Shirah's turn, and again, she closes her eyes, kisses her hand, and blasts the ball into the other side. A player on the other team bumps it, but it rockets out of bounds, straight at my eyes.

BLAM!

Pain shoots up my nose, and I see stars. My glasses are knocked clean from my face. I'm stunned, and I feel something warm and wet welling up in my nostrils.

"Holy crap," says Max. "You're gushing blood. I think you need a tourniquet."

There is a minor commotion around me. Adult faces, contradicting advice: *Tip his head forward! Tip his head back!* A coach with a whistle and a white first-aid kit, some gauze, an ice pack.

Then I see Shirah looking at me from her spot on the court. I'm pinching my nose as I was instructed, and the ice pack blocks my eyes, but I can see her face. With my free hand, I wave. Shirah doesn't respond. Her expression is blank.

I hear an adult yell, "Yo, let's go! We gotta finish this game!"

With my head back, I can hear but can't see most of what happens next. There's silence; the hollow thump of the ball. The other team cheers and then more silence. The pop of the ball, and the Purple Martens' fans cheer. Max cheers the loudest: "Go, Purple Martians! Go Shirah!"

I turn to Max. "What are you saying?" I ask.

"'Go, Purple Martians,'" he says.

"You know that our mascot is a *marten*," I say. "It's like a weasel. Not a *Martian*."

"Oh," he says. "I always thought a purple Martian was a weird mascot."

Then the entire gym drops into silence.

"Dude," Max hisses. "This is it. Game point. Shirah's serve."

I twist my head to see as Shirah, again, closes her eyes and kisses her fist. I feel a surge of inexplicable energy inside me. I want her to win. I want her to win so badly that for a moment, I don't exist. There's just Shirah and the ball—the ball that is now midair, and her fist that flies at the speed of light. The thing that streaks across the net is no ball—it's the full force of Shirah's will. The ball hits the ground before the other team can even move.

The Purple Martens cheer, and the players form a circle around Shirah. Her blank expression melts, and I see her take a big breath, but that's all. No huge smile. No laughter. No fists in the air. It's the same face I saw her make as she finished her Bat Mitzvah speech. It's the face of someone who knows she's done her best.

• • •

While the team climbs into a van, Shirah comes over to where Max and I are standing. Max is trying to balance-beam along a chest-high brick wall, and I've been replaying Shirah's rallying moment in my head: the fist, the kiss, the blast of power.

"Can I talk to you?" she says to me. She grabs my arm and pulls me away from Max. "Why did you bring him?" I can hear the contempt in her voice. She looks irritated, and she's breathing hard.

"I didn't bring him," I say. "It was his idea to come. He didn't want you to be alone at the game."

She opens her mouth, as if to add another harsh comment, but instead, her expression softens. She glances over at Max where he's walking heel to toe on the back of a bench.

"He wanted to see me play?" she asks. "Really?" She seems to consider this for a second. Then she turns to get in the van.

"Wait," I say, and she stops. "Why do you close your eyes and kiss your fist before you serve?"

"Why do you want to know?" she asks, climbing in the van's front passenger seat. "Why do you even care?"

How can I explain that she inspired me? How can I tell her that I wish I had power like hers? How do I say that I wish we could go back to the way things used to be? I can't, so I say nothing.

"It's private," she says, and shuts the door.

CHAPTER 43

THE LEAVES HAVE STARTED CHANGING. THE BACK 40 IS no longer a wide wash of green. The final flowers of autumn, waving like stubborn flags, and the droning chirrup of crickets in the thicket are signs of life all around. And yet, there's a feeling in the air: everything knows that the cold is coming. I wonder if this is the last winter in the Back 40. Next year, will this be a bunch of houses? Lawns? Driveways?

The excavator Max was climbing on back in September has been joined by a bulldozer and a backhoe. There's a giant mound of dirt, beginning on the other side of the fence, leading to a squat row of trailers. There's also a scattering of garbage: soda cans and Dorito wrappers, a few cigarette butts.

I head down to the pond, the pond where I failed RJ. I look down into the brown water. Standing here, I'm hit by a cold breeze, and the leaves rustle around me.

The turning of the seasons brings a memory—not to my mind, but to my body. I can actually *feel* it.

I'm a little kid. I'm walking in the woods with Dad. Maybe right here, right here in the Back 40. Leaves on the ground. Cold hands, cold nose. Now I'm up high, bouncing along on Dad's shoulders.

That's it—as fast as it comes, the memory is gone.

I bike home as fast as I can. Mom is watching TV.

"Hey, honey," she says. "Dinner's in half an hour. Where are you coming from?"

"When I was little," I gasp, breathless, "did Dad ever take me to the Back 40?"

"The Back 40?" she says, confused. She changes the channel on the TV and then changes it again. "He died before we moved here, Will. You know that."

"I had this memory of being on Dad's shoulders. I'm sure it was right there in the Back 40," I explain.

"Memory can be funny like that," she says. She turns away from me and rubs the back of her hand over her eyes. When we talk about Dad, Mom sometimes cries a little. It makes me feel bad for bringing him up.

"Okay," she says, getting to her feet. "Enough of that."

"Why do you always change the subject when I talk about Dad?" I ask.

"I don't change the subject."

"Yes, you do. I say the word 'Dad,' and you're off to get

ice cream. You said we're having dinner in thirty minutes! I think you don't want me to know about him!"

"Will!" she shouts, one hand raised, as if to block a punch, eyes squinted and brows furrowed. Then she closes her eyes and takes a deep breath.

"We lost your father," she says. "And we miss him. But we have to move forward in life. We can't spend it looking backward. I know I'm not a perfect mom, but I've been on my own for eight years now, and this is the only way I can manage."

Before I can say another word, she turns and goes into the kitchen. She leaves an absolute silence, a silence so repelling, it pushes me upstairs and into my room. I shut the door as quietly as I can.

CHAPTER 44

ON THE DRIVE TO THE HOSPITAL, RABBI HARRIS TELLS me that I'll need to wear the booties, a sterile gown, and head cover again.

"And I need to give you the update on RJ's condition," he says.

I nod.

He explains that the infection has caused swelling in his abdomen. It's putting pressure on RJ's organs. He's on medication, but he's in a fair amount of pain. Later in the week, he's going to have an operation to reduce the swelling.

I open Rabbi Harris's glove box, and I pull out two fruit pies. I hand one to him and open one for myself.

"If he's in pain," I say, "are you sure he wants me to visit?"

Rabbi Harris turns and flashes me a kind, sad smile.

"The day before you come to visit," says Rabbi Harris, "he perks up. And for days afterward, he has more life in him. I don't know what you guys do when you visit, or what you're talking about, but whatever it is, it makes a big difference. He's much happier because of you."

On some level, I already knew this, but hearing Rabbi Harris say it out loud makes me want to cry. I take a huge bite of lemon pie, barely chew, and swallow hard. The bucket list is no longer only a promise I've made to RJ. It's a promise I'm making to myself.

I resolve to do the next task without a word of complaint.

. . .

"Talent show?" I say. "No. No way. Please. I don't have any talent."

"Yes!" RJ says excitedly. *"Halloween Spooktacular!* This coming Saturday night! I saw it on the school website. All you have to do is put your name on the list, find a costume, and get onstage! You've been practicing, right?"

"Yes," I say. "But—"

"Look, man," RJ interrupts "I'm a drummer, and I've never played for a live audience. I really want to know what it's like to be onstage. Where my music really counts."

RJ has the blankets pulled up close to his neck, and despite the fire in his voice, he looks frail and weak, and the veins in his neck bulge when he talks.

"I've been onstage before," I say. "We had a school musical in fifth grade. I can tell you all about it."

In reality, Mom wrote a note to excuse me from participating, but I could probably come up with a convincing story.

"Stop trying to get out of it," says RJ. "You've already used your free pass since you basically refuse to go swimming."

I look away from him and sigh. On the one hand, he's right. There's no way out of this. On the other hand, people looking at me—especially a big crowd . . . That's the scariest thing I can imagine. That's even scarier than swimming in a murky pond. I sit there in silence.

"I don't have drums," I say. "All I have is the practice pad, and that won't sound good."

"Go lift up the towels off that box," he says, pointing to the corner.

I go over to a large cardboard box in the corner, near the turtle, and lift a couple of folded white towels. Underneath is a crumpled red bow.

"Sorry about the crappy wrapping job," he says.

I have a very bad feeling about this. I open the box's flap, and the second I see inside, I am filled with incredible excitement and sadness, all mixed together.

It's RJ's drum set. Pots, pans, clipboards—everything.

"No, no," I say. "No, no, no, no."

"Yes!" says RJ. "I don't play them anymore. You have to take them."

"Why wouldn't you play them?" I demand.

"I can't really grip the sticks," he explains. "The circulation in my hands is so bad, my fingers are numb. I don't want to play like that; I'd rather not play at all."

"You told me that drums are the only way you can escape this place," I say. "You need the drums to escape."

"No, I don't," he says. "Now I have something better."

"What?" I say. "What's better than drums?"

"In the past month," RJ says slowly, "let's see"—he counts on his fingers—"I finally got my own pet, I've gone to see Dog Complex, I've been to a school dance—I even got a slow dance—I went on the biggest roller coaster in Wisconsin, and I got a pair of sticks from my favorite drummer."

He points above his head, where the sticks lie on a shelf.

"Believe me," he says. "Every time we check something off the bucket list, I can see it. I can feel it. It belongs to me. I'd rather have *that* than a bunch of dented pots and pans."

There's nothing I can say to this.

"I'll do it," I say. "It's just . . . I hate people looking at me."

"I know," says RJ. "Here."

He pulls a frilly green-and-silver mask out from under his pillow.

"It's from Mrs. Barnes. I traded it for a giant bag of Funyuns. I had a feeling it would come in useful."

It's Manzilla—the wrestler Mrs. Barnes and I cheered on during my second visit to RJ. That feels like a million years ago.

"Wear it," he says. "And put together a drum solo and beat the crap out of those pots and pans and come back and tell me about it."

"What if I'm not good enough?" I say quietly.

"You don't have to do it perfectly," he says. "You just have to do it."

CHAPTER 45

WHEN I GET HOME, I PULL RJ'S BASS DRUM PEDAL OUT from under my bed. It has a thin layer of dust on it. I've been using the practice pad, but I haven't touched the pedal since he gave it to me.

I detach the mallet from the pedal housing. If RJ can make drums out of pots and pans, I can make a bass drum out of . . . *something*. I'll know it when I hear it. I move around my room, knocking the mallet against random objects: boxes full of books and a Tupperware bin full of terrarium parts. They sound dead—no resonance, no vibration, no *thump*.

Mom's room has nothing to offer: just her clothes, neatly hanging on the bar, and her shoes, side by side in a shoe organizer. Desperate, I even check the garage; maybe there's something solid but hollow sitting out there.

Nothing.

I stand at the door to the basement. I don't like to go

down there—It's dark and cobwebby and creepy—but I have no choice. It smells of mildew and mold, and I can feel my allergies flaring in the back of my throat. I walk around, hammering the mallet on whatever I can find. *Bap-bap. Bip-bip. Bup-bup.* Nothing sounds right. I try the box that an air conditioner came in: *boom-boom.* It sounds good, but it's way too big. A metal filing cabinet: *bang-bang.* Wrong sound. There's a box that says PASS-OVER. Inside, I find some pie dishes, a Bundt pan, and a serving tray.

The serving tray could be useful as a platform for all of RJ's metal pots and pans, but still, I need a thumpy bass drum. I continue to rummage as my allergies get worse and worse, my throat tightening and my eyes watering. Maybe I won't have a bass drum.

I'm about to head back upstairs when I notice an old hard-shell suitcase, light blue with white trim. It looks like an antique. It doesn't even have wheels, just a handle. I knock on it with the mallet, and it's just the right bounce. It's got two metal latches.

Pop-pop.

It's full of random junk: a dry-cleaning ticket, a pine cone, a very beat-up baseball hat, a menu from a Chinese restaurant. I look around for somewhere to dump the contents. There's an old wicker laundry hamper. I empty the suitcase, close it, and give it a few quick raps with the mallet.

Bump-bump-bump.

Perfect.

I grab the suitcase, along with a roll of silver duct tape from the kitchen closet, and bring it all up to my room.

There, I strap the board to the suitcase with a couple of leather belts. I arrange the pots and pans, copying RJ's setup, and with long strips of duct tape, I attach everything to the serving tray. I place the drum pedal in front of the suitcase, propping it in place with a plastic box that once contained frozen feed grubs for my turtles. I sit down and pick up the sticks.

I begin with a simple rhythm on the clipboard, and I hear RJ's voice in my head: *You can't play it if you can't say it.*

Left, right, left, right. Left, right, left, right. Left, right, left, right. Left, right, left, right.

It's a crisp, dry sound; the pace of marching feet. Now I double my speed, repeating in my head:

I can do it I can do it I can do it I can do it I can do it I can do it

It's the chugging of a train engine. I play this for a while, and then I wonder: Could I double the speed again? Is that even a thing? Twice as fast? I loosen my grip on the sticks and lean forward, furrowing my brow in concentration, and I count off in my head: *one, two, here we go!*

Lemme at 'em Lemme at 'em Lemme at 'em Lemme at

'em Lemme at 'em Lemme at 'em Lemme at 'em Lemme at 'em Lemme at 'em Lemme at 'em Lemme at 'em

It's the buzz of a hornet. I add the bass drum, and additional fills and ruffs and accents.

I practice most of the night and after school the next day. I begin wearing the mask so I can get accustomed to playing without glasses. My hands and wrists and back are sore. The sun has set and my room is dark, but I haven't stopped. My arms and legs are moving, flapping, flying independently, and just as I start to feel like I'm lifting clean off the ground, propelled on wings of sound and rhythm, I make the stupidest of all mistakes. I look down.

What if everyone gets bored? What if people yell for me to get off the stage? What if Jake and Spencer start the Turtle Boy chant?

I stop playing. This was a terrible idea.

I want to erase my name from the talent show list tomorrow, before it's too late.

The smell of nut loaf wafts under my bedroom door. I hear Mom calling me for dinner. I slump down over my pots and pans. I can't eat. I can't get up.

A few minutes later, there's a knock on the door.

"Will?" says Mom. "I've been calling you for dinner. Why are you sitting in here in the dark? And what's on your face?"

"It's a mask," I say, pulling it off and replacing it with

my glasses. "It's for the talent show. *If* I play in the talent show."

"Talent show?" she says. "Absolutely, Will! You should—you sound amazing! I'm so impressed! I think you should lose the mask, though. Put together a costume that won't cover your face."

"No," I say. "If I do this, I want the mask."

"Ooh, and I could help," she says, excited. "Remember when we made that adorable news reporter and newspaper costume? You were *such* a cute little newspaper."

"Mom!" I say. "You're not *listening*! The exact point is to cover my face."

She looks at me sadly. "Oh, Will . . . Why would you want to cover your face? You have a beautiful face."

"Yeah?" I demand. "Then why do I need surgery to fix it?"

"You know why," she says, as if it's obvious, as if we've discussed it a million times. "So you won't have problems breathing when you sleep."

I shake my head. "No, that's why *the doctors* want me to do it," I say. "But that's not the real problem. The real problem is I look like a turtle."

"Don't say that, Will," she says. "You're perfect the way you are."

"I don't think so," I say.

"I *know* so," she says. "When I look at you, you know what I see? I see that you're turning into a very handsome young man. You're far too handsome to wear a lizard mask."

"Maybe after my surgery, I'll get up onstage in front of people and show my face," I say. "Until then, I'm wearing a mask."

Mom takes a deep, resigned breath.

"Look, Will, I need to tell you something," she says. "The surgery's going to do some very good things for you. It'll be easier to eat, and it'll correct some speech issues, and hopefully, you won't need to wear that breathing machine while you sleep. But it's not going to change who you are. Or how you feel about yourself."

"How do *you* know?" I say, annoyed. It's bad enough that she's making me go through with the surgery. Now she's telling me it won't fix my biggest problem?

"Because feeling good about yourself doesn't come from changing how you look," she says. "It comes from changing how you see yourself. Learning to see yourself the way the people who love you see you."

"I need to worry more about how the people who *don't* love me see me," I say. It's true. If Jake and his friends were to interrupt my act with the Turtle Boy chant, it would actually crush me.

"Will, what other people think of you isn't something you can control, so there's no point in worrying about it."

"No point in worrying about it?" I repeat. "That's easy for you to say. You're not the one who's deformed."

Mom winces. "You are *not* deformed," she says. "Don't use that word."

"What, *'deformed'*?" I say. "Deformed, deformed, deformed."

"Stop it!" says Mom.

"It's my face," I say. "I can say what I want about it."

I grab my sticks and start singing, playing along on the drums: *"Turtle Boy is who I am, more deformed than Elephant Man."*

"You're being ridiculous!" she shouts. "I'm going down for dinner."

She leaves, slamming the door behind her, and I'm laughing, loud and bitter, and before I realize what I'm doing, I've thrown a drumstick at the closed door. It hits the wood with a loud bang and clatters onto the floor. I cry for just a second, scared and choking on my anger, my loathing. I can never win. Either she tries to make me feel better about things that are broken and hopeless, or I block her out; I chase her away.

I don't know what I want from her. I don't know if there's anything she can do for me.

CHAPTER 46

Two days later, I sit next to Shirah on the bus. "I'm thinking about performing at the talent show."

"Seriously?" she says. "You? I've never seen you voluntarily stand up in front of anyone."

"Thanks for the support," I say.

Shirah looks at me for a moment, and her eyes widen. I can see the rim around each hazel iris. "Wait, is this another thing for your friend in the hospital? The one you got the drumsticks for?"

I nod.

"Will!" she says. "That is so sweet! You're really going all-out for that kid!"

"Yeah, well," I say, suddenly shy.

"So what's your act?"

"It's a secret," I say. "You'd come, though. Right? If I get onstage, you'd be there?"

"Yes, dummy!" she says. She chucks me in the arm and a wave of warmth travels up to my shoulder. "You were there for me; I'll be there for you! That's how it works. And Max . . . he'll come too. He actually apologized for what he said. I think he's working on being a better friend."

I heave a quiet sigh of relief—a little for Max and a lot for myself—and out of the corner of my eye, I can see Shirah shaking her head.

"You are such a ridiculous dork," she says.

Amazing, miraculously, right now, *that* is the most wonderful thing she could say.

· · ·

Saturday comes, and I load the trunk of Mom's car with the suitcase full of pots and pans.

"We're going to pick up Shirah and Max," I tell Mom.

"Really?" she says. "Are you guys all friends again?"

"We've always been friends," I say. I decide to leave it at that.

First, we pull into Max's driveway. He's waiting outside, clearly excited, dressed in his Halloween costume: a black tracksuit, white face paint, and black circles around his eyes.

A minute later, we pick up Shirah. She's wearing a lab coat, stethoscope, and vampire teeth. Her hair is spray-dyed black, with white tips.

"Will, where's your costume?" Shirah asks.

"In here," I say, patting my backpack. "It's a secret."

"When will you tell us what you're doing for the show?" Max asks.

"That's *also* a secret," I say.

"Will's got a lot of secrets about his act tonight," says Mom. "But we can be sure he'll go out with a bang."

"Mom!" I yell.

She smiles, pleased with her inside joke.

When we arrive at school, I grow more and more nervous, and by the time I open the trunk to get out my equipment, my hands are slippery with sweat.

"You sure you don't want me to stay?" she asks.

"I told you, no parents." I don't specify that this is my own rule. I can't have her up there in the bleachers, watching me. It's too much. Too much Mom. She takes a breath, like she's deciding to play along with my little fabrication.

"Well," says Mom, slowly, as if I were climbing into a rocket ship and not heading into a talent show. "Good luck in there. See you in a few hours?"

"Okay, bye," I say.

"Beep?" she says, almost asking as a question.

I don't return the beep. I wave, and the three of us head to the school. Before we go in, I remove my glasses, open my backpack, loosen the laces on the back of the mask, and pull it down over my face.

In the school lobby, crepe-paper pumpkins and ghosts hang from the ceiling, and black and orange streamers twist every which way. The gym is noisy with excitement and nervous energy. Though plenty of kids look at me, no one sees me. I'm not scary or gory or elaborate. I'm just a kid in a mask.

Max and Shirah guide me to the bleachers, one sitting on my left and the other on my right.

"Shirah!"

About six rows up, Shirah's volleyball friends wave to her, coaxing her to join them. She doesn't. She stays with me.

That feels good, but it doesn't last long. My stomach is starting to churn. Max and Shirah are talking about something. I hear Max say, "I'm really sorry," and they go back and forth for a while. It seems like a really serious conversation, but I'm not listening. I can't. I'm too freaked out. Forgetting that there's anyone else around me, I let out a long, low groan.

"You okay?" Shirah says to me quietly.

I nod and lean forward, dropping my head between my knees. A minute later, she joins me, her head between her own knees.

"Anything I can do to help?" she asks.

"I feel like I'm going to puke," I say.

I feel her hand lightly rub my back.

"So, can I tell you something?" she asks. "Remember when you asked why I kiss my fist before I serve? Still want to know why?"

I nod, which, in this position, is more like wiggling my head.

"I do that when I'm about to do something I'm afraid of, something I really need to do."

I can't believe that Shirah would ever be afraid of doing anything, let alone something on a volleyball court.

"Okay, well, I've never told anyone this," she continues. "I used to be really close to my grandma, my *bubbie*. She was really tough; born in a refugee camp in Poland after the Holocaust. I don't know if you remember her— she lived with us for a while when we were in third grade. She used to have this thing she'd say to me when I was nervous—before a big game or a test. She'd say, '*Shirah, is the heart willing?*' And I was supposed to repeat, '*The heart is willing.*' And then she'd say, 'Come what may?' And I'd have to repeat, 'Come what may.'"

Shirah looks at me and laughs. "Elaborate, huh? It sounds a little silly to say it out loud. Maybe something was lost in translation."

It reminds me a little of the *"beep"* thing I do with Mom, but I think it's much, much better, because it's like a magic formula from long ago and far away, born in darkness and shadows. Crawling like a turtle through time.

"After she died," Shirah continues, "I started saying

it alone, by myself. Now I save it for really big moments. Moments that really count. I was thinking you might want to try it."

"Does it work?" I ask.

"It's *never* let me down," she says.

CHAPTER 47

THE LIGHTS FLICKER, AND EVERYONE CHEERS AND screams. A gorilla walks out in front of the audience, stands in front of the microphone, and pulls off his mask.

"Prairie Marsh!" he says, popping his glasses into place. Even without my glasses, I can tell from his posture and his voice, it's Dr. Monk, our principal. "Is everyone ready for our 'spooktacular' talent show?"

Everyone yells and claps. I begin to feel the buzz of adrenaline as my fear escalates.

"Our first act is Tracey Newman and Tina Piloski, singing 'A Whole New World.'"

Tracey and Tina go onstage, unroll a small carpet, and stand together in robes and turbans. They squeak through a song. Everyone applauds except me. "Looks like cultural appropriation to me," says Shirah, but I can't reply. The buzz in my veins has turned into a swarm of bees, jostling and crawling inside me.

"OW!" says Max. "What gives!"

I look down and realize I'm clenching his upper arm. I let go immediately.

Three more people perform their acts. I begin to plan my escape. Maybe I'll head to the bathroom and miss my turn. Then Dr. Monk says, "Next up, we have a mystery act. I now present to you . . . Manzilla!"

My body switches to autopilot, and without willing it, I'm lifting my backpack, grabbing the suitcase, and climbing down from the bleachers. I can hear my own breathing under the mask.

Here, in the center of the gym, I'm bathed in blue light.

It's blinding, actually. I squint, trying to see through the eyeholes of the mask. It's useless. I construct my drum set by sense of touch, hands trembling. I tip the suitcase on its side, wedge the pedal in place with a book, and flip the Passover serving tray onto the edge of the suitcase, pots and pans all facing up. I hear people say, *"Who is that?"* and *"What's he doing?"* but otherwise, it's silent. I can almost hear two hundred kids breathing.

I pick up the sticks. I can hear the hiss of the microphones.

I'm starting to panic. People are staring at me.

Then, from somewhere within me comes the question: *Is the heart willing?*

• • •

One kick on the bass drum.

BOOM!

I can see the audience jolt.

It's super-loud. But it felt good. Powerful.

Two thumps: *Ba-boom!*

Now it's time to add the metal pot.

Ba-boom CRACK!

The sound echoes across the room.

Again: Ba-boom CRACK!

I take a deep breath, close my eyes, and float down under the sea, allowing my arms to begin to work on their own. *You can't play it if you don't say it.* I say it in my head, and I play along: *I can do it I can do it I can do it I can do it I can do it I can do it I can do it I can do it*

Then I add the boom of the bass and the *crack* of the metal pot, and I keep it rolling, this marching rhythm.

B'boom! Crack doom-doom crack!

Doom-crack! Doom-crack!

Tick tick tick . . .

I play it two more times, and the last time.

Boom! Crack doom-doom crack!

Doom-crack! Doom-crack!

Tick tick tick . . .

I don't finish it—I stop, motionless. I hold the room in silent suspense.

I count to myself . . . One, two, three, four, five, six, seven, eight—

And on eight, POW! I throw my sticks into the double-time, hummingbird beat.

Lemme at 'em Lemme at 'em Lemme at 'em Lemme at 'em Lemme at 'em Lemme at 'em! Lemme at 'em Lemme at 'em!

And onto that, I layer first the drum . . . *DOOM DOOM DOOM DOOM! DOOM DOOM DOOM DOOM!*

And then I add the pan: *Lemme at 'em! CRACK-EE-AT-'EM! Lemme at 'em! CRACK-EE-AT-'EM! Lemme at 'em! CRACK-EE-AT-'EM!*

I can see two hundred heads bobbing, mesmerized by the rhythm. Now and then, little squalls of applause erupt from the left or the right. My sticks speed up, and I start throwing in extra accents—jabs and punches and extra kicks on the suitcase–bass drum.

My sticks are now in a frenzy of flight. I'm playing faster and louder than I ever have before—an explosion of sound and power—and it's just at this moment that the mask starts to slide forward over my face. My repetitive head bobbing has been causing it to inch forward and down. It's picking up its momentum, and soon it will fall straight off.

I have to make a choice.

I can stop my flow to fix the mask. It will drain all the energy I've been building.

Or I can shrug the mask off and confront the audience with my naked face, my bare turtle face. I have to decide. Now.

The heart is willing.

Come what may.

I speed up the tempo, whipping the rhythm into a hurricane of noise, and I start to count: *five, four, three, two, one.*

On one, I fling one arm out and flip the mask clean off. I return to the rhythm I began with. It's the same marching rhythm—but now, rather than building energy, preparing to storm the castle, it's the proud march of victory. The whole audience is clapping along, and I can feel the hot stage light on my face. It glints off the sweat on my eyelashes.

I roll this rhythm until it's strong and proud, and then I end it.

Ba-boom! Crack doom-doom crack!

Doom-crack! Doom-crack! Doom-crack DOOM DOOM!

I freeze. The lights turn dark, and the audience is silent for a moment and then erupts into applause.

And it's over.

Dr. Monk comes over and says, "Let's have another round of applause for Manzilla!"

I dump the pedal and book and sticks into the suitcase, my hands shaking so badly, I can barely hold anything. I grab my gear and wobble toward the bleachers.

The next thing I know, I'm sitting on the edge of the bench, shaking, while two kids lip-sync a rap. Shirah grabs my arm and pats me on the back while Max leans over and tries to say something, but he's so excited, he shouts it in my ear, "Dude! I didn't know you could do *that*!"

That's when I realize that the hornets and bees in my veins aren't terror after all.

They're pure, liquid thrill.

CHAPTER 48

I CAN'T WAIT UNTIL MY NEXT USUAL VISIT TO TELL RJ about the talent show, so Mom drops me off on Saturday morning.

"Have fun," she says. "Beep."

I ignore the "beep" and hurry through the atrium and up the elevator. I run down the hall, fast as I can, blazing with excitement. As I pass the nurses' station and head toward RJ's room, I'm seized by a terrible feeling. RJ's door is wide open. Roxanne sees me and shouts, "Will, wait!"

She's rushing toward me, but it's too late. The bed is empty, stripped clean. No blankets, no sheets. The shades are pulled wide, and cold light floods the room.

RJ is gone.

My legs turn to rubber; my head swims; my vision goes grainy.

Hands grab my shoulders. It's Roxanne.

"RJ!" I say. "Is he . . . is he . . . ?"

In the moment before the answer, my heart stiffens, cracks.

"Will, listen to me," says Roxanne. "RJ is alive. He's in intensive care. The infection has taken a turn for the worse, but he's getting the best care possible."

First, I'm filled with relief. RJ is alive. But quickly, that relief darkens, shrivels, and in its place, I'm filled with terror. I'm gripping the knees of my pants.

"I can't breathe," I gasp.

"Breathe with me," says Roxanne. Her voice is firm: a command. *"In* . . . two, three, four. *Hold* . . . two, three, four. *Out* . . . two, three, four."

We do this for a few rounds until my first-ever drum-beat settles into place, ordering my breath and my pulse to *Boom, pack! Boom-boom pack! Boom, pack! Boom-boom pack!*

"I'm going to take you down to the cafeteria," Roxanne says. "Rabbi Harris will meet us there."

I can't think. I can barely walk. Roxanne leads me down the mile-long hallway, the walls swaying and wobbling around us.

• • •

Now I'm sitting in the cafeteria, my hands around a hot chocolate. A cup of chamomile tea steams in front of

Rabbi Harris. My shirt is soaked, and I'm swimming in sweat, and yet I shiver underneath my winter coat.

"I'm really sorry," says Rabbi Harris. "The receptionist was supposed to stop you so you wouldn't get spooked like that. Did Roxanne explain what's going on with RJ?"

"He's on a breathing machine," I answer.

"The doctors are keeping him asleep while he fights the infection," he adds. "We're hoping he'll pull out of it. But, Will, there is no way to know."

This brings back the feeling from before. Woozy dizziness. I turn away from Rabbi Harris and lean down, putting my head between my knees. "Keep breathing, Will," says Rabbi Harris. "Slow and steady. When's your mom coming back for you?"

"She'll be back in"—I look at my watch—"forty-seven minutes."

"Okay," he says. "This is going to sound far-out, but we're going to review your Torah portion."

"Now?" I ask. "Here?"

"Yes," says Rabbi Harris. "Very much now and here."

I don't have enough energy to object. From memory, and at a volume low enough that the doctors in their scrubs walking by with trays of food won't hear me, I begin to sing the words of my *parashah*. The Hebrew and the repetitive melody calm me a little.

"You want me to call you once RJ is out of intensive

care?" Rabbi Harris asks, after I finish. He stands up to throw out his trash. "I know he'll want to see you right away."

That reminds me: if RJ is in intensive care, there's no one to take care of the turtle. Turtles shouldn't go for more than three or four days without eating.

"I have to go back to RJ's room," I say. "I . . . I need to water his palm tree. I told him I'd take care of it."

"You want me to go with you?" he asks.

"No!" I blurt out. "No, thank you. I can do it."

We walk together to the elevator, and we push the buttons for floors seven and three. Rabbi Harris gets off before me and waves goodbye as the doors close.

Now I'm riding the elevator alone, and with every successive floor, and as I walk the hall to RJ's room, dread descends farther on me.

His door is still open. I go inside, shut myself in, and pull back the curtain where the terrarium is.

The turtle is basking under the heat lamp. It lifts its head as soon as it sees me, wagging it from side to side; it's hungry. My hands shake as I open the container of freeze-dried crickets. *Will,* I say to myself. *Relax. Everything is fine.*

I drop three crickets into the terrarium, and one falls on the floor. I bend over to pick it up, and I can't get my fingers around it. I gnash my teeth and command my hand into position like the pinchers in a claw machine game. On the third try, success—I throw the cricket into the tank. The turtle scrambles over and snaps it up. I replace the curtain over the terrarium, step back, and take in my surroundings—a hospital room, alone. The bed, empty.

A flash—not a memory, but a glimpse of the future: me in a bed like that, bloody bandages all over my face, and my jaw wired shut.

Alone.

• • •

I'm confused. I'm aware of sensations in my fingertips. I'm looking up at a face. It's Denise, the grouchy nurse who takes RJ's blood.

"What happened?" I ask.

"You passed out," says Denise. "Hold out your arm."

I do as I'm told, and I feel her sliding something—a blood pressure cuff—over my hand, wrist, and then upper arm. Pressure, pulsing, tingling.

"Looks like you're alive," she remarks. "Hold this against your head. You took a bump when you fell."

She takes my hand and presses it against a crinkly cold pack on the side of my head. The sting of the ice collides with the dull ache in my skull.

A minute later, Mom is there. She hugs me. Denise

brings me an orange juice, the same kind that RJ freezes to make slushies, and gives Mom a few extra ice packs.

"Ice twenty to thirty minutes, every three to four hours," she says.

"Let's get you home," says Mom, taking my arm to lead me away.

CHAPTER 49

It's dark in my room. Mom comes in and says it's time to come down for dinner. I don't want to go.

"Will, you can't hide up here," she says. "You're coming downstairs, and we're going to talk."

She says it firmly, and I don't feel like fighting. I follow her downstairs. We're silent through half the meal. I don't eat much. Finally, she speaks.

"Someone had a rough day today," she says, way too brightly. "The last time you passed out like that was when Dr. Haffetz told us about the surgery."

"Can we not talk about the surgery?" I ask.

"Hospitals can be scary places."

"*I said,* I don't want to talk about the surgery." I drop my fork onto my plate with a clank. Then I go further: "I don't want to do it. The surgery. I can't do it. No more hospitals."

"Will," she says, "you've been visiting RJ since the start of the school year. Until yesterday, you've been absolutely fine, and you'll be okay in December too. You had an upsetting experience, but you'll move past it."

"No, I won't," I say. "I can't do it. No surgery."

My legs are starting to feel rubbery. I need to get to my room. I hurry for the stairs and haul myself up by the railing, hand over hand.

"Will! Stop!"

"Leave me alone!" I shout, slamming my door.

A moment later, a loud knock. "Will, I'm coming in."

She opens the door.

"Get out!" I yell.

She's standing by the bed, next to where I've thrown myself.

"We have to stick together, Will," she says. "Stay with me here, okay? What's happening to RJ is scary. I understand that. And the surgery is scary. But you are going to be all right."

"Dad wasn't all right," I say. "He went into the hospital to have a stupid hernia operation, and he didn't wake up!"

"Is that what this is about?" she asks. "You're afraid something bad will happen to you?"

"People go into the hospital and they don't come out," I say.

"Yes, they do come out," says Mom. "They do all the time. We'll never completely understand why your dad didn't make it out of surgery, but that kind of thing is really, really rare, Will. It's so rare, it almost never happens. It won't happen to you, I promise."

I can't handle this. I turn my face and push it into my pillow.

"Will, listen," Mom says. "This isn't like a dentist appointment you can just cancel and reschedule. It needs to be during your winter break so you can heal and get back to school."

"I don't care, cancel it," I say, my face still smushed into the pillow. "Cancel it."

PART THREE

CHAPTER 50

RABBI HARRIS STOPS ME ON MY WAY INTO HEBREW class to tell me that RJ has stabilized. He's out of intensive care, and he's taking visitors.

"He asked about you, Will," says Rabbi Harris, maybe seeing something in my expression. "He'd love to see you."

I nod and head to my desk.

Idiot, I tell myself. My friend is alive, but I'm afraid to go see him? What kind of person am I?

• • •

An hour and a half later, Rabbi Harris and I are riding the elevator to RJ's room. I know this isn't going to be easy. Rabbi Harris ate three Hostess pies on the way to the hospital. I've learned to tell how RJ is doing based on how many pies Rabbi Harris eats; when he reached for the third pie, my pulse quickened and my stomach began to swirl.

Now we're at RJ's door. We go inside without knocking.

RJ's head is on the pillow—eyes closed, mouth open. A new bank of monitors shows moving lines, climbing and falling. His glasses are gone.

Immediately, I'm struck by a powerful memory like a punch to the gut. It fills my whole body.

I see Dad, lying in a hospital bed, tubes and wires all over. He's holding Mom's hand. I'm small—small enough that my face is bed-high. Mom brings me forward, closer to Dad, tugging on my arm.

Then, just like that, it's over. I'm back in the room with RJ and Rabbi Harris.

I watch as Rabbi Harris leans over RJ and puts a palm on his cheek. RJ stays asleep. Rabbi Harris gestures to the cake-chair. Obediently, I sit down. I'm still rattled from the memory.

Or is it something I made up?

I lean forward over my lap, my arms clenched around my stomach. Rabbi Harris drapes his coat over the back of a rolling chair. The chair has never been here before; he must be spending more time in the room with RJ.

I wonder if I can sneak a peek at the Blanding's turtle without Rabbi Harris noticing.

I pull back the curtain. The turtle ambles toward the

light. I won't be able to clean out the terrarium while Rabbi Harris is here, though.

"How's the turtle?" asks Rabbi Harris.

His voice startles me so badly, I flinch and drop the curtain back into place.

"What?" I ask. "What turtle?"

"The one you generously provided RJ with," he says, without looking up from his book. "He told me about it, back when he was going in for surgery. He needed someone to know that he has a pet hiding in here."

"Am I in trouble?" I ask.

"No," says Rabbi Harris, now looking at me. "RJ's morale is more important than whatever rules they have here about pets. I'd say he *needs* to know it's there."

"RJ *needs* the turtle?" I ask, incredulous.

"Absolutely," he says. "And I'll tell you a secret. RJ isn't religious in the typical sense. But he confided in me that he feels like the turtle is a guardian angel."

This is the strangest thing I've ever heard.

"He even talks to it," says Rabbi Harris. "Sometimes, just before I open the door, I can hear him, deep in conversation. When you're as sick as RJ is, it can be very comforting to feel like something good and pure and sweet is watching over you."

"But it's just a turtle," I say. "It can't do anything for him."

"I know that," says Rabbi Harris. "And RJ knows that.

But the thing that's *actually* watching over RJ isn't the turtle at all."

I believe in science. I don't believe in angels. I'm not sure I believe in God. How does a turtle in his room make him feel like there's something good watching over him?

"It's not the turtle," says Rabbi Harris. "It's the person who gave him the turtle. The turtle is just the reminder."

He stops talking, and it takes me a moment to realize he means me. I'm the one who's watching over RJ.

I'm the guardian angel.

This is too much for me to handle.

"I need the bathroom," I say. I leave the room fast and walk down the hall.

I'm not an angel.

• • •

A while later, after walking up and down every hall and guzzling five cups of water, I return to RJ's room. He's awake. He's sitting up, but his glasses are still off.

He looks terrible, and that makes me scared—gray in the face, and his voice is dry and quiet. He has a breathing tube in his nose.

"I'm going to let you guys hang out," says Rabbi Harris. He steps closer to me and says quietly, "Ten minutes."

He leaves and closes the door behind him. I want to

tell RJ about the talent show, but he looks so tired, so weak, I'm not sure he would even care.

"Hey, RJ," I say, testing the waters. "We can cross another thing off the list. I did the talent show."

"Really?" he asks quietly, his eyes widening. He sits up in bed, grabs his glasses, and puts them on. "Did you use my set?"

"Yes, and I added a few of my own things," I say, growing more excited. "A suitcase for a bass drum."

"Tell me everything," he says. "Here, help me with this pillow."

"Well, I was maybe fifth to go," I say, adjusting the pillow while RJ leans forward. "I was totally nervous, but my friends Max and Shirah were there. When my name got called—Manzilla—I went down to the stage and set up the drums. I had Mrs. Barnes's mask on."

"Awesome," says RJ, clearly amused. "The audience must have been like *'What the hell is going on?'*"

"Totally," I say. "They turned on the microphones, and when I hit the bass drum, you could feel the kick, right in the chest. The pots and pans sounded awesome, too— really sharp and clear."

RJ is listening and nodding, and his mouth is locked into a kind of half smile, half "wow." He sits back in bed, blinking toward the ceiling, as if savoring the talent show within the muscles of his own body. As for me, I'm reliving the moment when the whole audience saw my face.

If not for the drums, for the shield of noise that protected me, I probably would have fled.

"It's done," I say after a few moments. "We can cross it off the list."

RJ nods and says, "Yes. That is so amazing."

This makes me really happy. I've now helped RJ with five things on his list. I wonder how many are left, and with a nervous flush, I worry that maybe the list is complete.

RJ tips his head back against his pillow and seems about to say something, but then he pauses, coughs twice, and says, "I'm gonna catch some z's, okay?"

Before I can say another word, he's quiet and still. If there is another task, I won't learn about it today.

CHAPTER 51

IT'S THE LAST DAY OF SCHOOL BEFORE THANKSGIVING break, and it's snowing. When the first flakes fell from the mess of gray overhead, kids jumped out of their seats and ran to the window. Mr. Firenze yelled at them to sit down. I didn't bother getting up. Who cares about snow when your friend is dying? I have no hope for RJ. The only thing I could ever hope for is the Back 40, and even that might be lost.

The minute the final bell rings, I grab my coat and backpack. I need to be alone. I need the Back 40. I run down the stairs and out the back door toward the parking lot. I'm hit by the polar blast of the winter wind.

The chain-link gate is open. That's odd. I run through and clamber up the dirt mound which is frozen solid, and I can see straight down to a row of construction trailers. Someone's down there, dressed in a heavy coat and a hunter's cap.

Instantly, I'm running down the hill, shouting, "Ms. Kuper!"

She looks up at me and waves a gloved hand.

"What's happening" I ask, breathing hard. "Did you save the Back 40?"

"I met with officials in Madison," she says, "to see if I could convince them that the Back 40 is essential to our science program."

"And?"

"I did my best, Will," she says. "But it didn't work. They want to proceed with the sale."

"No," I say in disbelief.

We're both quiet for a very long time. Somewhere, a couple of cardinals are calling to each other: One cries, "Cheer, cheer, cheer," and the other replies, "Birdie, birdie, birdie." It strikes me as tragic that they should have such a happy song when their home is about to be demolished.

"Isn't there anything else we can do?" I ask.

At that moment, a rustling comes from the trees, and from between the leafless trunks near the pond comes a figure, limping. It's Mr. Firenze in a heavy green parka with a fur-trimmed hood.

"Can't say you didn't warn me," he says. "Slipped on the ice." He lifts his head so the hood isn't blocking his eyes. "Hello, Will. Didn't see you there."

"I'm giving him the update," says Ms. Kuper.

"Well, yes," he says, rubbing the side of his leg. "It's not a rosy one."

"We do have one last shot," says Ms. Kuper. "The county has made up its mind to sell the Back 40, but there are state and federal laws that would protect this land in a very specific set of circumstances."

I have no idea what she's talking about, and Ms. Kuper picks up on that.

"We'd need to prove one of two things," says Ms. Kuper. "First, we could prove that this area is a corridor for migration—that wildlife uses the Back 40 to migrate from one larger area to the next."

"Well, that's never going to happen," I say. "It's basically an island—it's not connected to anything else."

"And the second possibility," she continues, "is that we prove the Back 40 is home to an endangered species."

Endangered species?

"Ms. Kuper," I say, knowing she'll be upset with me. "Back in September, Max and I were out here, and we caught a Blanding's turtle."

Mr. Firenze looks at Ms. Kuper for a reaction. Her face is blank.

"A Blanding's turtle," she says. "You're sure it was a Blanding's turtle?"

"Hey," I say, putting up my two palms in a gesture of pride, as if to say, *Am I Turtle Boy or not?*

"And what did you do with this Blanding's turtle?" she asks.

I don't say anything. She knows.

"So, Will, are you telling me that your illegal wildlife collection included an endangered species?"

"Yes," I admit.

"And I'm guessing that even though you and I supposedly released all your illegal turtles, you disobeyed and kept this endangered turtle, am I correct?"

"Yes," I say.

"And where is this turtle currently?"

"Uh," I say, aware of how ridiculous this will sound, "it lives on the seventh floor of Horicon General Hospital."

"And why is this turtle living in a hospital room?" says Ms. Kuper, with forced patience.

"Because my friend RJ is dying from a mitochondrial disease, and he needed a pet."

"Endangered, wild turtles are not pets," Ms. Kuper says crossly.

I roll my eyes.

"Do I need to worry about this Blanding's turtle's well-being, Will?" she asks. "It's too cold to release it now. Have you been going over there and caring for it every day?"

"Yes," I lie.

Obviously, I don't mention the lesions or the soft

spots on its shell. Or the fact that a rabbi has been feeding it crickets.

Mr. Firenze and Ms. Kuper look at each other.

"Will, would you excuse us for a second?" says Ms. Kuper. She pulls Mr. Firenze aside. For a moment, I watch them gesturing and talking and even pointing to the tree line of the Back 40. Snow is gently settling around us, soft and fluffy, with flakes so large I can hear them landing: *thup, thup, thup.* The sun gleams through the clouds and around the jagged edges of the trees. A bit farther down, the pond must be close to frozen, dusted with snow, jagged with cracks, brown and mysterious and terrifying.

"Okay, Will!" calls Ms. Kuper. "Let's get out of this cold and talk. The county is supposed to sell the land to the developers in a week or so. We have some important planning to do, and we think you can play a significant role."

CHAPTER 52

RABBI HARRIS AND I WALK INTO RJ'S ROOM, WHERE HE'S lying back, eyes closed. I'm glad to see that the bank of monitors and breathing tube are gone, but still . . . I'd hoped he might be awake, maybe looking a little better. Instead, he looks exhausted, thin, almost brittle. Someone has tried to cheer up the room with a plush Thanksgiving turkey, dressed as a pilgrim. It isn't working.

Rabbi Harris puts his hands on RJ's cheeks for a second, then sits down and pulls out a thick book with tiny Hebrew print and starts to read.

"Can you keep an eye on the door?" I say to Rabbi Harris. "I need to clean the tank."

Rabbi Harris nods but keeps reading. I use a small scoop to remove some cricket carcasses and half-eaten vegetables. With my head closer to the terrarium, I catch that bad smell again. I wonder—is that the smell I remember from Ms. Kuper's bio lab? She was treating a turtle for shell rot, trying to catch it before it spread from the shell to the body cavity. Once that happens, it's hopeless. I'm pretty sure Grampy doesn't have shell rot, though. I look closer, and I also see a few small lesions on the turtle's neck.

"Who's there?" asks RJ. "Will?"

That startles me. He spoke without moving. I drop the curtain and straighten up.

"It's Will and your favorite rabbi," says Rabbi Harris. "How are you feeling today?"

"Not—so good," says RJ. "Rabbi Harris, did you hear— from the doctors?"

He speaks slowly, and he's having trouble getting through sentences.

"I did," says Rabbi Harris.

I don't know what they're talking about. Usually, Rabbi Harris gives me the update on RJ on the ride to the hospital, but today, we only reviewed my Torah portion.

"I'm scared," says RJ.

I realize now that I've risen to my feet.

"I know you are," says Rabbi Harris. "You're not alone. You're never alone. People who love you are with you all the time, okay?"

He's holding RJ's hand, and the fainting feeling returns. I sit back down and put my head between my knees.

"Did you tell Will?" asks RJ.

"Last time we talked, you said you wanted to tell him yourself," says Rabbi Harris. "Did you change your mind?"

RJ shakes his head a little.

"I forgot," he says. "Hey, Will."

I look up, and Rabbi Harris motions for me to step closer. I do. I wish he would put his arm around me. Just as I wish it, he does that exact thing: he puts his arm around me, and it feels like the safety bar on the roller coaster.

"Will," says RJ. "Pretty soon I'm going to check out of this crappy hotel."

I understand immediately what he means. He's going to die.

"It could be a month or so," he says. His voice is flat. Matter-of-fact. "Maybe just a few weeks. My kidneys and my liver and pretty much everything else is messed up."

He doesn't say anything more. Then he starts to cry.

I don't know what to do with myself. I can't handle the sight of RJ crying. Rabbi Harris holds me a little tighter and hands RJ a tissue with his spare hand.

"I want to give you something," says RJ, wiping his nose. He reaches over and picks up his headphones.

"These are for you," he says. "I want you to have them."

I feel their weight in my hand, heavier than I expected,

and when I put them around my neck, I can feel them pulling down on me, pulling down on my heart.

"And, Will, I have one last thing on the list," he says. "And please don't say no."

"I won't," I say. I realize now that I'm crying as well, with no sound and no motion. Just tears on my cheeks, gathering on my eyelashes, making my eyes burn.

"Okay," says RJ. "The list. I've never been out with a girl. I want to go on a date. And I can't leave the hospital, so it's got to be here, which sucks, but that's the way it is."

I force myself to look at RJ. His face is all hope, fear, trust.

"Can you help me?" he asks.

"Sure," I say immediately. "Of course."

CHAPTER 53

"HOW WAS YOUR VISIT?" MOM ASKS. I WALK PAST HER and hang my coat on the hook by the basement stairs. She's stirring a pot on the stove.

"Fine, I say. "Good."

"Any change?" she says.

"With RJ?" I say. "About the same."

"Okay, so that's good," she says. "We'll have to keep sending our hopes and prayers. Would you set the table for soup and salad? Bean soup with leftover turkey and stuffing."

Mom goes on about how Thanksgiving food is better as leftovers, but I'm not listening. I put the bowls and napkins out, and then I stop, spoons in my left hand, forks in my right. I can't go on.

"Actually . . . ," I say.

My throat tightens. Mom immediately realizes what's happening and turns off the stove. She comes over and guides me by the elbow into a chair. She sits down next to me and puts a hand on my shoulder.

"What is it?" she asks. "Tell me."

I shake my head.

"Will," she says. "Please let me in. Please tell me what's happening."

"RJ, he's . . . he's getting a lot worse. . . ." I'm forcing the words; my instinct is to run away, to block her out. But maybe this isn't a time for instincts. If I don't let go of some of this pain, I'll crack. "He says his kidneys are messed up, and . . ."

I'm struggling to breathe.

She reaches out and touches the huge headphones around my neck.

"Are these his headphones? Did he give them to you?"

I nod.

"Is he starting to say goodbye?" she asks.

I nod again.

"Oh, Will," says Mom. She pulls me in for a hug, and I'm crying. I haven't cried in front of Mom since the visit to Dr. Haffetz, when I found out about the surgery and passed out. I take a deep, trembling breath.

"It's hard," Mom says in a soothing voice. "It's hard to learn to love someone and then have to say goodbye."

I know she's talking about me and RJ, but it sounds like she's talking about Dad. Maybe she said goodbye to him, but I don't think she ever let him go. It's as if speaking his name would cause him to drift farther away, to recede into the past.

As for me, I never got to say goodbye. I was too young to understand.

"Will, I want to tell you how proud of you I am," Mom says. "You've already lived through enough loss for one lifetime, but you found the courage to go and connect with someone who needs you. You've given him such a gift."

What gift? I think. The bucket list is incomplete. *And what courage?* Courage is swimming in a murky pond, even when you're afraid. Courage is taking opportunities that come along, not running from them, not hiding. But I run. I hide. I won't swim. I'm still a coward.

"There's still things I haven't done," I say, wiping tears from my eyes.

"What?" she asks. "What haven't you done? You've been his friend. That's all he needs right now."

I don't want to tell her about the bucket list. Now, more than ever, the bucket list is something private between me and RJ. But then a thought bubbles up: *What if RJ dies before I finish?*

I can't leave the bucket list incomplete.

• • •

After school the next day, I take the bus to Herb's Herps. Gwen is talking to a customer, explaining how to feed a snake.

"Snakes will pretty much eat anything smaller than they are," she says. "You could do grasshoppers, but mice are really the way to go."

"Mice?" asks the customer.

"And sure, you can waste your money on frozen mice," she says. "But why do that when you can breed 'em yourself? Grow your own snake food."

"Cute little mice?"

"Yummy, nutritious little mice," says Gwen, a bit condescendingly.

The customer thanks her and heads off to another area of the store. Gwen turns to go back to work, when she sees me.

"Oh great, it's the King of the Turtles," she says. "Here to argue about turtle habitats? I don't have any free gear for you today."

I can feel my face flush, but this is no time to give in to shyness. I take a deep breath. I want her to meet RJ, but I don't want her to do it out of pity. I'm going to have to swallow my pride.

"I have a friend with a turtle that's got an infection, and I can't fix it," I say quietly. "I was wondering if you could help."

She looks at me funny. I'm afraid she's going to tease me, but she doesn't.

"Sure," she says. "Tell him to bring it in and we'll look at it. If I can't fix it, my dad can."

"He can't bring it in," I say. "Can you come see it?"

"Okay, where is it?" she asks suspiciously.

"In the hospital," I say.

"Wait a minute," she says. "Is this the same 'friend' who needed Medi-Eye for his turtle about two months ago?"

I nod.

She crosses her arms and purses her lips. After a moment, she looks down and kicks the side of one boot with the toe of the other and talks to herself, as if running a complex calculation.

"Unusual situation," she says, counting on her fingers. "Nothing else interesting going on in this town. Demands my expertise. Possible college application essay subject."

She looks at me. "Sure. You got it."

CHAPTER 54

GWEN AND I ARE ON THE BUS. SHE HAS A PHONE, SO I BOR-
row it to call RJ.

"Hey, it's Will," I say when RJ answers. "I'm bringing
a friend. Be ready."

"A friend?" RJ is quiet for a minute; then, in a hushed
voice, he says, "Will, is this what I think it is?"

"Is there a room we can use that's good for . . . hanging out?"

"How about the family room? It's like a lounge with
chairs and stuff. It's on floor six."

"Great," I say. "You have any food? Snacks?"

"Snacks," he says. "I'll see what I can do."

Twenty minutes later, we're in front of a door labeled
FAMILY VISITING ROOM. I knock and open the door. RJ is
sitting in a big chair. His hair is combed. He's wearing a
T-shirt—THE CLASH: LONDON CALLING—and green sweat-
pants. On his wrists, he's wearing his bracelets—woven
brown string and colorful beads. It's exactly what he wore

the first time I came to visit. There's no way he made it here on his own. Roxanne and Denise must have helped him.

"Gwen," I say, introducing her, "this is—"

"Ralph?" she interrupts.

"Who's that?" he asks. He's squinting toward her.

"Gwen!" she says.

"Marching Band Gwen?" he asks.

"Well, I prefer *regular* Gwen, but sure."

I've seen people do double takes in cartoons, but I've never done one myself until now. I gawk at her, then him, then her.

She goes over to RJ.

"Dude," she says. "I haven't seen you in a million years!"

"I know," says RJ. "We moved up north to Baraboo halfway through sixth grade, but then I got sick, and we came back because of the hospital."

I can hear that he's straining to complete his sentences without pausing for a breath.

"Wait, what are you sick with?" she asks. "What's the matter?"

I look at RJ. His lips part, as if he's considering what to say. I've never seen him at a loss for words before.

"Oh, it's nothing," he says. "I'll be out of here really soon."

For a second, I think I see his eyes dart over to me, but I know that's impossible: he can barely see.

"Hey," he continues. "I was just having a little picnic here. Want to join me?"

On the floor, he's spread a green and white hospital blanket and about ten bags of chips, all of which I recognize from the vending machine. There's also a few bottles of lemonade.

I'm filled with a strange mix of emotion: RJ has a kind of energy that I've never seen before. And I'm happy that he's reconnecting with an old friend. But I'm a little jealous, as if I don't want to share him. I know I should be happy for him. RJ doesn't belong to me.

"Funyuns!" says Gwen. She plops down cross-legged on the blanket and tears open a bag.

RJ is clearly thrilled and trying to play it cool. He's slouched back in his big chair, as if a visit from someone like Gwen is an everyday occurrence. His face is radiant. He hasn't asked me to leave, but I'm starting to feel weird standing here. Should I remind them that I've brought her here to look at the Blanding's turtle? Somehow, this doesn't seem the time for it. I decide to wander the halls.

As I pass the nurses' station, Roxanne turns around from her computer.

"Well, hello, Will," she says. "Did you have a nice Thanksgiving?"

"Yeah, it was good," I say.

"What are your plans for winter vacation?" she asks. "Traveling somewhere tropical, I hope?"

This catches me off guard. Ever since this summer, the plan was for me to have the surgery during winter break. But all that changed when I told Mom I wouldn't do the surgery. We haven't talked about it since. I guess that means winter break is in limbo, but I don't feel like explaining any of that.

"Nothing special," I say.

. . .

A long while later, I go back to the family room. The door is closed. I reach my hand to open it, but something makes me think that I should knock first.

"Come in," calls a voice. RJ's voice.

I don't know why, but I'm hesitant to enter. I open the door, and they're sitting on the sofa. RJ is leaning back with his legs on Gwen's lap. His socks are off and she's rubbing his feet.

"Reflexology," she says abruptly. "Very good for the renal system."

Reflexology? I have no idea what she's talking about. I don't understand what's going on with them: they're making a connection that doesn't involve me.

"I need to go home," I say to Gwen. "Do you want to see the turtle or not?"

She looks at RJ, and he nods.

"I'm going to stay," she says. "I'll look later."

Without another word, I grab my bag and walk into the hall.

CHAPTER 55

IT'S ABOUT EIGHT-THIRTY. WHEN I CAME HOME FROM the hospital, I closed myself in my room, and since then I've been rehearsing my lines over and over, preparing for tomorrow's action to save the Back 40. It's only four sentences, but every time I learn one, I forget the one before it. I drop the page of notes and cover my eyes with my hands. How did I get myself into this?

The phone rings, and a minute later, there's a knock on the door.

"For me?" I yell.

Mom opens the door and mouths the words, "It's a girl!"

She knows Shirah's voice, so it's definitely not Shirah. What other girl would call me at home?

I jog downstairs and grab the phone.

"Dude!" a girl's voice says sharply. "What were you thinking, giving Ralph a Blanding's turtle?"

Oh great. It's Gwen.

"I can explain," I say, though really, I can't.

"Ralph said he wanted a pet, and *that's* what you brought him?"

"It's not a pet," I say. "Turtles aren't pets."

"You took an endangered species out of the wild and gave it to a guy in the hospital!" She's practically screaming. "That sounds like you turned a wild animal into a pet, *doesn't it?*"

I can feel my arms going numb with fear.

"You've put an endangered turtle in actual danger," she says. "It can't stay in that terrarium. It has lesions and a bad case of shell rot. Is that what you want?"

"It does *not* have shell rot," I say, though I know she's right.

"Listen to me," says Gwen. "You haven't been changing the water enough; it doesn't get enough sun; the terrarium is too small; and it's getting lesions all over its body! We have to transfer it to something clean right away, or it's going to get even sicker. And we can't release it into the wild because it'll infect other turtles."

At this point, I'm so overwhelmed, I just want to hang up, go to my room, and curl up under the blanket. I'm flooded by guilt and shame.

"But RJ loves it," I say.

"Who's RJ?"

"Ralph," I say. It feels so weird to say his actual name. "He loves the turtle. We can't take it away."

She pauses for a second. She knows this is true.

"This is what we're going to do," she says definitively. "I'm going back tomorrow. I'm going to clean off the rot and apply antibiotic and change the water and install proper lighting and a better dry area for it to bask."

"Don't let the nurses see you," I say.

"Or what?" she asks. "They'll make me take it home?"

I have nothing to say to that.

"And we'll divide up the work. I'll go and put antibiotic on its shell and clean the tank on Mondays, Wednesdays, Fridays, and Saturdays. You go on Sundays, Tuesdays, and Thursdays. We'll keep it clean through winter, and in spring, we'll let it go."

"Good plan," I say. She'll be visiting one more day a week than I will, but it doesn't seem like a good time to argue.

"Maybe we'll just switch the turtles in spring," she says. "I'll source an ethically raised turtle: a box turtle or musk turtle, one that isn't endangered. Knowing Ralph, he won't even notice the difference. And once he gets out of the hospital, hopefully, it'll be warm enough so that we can all let the Blanding's turtle go together."

Once he gets out of the hospital.

Gwen talks for a while longer, but I'm not listening. With every last nucleus of every cell of my heart, I want RJ to leave the hospital, but I know the truth.

303

He's only leaving that hospital one way. And it's not the good way.

We agree on the plan, and as I hang up, I'm hit by another chill: RJ didn't tell Gwen the truth about his condition.

And neither did I.

CHAPTER 56

IT'S FRIDAY. MS. KUPER HAS GONE TO MADISON TO TRY to speed up the process to declare the Back 40 a protected refuge. There are about twenty of us gathered behind the old bank in the freezing cold. We're going to catch the county officials when they arrive to sign over the property. Mom is here, along with Mr. Firenze, Max, and Shirah and a couple of sixth graders from Max's lunch table gang. The other adults are reporters from a couple of newspapers, including the one my mom works for; a camera operator; and members of various community groups: bird-watchers, ecologists, and a handful of adults who went to Prairie Marsh as kids. They hold posters saying SAVE THE BACK 40! and THE BACK 4OUR KIDS!

Mom puts her hand on my shoulder. I'm glad she's here. She wrote a note to the school, excusing me, red-inked in sharp, neat letters: *Will won't be in school today. He's going to save the Back 40.*

With the windchill, it's definitely below zero. I can hear the crunch of snow under forty boots. Just before noon, we hear a whistle. We begin moving rapidly, and as quietly as twenty people can move, to the side, then to the steps of the bank.

A gray-haired couple in a blue Prius arrives. The man helps the woman out of the car. They look like regular, nice people.

"*Those* are the government officials?" I hear a voice ask.

"What were you expecting?" someone else says. "Giants?"

"Excuse us," yells Mr. Firenze. "Can we have a word with you?"

The couple turns and looks at the approaching group with surprise and apprehension.

"We're not here to harass you," says Mr. Firenze. "We're actually here to save the county from making a very bad and very expensive mistake. We can prove that this land is home to an endangered species."

The crowd pushes forward to hear the conversation.

"Let me guess," says the woman. "You found the last unicorn back there."

Mr. Firenze doesn't smile. "I'd like to introduce to you one of Prairie Marsh's finest students, Will Levine."

My mother pats me on the shoulder, and I step forward. At least five phones and a camera are in my face, recording. My knees are shaking.

"This is the Blanding's turtle," I say, my voice quavering, holding Mom's phone up for the officials to see. "Latin name, *Emydoidea blandingii*. Notice the signature bright yellow chin and throat. And also, on the carapace, the upper shell, those yellow flecks on a dark background. My associate and I found this specimen in the Back 40."

I know turtles don't feel emotions beyond aggression and fear, but this one looks proud, with its snout up in the air, its eyes wide open, and its signature yellow chin by far the most colorful thing in RJ's hospital room.

I step back and feel a pair of hands clasp securely around my upper arms, supporting me on my trembling legs. Mom's hands.

"If you sell the Back 40," Mr. Firenze continues in a voice at once gentle and brimming with power, "you might be accused of intentionally dumping a federally protected wildlife refuge for a quick profit. Even children are asking you to stop. This is not going to look good come election time."

There's an excited chuckle from the crowd.

"We aren't irrational people," says the woman. "If there is an endangered species dwelling on county property, one that would block our ability to develop the land, we certainly want to know about it."

"Dolores, they're fleecing us," says the man. "Who knows where they found that thing."

"Let's give them until Monday," the woman replies. She turns back to Mr. Firenze. "We need better evidence. An endangered *population*. Not just one—we expect to see *multiple* turtles. Otherwise, first thing Monday morning, we're back here to turn the land over to the developers."

CHAPTER 57

Saturday was a wash. We got a late start because the hole under the fence Ms. Kuper and I have been climbing through was blocked with snow and ice and it took hours of digging to open it wide enough to enter the Back 40. Then, already exhausted, we looked and looked but found nothing.

Now it's early Sunday morning, and we have a much smaller crowd. "All right, gang," says Mr. Firenze. "This is our last shot, but no matter what, we have to stop when the light begins to fade."

"It's hopeless," I say. "Turtles burrow down into leaves and dirt. They could be right under our noses and we wouldn't even see them. They could be under the ice."

"We have to do our best, Will," Mr. Firenze says gravely. "You're one of Prairie Marsh's finest students. Your expertise is not to be underestimated. Plus, another graduate of our fine school will be joining us shortly. She's quite a herpetologist, I'm told."

"Wait a minute," Max says to me. He's been silent, taking this all in. "How can they live under the ice? Don't turtles have lungs? How do they breathe?"

"They do something called cloacal breathing," I say. "They absorb oxygen through a cavity near the end of their digestive tract."

Max's eyes widen, and he grabs me by both shoulders. "They breathe through their butts?!" He turns to the nearest sixth grader and says, "Turtles can breathe through their butts."

"Ah, here's our expert now," says Mr. Firenze.

A familiar figure climbs to her feet from the hole under the fence.

It's Gwen.

"Looks like everyone's ready," she says, approaching. "I'd say the best way to find a turtle is to think like a turtle. Let's go where you found the last one. Grab a stick and everywhere you see a mound of dirt or leaves, carefully move it aside and let's see who we meet."

Max gallops down the path to the edge of the pond, pulling Shirah along. I walk alone until Gwen trains her eyes on me. I get the feeling I'm in trouble, and in fact, she veers closer, intercepting me.

"Why didn't you tell me?" she hisses, her breath puffing like smoke in the frosty air.

Instantly, I know she's talking about RJ.

"You tricked me," she continues. "Why didn't you tell me he's *dying*? You and Ralph— No one told me! I finally got it out of him yesterday!"

"I was trying to help him," I say. "He was lonely. What was I supposed to do?"

"Tell the truth!" she says. "Tell people the truth!"

"I'm sorry," I say.

She looks at me and shakes her head. "I'm not sorry I reconnected with Ralph. He's a special person. Really special. I just . . . I wish it wasn't the way it is."

I keep my hands jammed in my pockets and we walk silently following the sixth graders until we reach the pond, the cold wind whipping between us, stirring up a cloud of fresh snow.

. . .

Over the next few hours, I watch Gwen. Her technique is fascinating. She stands and gazes at a number of spots, each for a long time. Then she walks to one of the spots, takes a quick look, as if checking her vision, and moves on.

"Guys," calls Mr. Firenze. "Gather up."

Everyone circles around him. The sun has begun to set behind the trees.

"I want to thank all of you for coming out here in the cold today," he says. Everyone takes a deep breath, as if they've given up and are trying to adjust to the reality of our failure. "We've done our best, but our hunt is over."

"No!" I say. "No! No! No! We are not quitting!"

My feet are on autopilot. I run from the group, and I'm shuffling leaves and digging down into rocks by the edge of the pond, and suddenly, there's a feeling like knives biting into my foot, gnawing up my leg, all the life draining out.

I don't know what's happening until I look down and see that my right foot has plunged through the edge of the ice.

"Don't move," says Shirah. She comes closer and steps up next to my shoulder. "Put your arm around me."

I lean on her, and she supports me as I yank my foot out of the ice.

"It's cold," I say, in shock.

"Here," says Gwen. She pulls her boot off. "I've got a spare pair of hikers in my backpack. Somebody get his wet shoe and sock off."

Max and Mr. Firenze unlace my wet shoe and pull it off, along with the sock. My foot is pink with cold, like a fresh piece of salmon. They slide Gwen's boot over my foot.

"That should keep it warm long enough to get inside," he says.

I hang my head. It's over. We've lost.

"Where's Gwen?" Mr. Firenze looks around. "Gwen!'

I look along the edge of the pond where Gwen, still as a statue, is staring out across the frosted ice.

"What's that, over there?" she shouts our way. "It looks like an island; maybe it's a sandbar?"

I hear Mr. Firenze speak to the remaining adults. "We're not going out there. Will just learned his lesson about walking on ice."

"Turtles love sandbars," Gwen calls. "And that's one place we haven't looked."

"Maybe there's some fallen trees," says Max. "Like a bridge?"

Max takes a few steps down to the edge of the pond and jogs toward Gwen.

"Will, come on," he calls, and I gallop over the best I can in my mismatched boots.

"Look," he says, pointing. A huge fallen tree is frozen into the ice. The trunk is thick, and then it narrows as it reaches out toward the sandbar.

"You have to come with me," says Max. "I don't know what to look for."

"You're out of your mind," I say.

"I'm going," says Max. "I hope you're going to come with me."

He grabs onto a few of the larger roots of the fallen tree with his gloved hands and pulls himself up and begins to balance along.

What the heck? I tell myself. I'm doing this.

I climb up—not as nimbly as Max—and I follow the path he took. He made it look easy. It's not easy. It's really slippery. The bark of the tree is filled in with ice. The rest of the group has run over to the roots of the tree, but now I'm about twenty feet out.

"The tree ends here," Max says. Up ahead, there's a smaller tree, also fallen, thinner and longer than the first. It stretches out farther toward the sandbar, but it's hard to tell whether it makes it all the way.

Max looks at the lower tree, takes a deep breath, and leaps off the side of the trunk we're standing on, landing in a crouch on the second, longer tree. He follows it along and comes to the edge of the sandbar.

"I made it," he says.

I'm starting to panic.

"Come out to the edge," says Max.

I inch a little more, a little more, holding onto whatever branches I can, my gloved hands trembling with fear.

"Keep your center of gravity low and keep creeping forward," says Max.

Pretty soon the second tree is just a few feet away.

"Okay," he says. "Now I want you to jump to the second tree. I'll be waiting to grab you."

I look at Max. This is Max, who never considers the consequences of his actions. If I jump, will he catch me?

"It's getting dark," says Max. "Stop thinking about it and do it. Do it for the turtles!"

That's exactly what I need.

I leap.

. . .

We find the first Blanding's turtle under a clump of dirt and leaves.

"Well, what have we here?" asks Gwen, leaping from the long tree in her mismatched footwear and squatting by a mound of dirt and dead reeds. She gently digs her gloved fingers around a sluggish turtle. "Our treasure, Blanding's turtle number one."

Not a minute later, we sift through another pile of leaves and find another—speckles on the shell, golden chin and throat.

"A female. A mating pair," says Gwen.

"Max," I say, "can you get a video?"

He pulls off a glove and pokes at his phone, finally saying, "Okay, action. Everyone say hi." He sweeps the camera around, capturing our setting—proving that we're right here in the Back 40. He then zooms in on the two Blanding's turtles.

"What if this isn't enough?" I say. "We need evidence of a *population*."

It's getting dark now, for real. We're down to our final minutes of light, but I'm not satisfied we've completed our task. I don't want the minimum. I want one more. One more turtle makes four.

"Hey, Turtle Boy," says Max quietly. "Come look at this."

Gwen and I walk closer to Max. He's pointing down through the ice, capturing it on video.

I don't know what I'm going to see. What is there to find on the other side of the line that divides this world and the underworld? But there it is. On the other side of the ice, on the opposite side of the universe, where living things die, *there it is*. Another turtle. Clearly a Blanding's turtle.

Drifting.

Drifting and swimming with the invisible current.

As alive as I am.

PART FOUR

CHAPTER 58

RABBI HARRIS PRESSES THE HOSPITAL ELEVATOR BUT-ton. On the way here, he told me he'd seen me on the news, saving the Back 40. He was really proud of me. Then we talked about the flashes of memory, how I've been seeing Dad from time to time. When it happens, it's a bit scary, and yet I want more.

That led us to talking about Mom.

I told him that she doesn't go out much, that her only friend is Aunt Mo, and that she won't tell me about Dad. He listened, but I got the sense that he already knew these things. In return, he told me a few things I knew, but didn't know I knew: he told me that Mom loves me, but she isn't always sure how to help me.

"She doesn't understand how badly you want to know about him," Rabbi Harris says as we get on the elevator to visit RJ.

"Oh, come on. Of course she knows," I say. "I ask her questions all the time."

"Sometimes we ask questions," says Rabbi Harris, "but we don't want to know the answers. She can see that. She doesn't want to hurt you."

"How can learning about Dad hurt me?" I ask. "I don't even know who he is."

"You know the saying 'What you don't know can't hurt you,' right?" he says.

I nod.

"Well, it isn't true," he says. "But we wish it were. It makes sense she doesn't want you to know. We all have our ways of protecting ourselves and the people we love from danger. I have my ways. You have yours. She has hers.

"You'll need to find a way to help her see that knowing your father and feeling the loss is better for you than living in the dark."

The elevator doors open, and Rabbi Harris gestures with an *after you*. He used to be the first one out of the elevator. Now it's me.

As I lead the way down the hall, I find myself hoping that Gwen won't be around. I miss how it used to be with just RJ and me. No luck: we walk in and she's here. She doesn't greet me with the usual sass, maybe because I'm with Rabbi Harris. Or maybe it's because of RJ. He looks much worse than last time. His breathing tube and monitors have returned. He's sitting up, but he's leaning back against the pillows, with no strength of his own. His face is blank, like he's there but not really there.

320

Gwen is sitting next to the bed, holding RJ's hand, the one with the wire running to his fingertip, the IV in his arm. More wires run to a bank of screens. Green dots zip across the monitors.

When Gwen turns and sees me, she gives me a little wave. She looks sad. RJ looks puffy, and his face looks weird, a funny color. Gone are the Clash T-shirt, the string bracelet, and the glasses. He's in a hospital gown. I look at Gwen, and then I look back at RJ. I'm sure of it. Gwen looks normal; RJ looks yellow.

There's something else too. Something different.

His mop of hair is cut, shaved to a neat buzz.

"Hi, Gwen," I force myself to say. "Hi, RJ."

Gwen looks at me and then at the clock.

"I'll give you guys some time to hang out," she says. "I'm going to get something in the cafeteria."

"I'll go with you," says Rabbi Harris. "They're having a special on grilled cheese sandwiches. Will? Want anything?"

I shake my head. Gwen and Rabbi Harris leave, and rather than sit on my usual cake-chair, I sit where Gwen was sitting, in the rolling chair next to the bed. RJ hasn't said anything since I came into the room.

"Nice haircut," I say.

"Pff," says RJ. "Denise made me do it. She said the 'rock star' do was getting too hard to keep clean."

"I hate her," I say.

"Don't," says RJ. "She's no fun, but don't hate her. See that container of baby wipes over there? I'm not going to tell you what she does with them."

I get it. I nod.

"Gwen told me about the Back 40," he says. He's really breathy, and he pauses between phrases. "And how you guys . . . you found some kind of rare turtle."

This is freaking me out. He can't even finish a sentence without pausing to breathe.

"Yeah," I say, trying to sound cheerful. "It was a close call. Actually, Gwen found the spot where they were hiding, and Max—"

RJ starts coughing, and I don't finish the sentence. Once he's done coughing, I decide to let the topic go. It doesn't matter. The details don't matter.

He doesn't say anything after that.

Should I tell him how I'm thinking about doing the surgery? I really don't want to bother him with any of that.

Drums. I could tell him that I want to take drum lessons. Real drum lessons.

But what's the point?

Whatever the topic, it doesn't feel right to bring it up.

And now I've missed my chance, because RJ has dozed off. His breathing is labored, like his lungs are wet sponges.

"Go on," he then says suddenly.

"RJ?" I say. "You awake?"

"I'm awake," he says.

We're quiet for another minute.

The bucket list.

"RJ," I say.

He waits a minute before he responds. "Yeah."

"Tell me about the next thing on the list."

He's quiet for a minute.

"That's it," he finally says.

"What?" I say.

"That's it."

"What's it?" I say. "*What's* it, RJ?"

He turns his head a little to look in my direction, but it's pretty clear that he can't see me.

"The list is done," he says. "No more."

I feel a blow to the center of my chest, as if I'd been kicked by a horse. That cannot be it. There must be more to do. More I can do for him.

"No, there's got to be something else," I say. "RJ, it's already December. I can . . . I can find you a Christmas tree. I can throw you a tree-trimming party."

RJ is silent, just shakes his head a little, side to side.

"RJ!" I say. I don't mean to yell at him, but I think I'm yelling. "Come on, RJ. One more thing!"

He takes another deep breath, enough to say a few more words.

"You did it," he says.

I don't say anything. I can't say anything because a cold hand has closed around my vocal cords; I'm not crying because everything's been frozen solid.

"It's done," he says. "The list is complete."

He seems to relax into his pillow. The white softness cradles and enfolds his head from all sides.

Then he adds one more word.

"Thanks."

CHAPTER 59

WHEN I GET HOME, MOM IS STANDING ON THE SOFA. She's hanging clear sheets of plastic over the windows to keep the cold air out. She usually does this around Thanksgiving. She's late this year.

"Hi, honey," she says as I walk in. "How was your visit?"

I push past her without a word and go up to my room. I stand in the middle, my arms wrapped tightly around myself. I feel like I want to scream. On the floor are the drumsticks. I pick them up, throw myself in front of my junk kit, and begin to play.

Lemme at 'em Lemme at 'em Lemme at 'em Lemme at 'em Lemme at 'em Lemme at 'em Lemme at 'em Lemme at 'em Lemme at 'em Lemme at 'em Lemme at 'em Lemme at 'em Lemme at 'em

I play louder and faster and louder still, but it feels like something's missing.

On the small table next to my bed are RJ's headphones.

I grab them. Then I start digging in the drawer next to my bed. Under packets of wax for my braces, some extra hoses for a turtle terrarium, and an extra bottle of Aqua-gel, I find a folded piece of paper. It's my forty-hours form. I stare at it in disbelief. I stopped keeping track of my hours a long time ago, after the fourth or fifth visit. I can't believe I ever thought of RJ as a chore I had to deal with, a way to get numbers on a sheet of paper.

I turn the form over, and it's covered in RJ's hand-writing. His music list—ten songs by ten different bands. The first song: "Clash City Rockers" by the Clash.

I open my laptop, search for the song, and find it with no problem.

I hit play.

Ner! Ner-ner! Ner! Ner-ner!

Ner! Ner-ner! Ner! Ner-ner!

I sit down at my drum set, headphones on, and the music fills me. Anger. Frustration. Power.

Dum-chack!

Dum-dum chack!

Dum-chack!

Dum-dum chack!

The drums kick in, and my head starts to bang up and down with the music as I stomp the pedal and slam the metal pan, again and again. The music has taken com-plete control, and I'm not even here. It's just the music.

When the song ends, it's like being jerked out of a happy sleep. I can't hit replay fast enough. I play with my full might.

I want to liquefy everybody gone dry

Or plug into the aerials that poke up in the sky

This is how I feel: caught between hating everyone around me who doesn't know what it's like to be filled with tears, and wishing I could connect to something far away, far up there. I play harder and harder, and then I hear a crack and see something whiz away, as if electrified. I pause the music. I'm in awe. Like the Dog Complex drummer, I broke a drumstick.

There's banging on the door.

"WILL!"

"WHAT!"

"Knock it off—you're driving me crazy!"

I feel a surge of anger, and when my bedroom door opens, I turn it on Mom as she comes in the room.

"I DON'T CARE!" I yell. "GET OUT!"

"Will!" she says. "You don't talk to me like that!"

I throw the sticks down onto the floor and sit, glowering at her. I'm breathing hard.

"What's the matter with you?" she asks. "Did something happen with RJ?"

"No!" I say.

"You're sad about RJ."

"I'm not sad!" I say.

"You're angry," she says.

"Would you stop telling me what I *feel*?" I say.

"But I know how you feel!" she says.

"No, you don't!" I shout. "You don't know. My friend is dying in the hospital, and I've been watching him get worse and worse, and you have no idea what it's like!"

"Yes, I do, Will," she says sternly, her voice getting louder and louder. "I know what it's like to lose someone. I went through it with your father!"

"Then why won't you actually help me?" I yell back. "All you give me is your bullcrap, your 'it's hard to say goodbye' bullcrap! I don't need to be told this is hard! Obviously, it's hard!"

"Then what do you need, Will?" she asks.

"Tell me about Dad," I say, looking her in the eye.

At first, I see the tiniest little shake of her head. But I can tell—she isn't saying no to me. She's actually saying no to some part of herself, a part that she's afraid of. She looks like she's about to speak, but then her eyes fill with tears. She puts both hands up to her face and sobs.

Shame spreads across me, as if I'm the cause of her sadness, and then *bam!* Just like that, for the second time, I'm four years old.

I'm in the hospital with Dad.

Mom is here too.

She's crying the same way she is now. I'm standing a few feet from the bed, clutching a stuffed penguin.

"Will, come tell your father you love him," she says. She leads me forward to the bed. Dad's eyes are closed, and the machines breathe in and out. I open my mouth, but no sound comes. No breath.

"Go ahead, Will," she says. "Tell him you love him. Maybe he can hear you."

I can't. I can't get the words out. I'm too scared.

I shake my head and push back, away from the bed, away from Dad.

I don't say "I love you."

Now the memory is gone. I'm here in my room.

"Whoo," she says, wiping her eyes with the tip of her sleeve. She breathes deeply for a moment, the way I did the one single time I jumped off a diving board and resurfaced, disoriented from the plunge, the noise, the bubbles, but back in the world I'd come from. I have the feeling that another dive lies ahead of the two of us. A higher jump, a deeper plunge.

"It's always been really, really hard for me to talk about your dad," she says. "But I know I need to change that."

She sniffles and looks around for something to blow her nose on. She digs in her jeans pocket and pulls out a crumpled piece of tissue.

"I didn't tell Dad I loved him," I say.

"What?" she asks. She blows her nose and looks at me. "When?"

"Before he died," I say. Suddenly, I'm crying too. "I couldn't do it."

It's my turn to cover my face with my hands.

"Oh, honey," she says, pulling me over to sit beside her on the bed. "Please look at me. You were only four years old! It's okay! He knew! Please trust me, he knew how you felt."

We sit in silence a minute. My breathing gradually steadies. I feel tingly.

"Has that always bothered you?" she asks. "That you couldn't tell your dad you loved him? Why didn't you ever tell me about that?"

"I just remembered," I say.

"You need to forgive yourself, Will," she says. "Dad wouldn't want you feeling bad about that eight years later."

I nod.

"You know, hospitals can be really strong triggers for memory," she says. "I wonder if what's going on with RJ is bringing up old stuff about Dad."

"Rabbi Harris said this might happen," I say. "I didn't believe him."

"Rabbi Harris knows a lot more about life than he lets on," she says. "Don't let his hippie-dippie act fool you."

She's quiet for a second.

"Look, Will," she continues. "After your father died, I gathered up some of his—not special things, just everyday things. I thought when you were a little older, you might want them. Are you ready to see them?"

I nod.

Without another word, she disappears from my room. I hear her footsteps on the stairs go down. A minute later, she comes in the door with the wicker hamper from the basement. The place I've been avoiding since the day Mom and Aunt Mo moved the boxes down there six years ago. The place where I went to excavate for a bass drum and found an old suitcase full of odds and ends.

"It looks like you got into this already," she says. "I thought I recognized that suitcase."

"That's *Dad's* stuff?" I say, horrified at how unceremoniously I dumped it into the hamper. "I—I didn't know!"

"It's okay, Will, relax."

She sets it on the bed; then she takes a breath—not a big one. Anyone but me would have missed it. But I know what that breath means. I can see that what's about to happen is big for her. Really big. Bigger than jumping into any pool, no matter how deep, or any pond, no matter how murky. I imagine it's more like leaping into the ocean—endless blue below and crashing waves above.

"Everything in here has a little story attached," she says gently, almost sweetly. "Nothing big, all little stuff. Some of it might help you feel more connected to Dad."

I reach into the box and pull out the baseball hat.

"This was Dad's?" I ask.

"Yeah," Mom says. "He was a big Oakland A's fan. He grew up in Oakland. Put it on."

I hold it in my hands, but I don't want to put it on. It doesn't seem right to wear his hat.

"What's the matter?" she presses. "You can wear it."

This hat was once on Dad's head. If I could run backward in time, one hand on the hat, eventually, I'd find my father there. Here. He'd be right here.

I go back to the hamper.

A Post-it note: *Went to get grozeries. See you in 1 hr.*

"What's 'grozeries'?" I say.

"That's how your dad and I used to say it," Mom says with a smile. "Grozeries. I don't even remember how that started."

I go back to the hamper and pull out a thin strip of paper.

"That's a sushi menu," says Mom. "I've never met anyone who could eat as much sushi as your dad. He would have been horrified at what passes for sushi in Horicon."

The menu has little Xs next to certain foods. A random

dinner on a random night. I wonder if I was there, a toddler or a baby or not yet born. I dig a bit lower in the box and find something odd: a bundle of red pens, held together with a rubber band. Before I can ask what it is, Mom sighs and lifts the bundle from my hand, cradling it in two palms.

"You know how Dad and I met, right?" she says. "We were copy editors at a newspaper in Berkeley. This part I've never told you. We were both hired at the same time, and we liked each other, but neither of us had the nerve to ask the other one out. So after a while, your dad would steal all my red pens when I was away from my desk, and when I'd come back to my desk, I'd be like 'Oh, shoot. I don't have any red pens. I'll have to go borrow some from the cute new guy.' I would visit him for pens like five times a day, and finally, we went on a date!"

She looks at me. "Isn't that *soooo* sweet?"

I shrug. "Dorky."

"You think that's dorky—our first Valentine's Day, he gave me a big, cheesy bouquet of roses and a really sweet card, written in red pen. And the first red pen was stuck down in the flowers. And every Valentine's Day, he'd give me another bouquet and card and another red pen."

"That's why you always write me notes in red pen," I say, realizing.

She nods, reaches into the box, and pulls out a thick manila envelope.

I can guess what's in it, and I know what she's thinking: maybe soon she'll be ready to open the envelope and read those cards. To face the feelings.

"Why didn't you show me this stuff a long time ago?" I ask.

"I wasn't ready," she says. "Maybe I waited too long."

"Yes, you waited too long!" I say. "I can't believe you just left all Dad's stuff sitting in the basement!"

"Will, I need you to understand something," she says. "Raising a kid alone . . . It's really one of the hardest things in the world to do. Even with a great kid like you. For a long time after your dad died, the only way I could make it through the day was to keep my mind on the two of us. Focus on you and me. I couldn't afford to think about Dad. I couldn't afford to be sad all the time."

This makes me feel bad, but it also makes sense.

"But maybe things are changing," she says. "Your Bar Mitzvah is just around the corner. You've gotten up on-stage alone; you've made friends besides Shirah; you've become a rock and roll drummer. You gotta admit, you're not the same kid you were two years ago. Or even last summer."

She's right. I don't feel different. But when I look back, I see that things have changed. *I've* changed. Maybe I'm ready to remember the past. Maybe I'm ready to try new things.

I put the hat on. It fits.

"Mom, I was thinking," I say. "About the surgery. I think I'm ready. I want to go through with it."

"Are you sure?"

I nod.

"I knew you'd come around," she says quietly. "I never actually cancelled it."

"Mom!" I say, as if I'm angry; she knows I hate it when she doesn't listen to what I say. But I can't be angry with her, not now.

She leans over and puts her arms around me, and she holds me for a minute, the way she used to do.

CHAPTER 60

I'M IN THE HOSPITAL BED, WAITING TO BE TAKEN INTO surgery. My room has a view of the Milwaukee River and the snow that's settling on the buildings and church spires and roads and little cars down below. I'm wearing a hospital gown—the kind that ties in the back, the kind that RJ was wearing the last few times I saw him. Also, I'm wearing Dad's hat. It's giving me courage. Mom is sitting here next to me, in a fold-up cake-chair, just like the one in RJ's room. I've been here for about an hour, but it already feels like a day. Mom and I drove three hours to Milwaukee yesterday and spent the night at a motel down the street so we could be at the hospital for intake at seven a.m. Before bed, I called RJ to say I'd visit as soon as I could, but he was groggy and distant. It was a short call.

My heart has been pounding for most of the morning, but once I changed into my gown and settled into my room, a nurse brought me a pill and a cup of water. She said it would help me feel calm and relaxed. Now she says she's going to put in the IV.

She has me lay my arm out, wrist up.

"Little pinch," she says.

It hurts. A lot. But then it's over.

She leaves.

"You okay?" asks Mom.

I nod.

We sit for a long time.

There's a knock on the door, and in comes Dr. Haffetz.

"Will Levine," he says brightly. "Any questions before we bring you in?"

I'm drowsy. I can't think of anything.

"Will, I know you're worried about your jaw being wired shut," Mom prompts. "Did you want to ask Dr. Haffetz about that?"

"Just to be clear," Dr. Haffetz interjects, "we're not wiring anything. We're going to use rubber bands, like the kind that are on your braces. They'll keep your teeth together, but there are not going to be any wires."

"But you told me—" I say.

"I said it was *possible*," says Dr. Haffetz. "Life is full of possibilities. Most of them never happen. I'm quite certain the worst of the swelling and soreness will be over in a week, and for a month, you'll eat lots of soup. No biggie. It's the only thing that's good to eat when it's twenty below out, anyhow."

There is one other thing. The sleep apnea that might have made Dad die. I've never forgotten that. "I have one other question," I say. He looks at his clipboard, then at me, and takes his glasses off. He's listening.

"Remember last summer you said that my dad might have died during his surgery because of heart damage from sleep apnea?"

Dr. Haffetz and my mom look at each other.

"We don't *know* that Dad had sleep apnea," Mom corrects me.

"Well, he might have, right?" I press.

"Again, it's *possible*," says Dr. Haffetz, raising both eyebrows. "You said he was a heroic snorer. It's possible he had the type of occlusion we're seeing in you."

"Well, the thing is . . . ," I say. "I snore. So could I have sleep apnea? Could I have heart damage? What if the same thing that happened to my dad . . ."

Mom puts her hand on my arm. She can see I've asked a really important question.

Dr. Haffetz comes over to me, pulls a penlight out of his jacket pocket, and looks in one ear, then the other.

"Mmm," he says. "Mm-hm."

"*What?*" I demand. "What do you see?"

"I see that your heart is fine," he says.

"You can see it in my *ear*?" I ask.

"No, that was for dramatic effect," he says. "The truth

is, even if you had very bad sleep apnea, you've only had it for a year or two. Nothing to worry about."

I look at Mom and let loose a long sigh; almost a laugh of relief.

Dr. Haffetz comes round in front of me. "Open," he says. He runs his thumb along the inside of my lip, top and bottom.

"Good," he says. "The braces really got you lined up. You're ready."

He pats me on the shoulder and says that the orderlies will come by with a gurney in about fifteen minutes.

The door closes, and it's very, very still.

The medicine is kicking in. I feel light-headed. My cheeks feel hot. Rather than being myself, I'm seeing myself.

I see that I'm about to go into surgery, the same way Dad did, the last day I saw him.

Dad, I say, inside my head. *If you're there, I miss you.*

The instant I say it, there's a knock on the door. Two men in white uniforms come in, pushing a gurney. They roll it next to my bed and help me shift myself onto it.

"Can you remove your hat, please?" asks one of the men. I take it off and hand it to Mom.

"I'll be waiting for you in the recovery room," Mom says, holding the hat, her voice almost fierce. She kisses me.

I feel the gurney start to move, and for a moment, despite the medicine to help me feel calm, a surge of hot adrenaline shoots through my body. The gurney is braced with two sudden but gentle jerks of the platform and then, total stillness. It's very bright in here. The masked face of Dr. Haffetz appears, along with the masks and glasses of other doctors. One says hello and tells me his name, but I don't catch it. He tells me to count down. I start at ten. I say nine. I forget what's next.

· · ·

Someone is calling my name sternly, like I'm late for school. I can't talk, and it's hard to breathe because my throat is bone-dry, and the muscles around my lips are numb. Like my face has fallen asleep.

I don't want to open my eyes, but the voice keeps telling me to keep my eyes open. Lights are sliding over me again.

Then I see Mom.

"Hi, honey," she says. "You did it. It's done."

What's done? I wonder. *What did I do?*

CHAPTER 61

I'VE BEEN IN THE HOSPITAL FOR THREE DAYS. I REALLY hope I get out tomorrow.

It's the winter solstice. The shortest day of the year. It's also the second day of Chanukah. I know this because last night, Mom and I lit birthday candles stuck to a piece of foil on my dinner tray.

After we lit the candles, Mom gave me my present for the first night. It was a little envelope like you'd attach to a bunch of flowers. I opened it, and inside was a little card with cartoon balloons and flowers. Mom decorated the inside like a homemade coupon.

Good for FREE drum lessons.

User must practice drums between lessons
or coupon is null and VOID.

"It's amazing that they sell those coupons in a hospital gift shop," she said.

"Ah dote have eddy drubs," I say.

"I know," she says. "We'll find you some drums."

I can't smile. I can't find my lips. And it's hard to talk. Partially because my teeth are banded together, but also because I have crusty, bloody bandages all over my face, stuffed under my lips, and up my nose. It's hard to breathe. I only talk when I have to. On top of that, my tongue hurts. If I move it the wrong way, an agonizing pain stabs all the way down my throat.

"If we end up having to spend another night of Chanukah here," Mom says, "I wonder what else they have down there in the gift shop. Maybe some other coupons?"

"A'duduh dight?" I say, showing my displeasure. "Ah wah go hobe. . . ."

"I know," she says. "But we can't rush it. It's not up to us."

...

I don't recognize myself in the mirror. My face looks like a purple jack-o'-lantern. My eyes are narrow slits; my cheeks look like I have an apple stored in each side; and the red-stained bandages look like something out of a horror movie. The bandages are starting to smell.

I stumble back to the bed.

"I wish I didn't do dis," I say to Mom.

"Do what?" says Mom.

I point to my face, irritated.

"You don't mean that," she says.

I turn as much as my stiff neck will allow. She's looking at me from where she sits on her cake-chair. It's just like the one in RJ's room. Maybe all the hospitals in Wisconsin buy their folding cake-chair/beds from the same store.

I lay my head back on my pillow. I don't want to watch TV. My eyes still strain to read. Outside, it's gray. I can't see the road or the little cars or the church spires from my bed. Just gray, and snowflakes banging against the glass.

Maybe I'll sleep more.

• • •

"Will."

Go away.

"Will, you should wake up, honey."

I open my eyes.

"Why'd you wake be up?" I say, annoyed.

I wish I could sleep for two or three more days and find myself magically at home, with my own face back.

It hurts. So. Much.

"Will, I just got a call," she says. "From Rabbi Harris."

Why would Rabbi Harris call Mom now? He knows I'm recovering from surgery. I'm going to see him for my Torah lessons in a week.

I turn to look at Mom, and she's not moving. Not talking. Her lips part, like she's got the words ready but can't release them.

"What!" I demand. "Why'd he call?"

"Honey," she says. "Your friend RJ . . . he died a few hours ago."

My face and tongue hurt too much to say anything. Instead, my eyes fill up fast and overflow.

CHAPTER 62

Max is on my left. Shirah is on my right. We walk down the cemetery path toward a crowd of people standing at a grave. Next to it is a mound of brown dirt, dusted with snow, and a pair of machines—jackhammers, I guess—leaning against a crate. A bit farther back are about eight rows of folding chairs, snow banked knee-high around them like a little frozen amphitheater.

We sit in the back row. Near the grave, I can see Rabbi Harris. He's wearing a long black coat. Instead of his usual knit *kippah,* he's wearing a white satin one like he wears on Yom Kippur. He's wearing sunglasses. Most of the adults are wearing sunglasses, even though there's no sun today.

More people fill in the seats. Two of them I recognize, though they look different without their blue scrubs: Roxanne and Denise. Roxanne has one arm around Denise, and both of them look like they've been crying a lot.

I look around at the faces of the people who stand off

to the side of the chairs. I see a few men in dark suits with flat expressions. Some older women are there too. Everyone is very quiet. Very still. A black car with a long back crawls down the road, followed by a black limo. The two cars pull up near the grave. People get out, dressed in black. I see the occasional puff of tissue, held to eyes, pushed under lifted sunglasses.

Some of the men from the limo go to the rear of the long car and open the back. Inside is a casket. The men roll it out, gripping a set of metal poles that run its length. The front of the coffin is supported by two big men. One is tall, built like a lumberjack. His eyebrows, his nose, the square of his jaw—in his face, I can see RJ.

It's RJ's dad.

He drove the truck that paid the bills, coming to visit RJ late at night, sleeping over and leaving early in the morning.

I want to meet him and talk to him. But I'm a little afraid. Afraid of his grief. Afraid I won't know what to say.

My eyes move to other faces and lock on someone I never expected to see. Certainly not at RJ's funeral.

Jake.

WHAT IS HE DOING HERE?

"Jake," Shirah calls to him, and points across me to a chair, two down on my right side. "You want to sit with us?"

I start to stand up in objection and realize that Shirah's arm isn't pointing. It's blocking. She won't let me escape.

Jake doesn't notice this, though. He crosses in front of me, wiping his nose with the back of his sleeve, and plops down next to me. His cheeks are wet with tears.

"My brother was really good friends with RJ back in fifth grade," he explains to Shirah. A few rows up on the other side of the aisle, I see a taller-looking version of Jake; obviously, his brother. "He used to hang out at our house a lot, before he moved away. We didn't know he was back. Or that he was so sick. How did you know him?"

Shirah points her thumb at me. She's telling me it's time to talk.

"We were friends," I say. My teeth are banded together, so when I talk, my lips draw back to reveal a pained smile, a sore sneer.

Jake nods and wipes his eyes. He starts to turn away and then whips back around to look at me: a classic double take.

"What happened to your face?"

I know he isn't talking about any improvement to my chin. It's too soon for that. My face is still swollen and puffy, and I have bruises under my eyes from the surgery.

"He had an operation," interjects Shirah. "Leave him alone."

"I was just curious," Jake says defensively.

"Drop it," says Shirah.

Jake turns back to the front. Shirah didn't need to come to my defense so aggressively, but still, I appreciate it. I'm not in the mood for Jake's interrogation. On the other hand, seeing him so devastated by RJ's death has caused some of my negative feelings about him to evaporate.

I see Gwen. She's standing off to the side, wearing a green coat and a knit hat with earflaps. She's standing by herself. Her face is blank. Frozen. I know how she feels. I carry my sadness inside me, too, a shell around my heart. I've always dealt with my sadness alone. But I know RJ wouldn't want her to be by herself. I rise out of my chair and wave to her. She sees me.

I motion for her to come over.

There's a seat in front of Shirah and Max and Jake and me. She walks over stiffly, half dead, and sits down. Shirah puts her hand on Gwen's shoulder.

The service starts. This is only the second funeral I've ever been to. The first was my dad's, but I was only four. I don't remember it. Except maybe I do.

Flakes of memory flutter around me. A mound of dirt. Shovels. The adults taking turns shoveling dirt onto Dad's casket, a Jewish tradition. Mom takes the shovel, her lip quivering, loosens some dirt, and shovels it into the grave. Then she hands the shovel to someone else, and she grabs my hand. The coffin is going in the ground.

Here, in the cemetery, with the ground broken open

for RJ, it feels like the line separating me from Dad is dissolved.

"Dad?" I whisper. "I'm okay," I tell him. "I'm really okay."

"You say something?" Shirah asks, leaning closer to me.

I shake my head. But I can feel it—my mouth is almost ready to tell Dad what my heart always needed to. But first, I remember the Mourner's Kaddish, the prayer for the dead, which my mom always says for Dad when we go to temple, the prayer I will begin to say once I've had my Bar Mitzvah. Right now, I'm still too young to say the Mourner's Kaddish.

But I can say the Drummer's Kaddish.

My mind says: *yitgadal v'yitkadash, shmei rabbah.*

My hands pray: *bappa dum, b'dada-bum, boom. Amen. B'dada-bum, b'dada-bum, b'dada-bum, b'dada-bum . . .*

I imagine sending the rhythm from my hands straight to RJ, wherever he is, then straight to Dad. Maybe they're in the same place, so I play this rhythm, over and over and over until it's done. And then, like Mom does as she completes the Kaddish, I bow: just the tiniest, most imperceptible nod—once to the left. Once to the right. Once to the middle.

And then my lips move.

"Dad, I love you."

CHAPTER 63

RABBI HARRIS GREETS ME AT THE OFFICE DOOR WITH A big hug. I follow him into his office and sit down across from him.

"It looks like your physical healing is coming along," he says. "You seem much less swollen. And I think the change is remarkable."

He's trying to be nice, but my cheeks and eye sockets look and feel like they've been bludgeoned.

"Are you happy with the results?" he asks.

The truth is, I've avoided looking in the mirror. I'm afraid of what I'll see. I'm not supposed to brush my teeth until the sutures dissolve in another week or so. Instead, I rinse with this intense green mouthwash at the kitchen sink: no mirror.

"I haven't been out much," I explain, talking through my banded teeth. "No one's told me how I look."

"Are you always going to let other people decide how you look, Will?" he asks.

I glance up at Rabbi Harris. He's looking at me kindly, but with one eyebrow raised a bit, as if he's proposed a riddle for me to solve.

"How's your heart?" he asks, changing the subject. "It hurts, doesn't it? Feels like a punch right here."

He points to the center of his broad chest.

I nod.

"You up for practicing your portion?" he asks.

I nod again.

I've been sitting at home with nothing to do for the past two weeks, so I've made lots of progress on my trope. On top of that, since the funeral, I haven't wanted to leave the house or see anyone. I basically sit in my room, going over my trope. I sleep a lot. I keep the blinds down.

Rabbi Harris and I work on my Torah portion, and when we're done, he closes my folder and slides it toward me, across the table.

"It feels weird," he says, "not to be heading to the hospital together."

It does.

"Anyway, before you go," he says. "I have something for you. It's from RJ."

I lean forward as he opens his desk drawer and pulls out an envelope.

"I helped him with the handwriting," he explains.

I open the envelope. Inside, there's a folded piece of notebook paper, the little spiral frills still attached.

Last Will and Testament of Ralph Jerome Olsen

Being of sound mind, I do hereby declare that this document is my last will and testament.

I nominate Rabbi Harris Goldberg, Executor of this Will, to serve without bond.

Hi, Will. This is my <u>will for Will</u>. Get it?

Will, you've been the best friend a guy could have. I wish I could give you way more than this, but I don't own much, so it'll have to do.

I leave you my three prized possessions:

(1) My turtle. I know it was originally yours, but now it's technically mine, so I'm giving it to you. Gwen will keep it for you until you're better from your operation.

(2) This, Rabbi Harris will give you.

(3) is a surprise. I'll have my dad bring it to your home.

RJO

I put the letter down. I can't believe RJ was thinking about me during his final days.

Rabbi Harris opens the drawer again and pulls out a small brown box. On the lid, it says *Will*.

I open it. I reach in and pull out RJ's necklace. I hold it up to my eyes. It's hundreds of tiny shell fragments, rough and irregular, strung together like the spine of some fantastic serpent.

"You want to put it on?" asks Rabbi Harris.

No. No, no, no, it doesn't belong on me. It's still his.

I hold it to my forehead. Part of me wants to put it back in the box, but the other part, the part that controls my hands, loops it around my neck, once, twice, then closes the clasp.

...

It's December 31, the last day of the year. My face no longer pulses with constant pain, but still, it's sore from the moment I wake up until I fall into bed.

Mom makes thick soup. Every night, it's potato soup, cheese soup, or tomato soup. Nothing tastes good. I also drink these gross protein things that come in a blue can. They taste like chalk, but I prefer them because when I drink one, Mom doesn't make me come downstairs for dinner. I stay in my room. I lie on my bed.

On my nightstand are RJ's headphones and the little brown box that RJ's shell necklace came in. I love the necklace. But I hated taking it off and seeing it at night, like an artifact of someone once great and living. So I decided I'm never going to take it off.

There's a knock on the door.

"Hey, honey," Mom says. "Did you want to come down for a little New Year's celebration? We can have ice cream. Or, hey! I can make you a shake! I promise, I won't sneak any protein powder in it."

I stay silent.

"Okay," she says. She comes over and tries to kiss me on my forehead, but I roll away. I don't want ice cream. I don't want anything good or fun or nice, not while RJ's gone. And he's gone forever, so maybe no more ice cream forever.

She leaves, and time passes. Maybe I should go to sleep. It must be close to midnight.

New Year's. Who cares?

CHAPTER 64

I WAKE UP, AND I DON'T MOVE. IT'S WEDNESDAY, THE first week of school after winter break. I've missed two days already—my face hurt too much to go to school.

Eventually, Mom comes to get me, but I won't get up.

"I will not allow you to stay home past Friday," she says. "You understand?"

She sounds angry, but I know she's only pretending. She's actually scared.

"And I think you need some grief counseling," she says. "I'm going to get a referral from your school."

I don't say anything, and I don't move.

She goes to work, and I stay in my room. Everything feels hollow and drained of life. I haven't touched my drums since before RJ died. Glass terrariums line the walls, empty except for the herp hotels, the pumps.

• • •

It's about 3:45 when the doorbell rings. It's Shirah, and she pushes past me, holding up two big cups. "Jamba Jews!" she says. "Get it? *Jamba Jews!*"

"Yes, I get it," I say. "Thanks. I am so sick of soup."

She hands me the cups and takes off her coat.

"How's the healing?" she asks. "Still a lot of pain?"

"It's not as bad as it was," I say.

"So you'll be there on Saturday, right?"

I look at her blankly.

"Max's Bar Mitzvah!"

Wow. I completely forgot about that.

"I'm not sure," I say.

"You *have* to come, Will," she says, her tone changing. "I know you're sad because of RJ, but Max really needs you. You have to be there."

"So, you guys are going out now, huh?" I say.

She nods. "I guess so," she says. "Is that weird?"

I shrug. I'm not jealous of Max, exactly, but the two of them together . . . it feels . . . odd. And a little lonely, like they've left me behind.

She looks at her watch.

"I guess I should probably get back to volleyball practice," she says. "I'm in some kind of rut and I need all the drills I can get. Here . . ." She takes a big sip of the Mango Tango. "I'll leave the rest for you. It's good."

Soon, she's headed to practice, and I begin thinking—

she didn't say anything about my face. I wonder: Is the change not noticeable?

I can't hold back any longer. I go to the bathroom and grab Mom's mirror and turn on the light. I take a deep breath. I count to three.

I look.

It's my face. My front teeth line up now, the top and bottom teeth banded together, touching. And my chin is a little different. The fold of flesh that surrounded my little turtle chin is gone. But essentially, I look the same.

I'm disappointed. Really disappointed.

CHAPTER 65

It's Friday night. It's dark out. I've been sitting in the room, one light on—too tired to read, too bored to do anything, too sad to play drums. I hear the sound of an engine in the driveway, headlights crawling across my ceiling. The new porch lights turn on; then I hear Mom talking from the door.

"Will!" she calls.

I come downstairs, expecting maybe to see Max. Or maybe Shirah. But it's neither of them.

It's RJ's dad.

I recognize him from the funeral. With his sunglasses off, I can see RJ got his burning blue eyes from him. He's very tall and thickly built, wearing a heavy plaid shirt, a puffy vest zipped over it, and a hunter's cap with earflaps and a brim.

"Can I make you tea or coffee?" asks Mom. "It's freezing out there."

"Oh, that's not necessary," says RJ's dad. "I'll only be here a minute." He turns to me.

"Will, I'm really sorry we didn't get to meet earlier. I'm RJ's dad. Glen."

He offers me his hand to shake, the way RJ did on the day we met.

"RJ gave me some really specific instructions," he says. "There's something out in the back of the truck he wanted you to have. Will you come have a look?"

I'm numb. I'm floating. I put on a coat and follow RJ's dad outside. We walk down the driveway toward a big white pickup truck. It's snowing, and the air is full of gentle movement.

There's something up there, in the back of the truck, under a blue tarp. A frosting of snow has settled into the folds. RJ's dad turns a knob for the truck's rear hatch to drop down. He grabs the corner of the tarp and lifts it off as a gust of wind comes along, billowing the tarp out like a sail.

It's a drum set.

Red. Sparkling under the porch lights.

"RJ's prized possession," says RJ's dad. "I really hope you'll take them."

The drums are beautiful. The bass drum, the big one, says SLINGERLAND. I remember that name from the very first time I visited RJ. He said he had a beautiful, vintage Slingerland drum set at home. I remember liking the sound of the name—like it's a faraway, happy place. Under the brand name, someone drew two very deliberate and bold letters: *RJ*.

For the first time since I finished RJ's bucket list, I want something. Deeply. I can't wait to set them up, grab my sticks, and pound the drums with all my might.

"Why don't you take the cymbals?" RJ's dad asks. "I can carry the shells myself." He hands me a black nylon case the size of an extra-large pizza delivery box, and with his two thick arms he lifts the drum shells off the truck bed.

I lead the way and hold the door for RJ's dad, and we march the drums toward the stairs.

My mom sees us from the living room.

"It's gonna get loud around here," she says.

"Very," I say, and find myself smiling for the first time in ages.

We go into my room, and immediately RJ's dad remarks, "That's a lot of fish tanks. I don't think there's even room for a drum set."

I look around from terrarium to terrarium to terrarium. He's right. They're taking up every corner of my bedroom. I only kept them because I thought I'd eventually catch more turtles, but I'm done with that.

"I'm getting rid of them," I say. "I don't need them anymore."

"I have the truck outside—you want me to take them off your hands?"

Moments later, we're moving the tanks downstairs and out the door to his truck. As he closes and locks the back, I notice my mood shifting; I feel lighter. Freer.

"RJ was a great guy," I say to Mr. Olsen. I know it's not enough.

I think he's going to speak because he opens his mouth, but then he swallows and clears his throat and claps me lightly on the shoulder. He nods and gives me the smallest of smiles, gets in his truck, and drives away.

CHAPTER 66

I'M AT MAX'S BAR MITZVAH PARTY. I WENT TO THE CER-
emony this morning. I didn't sit with the other kids from
Hebrew school. I sat way in the far corner. And I left as
soon as it was over, so I never talked to Max, but he saw
me; he was carrying the Torah down the aisles of the
sanctuary and our eyes met. His face ignited, beaming.
He brought the Torah a little closer, and he looked me in
the eye. I saw his joy, overflowing. I saw his pride. I also
saw sympathy and concern. It was more than I could
take, and I looked away.

I'm at his party, though I made sure to show up as late
as I could, hoping no one would notice me. My goal: to
wander around, find Max, say hi, and leave.

I'm feeling very self-conscious. I wonder if kids will
see my jaw under the flashing party lights and assume
the puffiness is a trick of the shadows. I've been very private about the surgery. My teachers know, and maybe a

rumor has gone around. So far, only a few kids have said anything: "Hey, Will—where'd you get the chin?" one yelled. I didn't answer. I turned and walked away, and I heard him call, "Can't you take a joke?"

A few more kids walk by and glance my way, and one says "Hey, Will, we miss you at school." But no one says anything more than that.

From where I'm standing, I can see Max and Shirah and the other kids on the dance floor. I'm happy for Max. Then the song ends, and it's a slow dance. I turn to get some punch, and I'm filling my cup when I feel a tap on my shoulder.

"Having a good time?"

It's Max. His forehead is beaded with sweat, and he's flushed and breathing hard. I'm happy to see him, but my mood has been so grim, I almost can't handle his joy.

"Your face looks good," he says. "The swelling isn't as gross, and your chin looks sort of *chinnier*."

"Thanks, Max."

"Shirah's over there," he says, thumbing behind him. "You should ask her to dance!"

"Wouldn't that be weird?" I ask. "You guys are going out, and it's a slow dance."

"Why would it bother me? Aren't you and I best friends?"

That's the thing about Max—he often doesn't think

before he speaks, but he's one of the most honest people I know. He has a truly good heart. I clap him on the shoulder and head over to Shirah, who is standing by a group of volleyball players. The music is loud and slow. Without talking, we get into the same position as we did at All *Lacrosse* the Dance Floor last October.

"You want to hear some good news?" she asks. "The chain-link fence is gone. You can just walk right into the Back 40."

"That's really cool," I say, but my mind is on other things. "Shirah, can I ask you something? Do I look different? Like, do you see any change from the surgery?"

"Change?" she asks, scanning my face while we rock side to side. "The truth is, Will, I never really saw what the problem was. Your face was always just your face."

"Okay, but I'm not asking about that," I say impatiently. "I'm asking if I look different."

She looks at me closer. I'm not sure what I want her to say.

"Smile," she says. "Oh, yeah—I can see it. I can definitely see it when you smile."

"What's different?" I ask, eager for answers.

"You look more like you," she says.

I'm standing here, smiling at Shirah like a total goofball—my face one foot away from hers in the dark of the dance floor. It's the saddest time of my life, at least that I can remember, but here I am, I'm smiling. Sure, it's because Shirah made me do it. But maybe there's just a tiny bit of smile left in me.

Maybe that's where RJ is.

CHAPTER 67

I'M GAZING INTO THE POND IN THE BACK 40. I HAVEN'T returned since the day we found the bale of Blanding's turtles—that's the word for a turtle group: a bale. It's been four months. The ice has melted, and the first light green buds of spring have arrived, speckling the branches of the trees. This morning, I rode my bike to Herb's Herps, where Gwen met me at the door with a turtle carrier.

"How've you been?" she asked.

I shrugged; not the usual *I dunno* shrug, but one that says *There's no words to describe the way I feel.*

"Me too," she said.

Now, duckweed floats along the edge of the pond in clumps, and here and there, my eyes catch the movement of water bugs coasting from sun to shade or a dragonfly zooming along the surface. All that's left to do is place the turtle in the water. It'll do the rest on its own—it'll swim away, and I'll never see it again.

"Hey, little guy," I say, pulling him out of the carrier. "I think you've been locked up long enough, don't you?"

I hold the turtle an inch over the water, and it occurs to me that this turtle saved the Back 40. There's no way to thank a turtle, though, except to let it go.

Bloop! and it's done.

As it swims away, a feeling of relief washes over me. For just a moment, it feels like I can breathe in a way I haven't been able to for a long while. Then, just as quickly, I'm hit by a terrible reality.

I never swam in the Back 40.

I didn't finish RJ's bucket list.

I could do it now. Shuck off my clothes, jump in, and be done with it. But that doesn't feel right, and I know exactly why.

RJ didn't want me to swim in the Back 40. He wanted me to swim in the ocean.

CHAPTER 68

I'VE NEVER WANTED TO HAVE A BAR MITZVAH PARTY, and one morning in May, as I'm gathering my stuff for school, Mom asks if maybe there's something else I want instead, some other way to celebrate the accomplishment of my Bar Mitzvah. Something other than a party.

"I want to go to Hawaii," I say.

I've never seen her go that still and that silent that fast.

"I don't know, Will," she says. "I feel funny about that idea."

I know what this means: *Dad.* She's upset about going on vacation, just the two of us, and it has to do with Dad. Even after all this time. Even after everything we've been through.

"We'll talk about it another time," she says, and kisses me goodbye as a way of ending the conversation, and without another word, I head out the front door into the humid spring morning. I'm halfway to the bus when I

368

realize that I've forgotten my essay for English class in the printer. I hurry home, open the door with my key, and hear Mom in the living room with Rabbi Harris on the speakerphone. I step closer to listen, staying out of sight.

"Will wanting to go is a *great* reason to spend a few days in Hawaii," says Rabbi Harris. "But it isn't the only reason."

"What else did you have in mind?" asks Mom. I can tell that she knows the answer, but she doesn't like it.

"Erika," Rabbi Harris says. "When we first met, your husband had been gone for a year but you missed him so much, you couldn't function, day to day. You couldn't look for work; you couldn't have fun with Will; you couldn't find any meaning in life. So what did we do?"

"Sat shivah," says Mom.

"Right," says Rabbi Harris. "Seven days of complete grieving, all the Jewish customs—even though Dan had already been gone for more than a year."

Dan. My dad's name. A name I haven't heard in forever. When Mom and I talk, it's always just "Dad" or maybe "your dad." Sometimes I forget he even had a name.

"You covered all the mirrors in the house with black cloth, and you sat on cushions on the floor, and you wore a black ribbon and people brought you meals for a week. After seven days, you'd completed sitting shivah—you got up from the floor, you took the black ribbon off your

369

shirt, and you went out and found your job. You started doing Saturday movies with Will. But I don't think you ever fully returned to life."

Saturday movies.

That's when we started synchronizing watches! For me, it had always been a silly joke Mom couldn't let go of. Now I see that it's a custom we invented during a painful transition; Mom's way of clawing her way back into the light.

"You've tried to move forward," says Rabbi Harris. "And you're doing an amazing job. But you're still holding on. You haven't let go. Am I right?"

I hear Mom sniffle. And suddenly, for the first time, I understand her. I know how she feels.

"It's time to take the black cloth off the mirrors, Erika," says Rabbi Harris. "Take Will to Hawaii. That's where you and Dan went on your honeymoon, right? Make peace with it. Have a fantastic time. And when you come home, return to life."

I slip out the door without making a sound, full of a new feeling, a blend of emotions that shouldn't be able to mix, and yet, here they are within me—two waves rolling in opposite directions: sadness and joy.

CHAPTER 69

EVERYTHING LOOKS DIFFERENT FROM UP HERE.

It's June 14, and I'm up on the *bimah*. I'm only a few solid steps up from the rest of the synagogue sanctuary, but it feels different with a sea of faces before me.

I'm not running the entire prayer service like Shirah and Max did. Mom and I made that agreement with Rabbi Harris, and it wasn't one of her red-inked "let Will off the hook" things. I have focused on school and memorizing my Torah portion and writing my speech. That was all I could handle, and Rabbi Harris understood. When I think about it, I've come to understand aspects of the values and kindness of Judaism I never knew. I'm not religious, but I do feel more connected.

Everyone sings as Rabbi Harris opens the doors of the Ark, and he hands me the Torah scroll. It's heavy, like the weight of a small child, and I grip it to my chest as I follow him down into the aisle between the rows of seats.

As we walk, people lean in to touch the Torah with their prayer books, kissing the covers as if the brief contact left a sacred residue. I work up the nerve to look the guests in the eyes. Many are older men and women who come to temple every week. Then, as we reach the back of the room, I see newer faces: a few of the kids from Thestrals, my grief counseling group. They aren't Jewish, but they smile and look fascinated and happy for me. I wish I could explain what's going on. I make a mental note to sit with them at lunch and answer any questions.

As I round the corner, I see Roxanne and Denise. Denise is singing the Hebrew along with everyone else. Funny; I didn't realize she was Jewish.

Continuing along the back row, I'm face to face with every kid from Hebrew school—even the ones whose Bar and Bat Mitzvahs I skipped because I was too sorry for myself, too angry, too sad for celebrations. They seem so happy for me.

Nearing the front row, I spot two faces: Gwen and Ms. Kuper. Instead of her usual overalls, Gwen is wearing a dress. She's even wearing makeup. Ms. Kuper is in a cool suit. They both flash me an expression of excitement, as if they're accompanying me to a ship that's about to set sail.

The final three faces I see before I return to the *bimah* are Max, Shirah, and Mom, and their faces blur together as my eyes inexplicably fill with tears. I can just make out their beaming smiles.

This blur continues as the Torah is unwrapped from its velvet cover, and soon the blessing has been recited and the silver pointer is in my hand. The Hebrew on the parchment froths in front of me, and I lower the silver tip to the first black, glossy letter to anchor it in place.

I begin to chant.

As my hand moves across the Torah, the melody unspools from my lips, long ropes of Hebrew connecting verse to verse, millennium to millennium. Once I'm finished, Rabbi Harris rolls the Torah scroll and we dress it in its velvet cover. Before he steps to the side to let me give my speech, he rests his hand on my shoulder and looks me in the eye.

"Go get 'em," he whispers.

I clear my throat.

"At the start of my Torah portion, the Israelites have already crossed the hot and deadly Sinai Desert," I begin, my voice shockingly loud. I move my face back from the microphone and continue, scanning my printed speech for the next line. "They stand at the border of the Promised Land. Not long ago, they were slaves in Egypt, dreaming about a future home where they could be safe, where they could be free. That dream could come true, just steps away. They dispatch scouts to determine what sorts of dangers might lie ahead.

"At first, the scouts present a realistic report. There will be struggles, for sure, but the Promised Land is a good land, and it will provide for all their needs. But then things turn sour. The moment the scouts' leader says the time has come for the Israelites to enter the Land, the rest of the scouts change their tune: they say the Land eats people alive. It's full of giants.

"The entire nation panics and revolts. They would rather return to slavery in Egypt than face the dangers ahead. The story ends in tragedy, with many lives needlessly lost.

"The first time I read this, I thought it was ridiculous. I thought: *There's no such thing as giants. There's no such thing as the ground opening up and eating people alive. There's no such thing as monsters.*

"But in the months that followed, I began to realize that I'd been incorrect. There are many monsters. The question is not *whether* they exist. The questions are *Where do the monsters live? And how will you handle them?*

"I'll come back to this later."

I take a deep breath. I'm swimming into deeper waters.

"I've been trying to open up about my friend RJ."

The second I say his name, I feel an ache develop in my throat. It's a bit like the ache that comes before crying, but it's tighter. Many of the people in the room know about RJ. I can feel everyone lean toward me like a slow-motion wave.

"RJ was an incredibly special person," I say, forcing out the words. "Our friendship only lasted four months, but he changed me forever, mainly having to do with how I've learned to think. And this came by watching how he lived his life. See, RJ had a lot to be scared and angry about. He was suffering from an illness that was stealing his future. It kept him locked up in a very small world: just a hospital room and the occasional trip to the cafeteria.

"And yet RJ constantly searched for new ways to send his mind and imagination outward. To widen the circle of his life. First by getting a pet. Then by going to a punk rock show. And a school dance. And on a roller coaster. There were plenty of times when RJ was sad and angry, but he never gave up his hunger for every taste out there in the world.

"For months, I couldn't understand this, but he asked me to help him. And I did. Each of those little adventures was terrifying, and it never got any easier. I couldn't understand what made RJ want to explore every mountain, every valley of the unknown.

"When I met RJ, I'd been having an awful time dealing with kids at school, and then I got scary news about my own health. The way I handled it was to close up into a shell. I wouldn't try new things. I kept to myself. I pushed people away. I shut them out. Everywhere I looked, there was danger—monstrous giants. I couldn't escape them. I couldn't hide from them. Everywhere I went, they were already there, waiting for me.

"Here's the moment things changed: I was playing drums in front of the whole school at Prairie Marsh's talent show. Me. Alone onstage. RJ pushed me to do it. He was relentless. I agreed, as long as I was wearing a mask. Well, mid-performance, the mask got loose, and it began to fall. I had to make a choice: save the mask or save the music. I let the mask fall, and I kept the beat, and I did this—as my friend Shirah always says—*come what may.*"

Out of the corner of my eye, I see Max gently punch Shirah's arm, and a giant smile blooms on Shirah's face.

"The moment the mask fell," I continue, "is when all the monsters became visible to me . . . as if a new light shone on them. I finally understood where they lived."

I pause and tap my right temple with my pointer finger.

"Inside my shell," I say. "Right here in my mind. The monsters were inescapable because I'd created them myself. And they seemed like giants only because they were so close to my eyes. Like the scouts in my Torah portion, who saw themselves as grasshoppers, I thought I was no match for my monsters. But once I tried stepping outside of my shell—just long enough to get on a roller coaster with my friend Max—I found that the monsters weren't as big as I'd thought they were. It's like it says on a car side mirror: *Monsters in mirror are smaller than they appear.*"

A good-natured chuckle passes through the room, and following his shout-out, I see Shirah turn and smile at Max. He doesn't smile back, though. His gaze is fixed on me, and for an instant, our eyes meet. I have the feeling that Max, someone I used to run and hide from, will be my friend forever.

"I've pushed myself," I say, glancing down at my speech. "In the past few months, I've gone to as many Bar Mitzvahs as I could, and I've gotten involved in Ms. Kuper's new Wild Animal Rehabilitation program. I teach other kids how to care for injured reptiles. And I've been talking more in class and in the halls at school. But I'm not out of my shell completely, which is fine, since that's not how growth works anyhow. Not all at once, but in stages and steps. And managing through sadness also isn't going to happen all at once."

I pause and take a breath. The ache in my neck is tightening.

"I know that mourning for RJ will take a long time," I say, my voice suddenly a croak. "Rabbi Harris says losing a friend is like a blow to the heart. I know I can't just bounce back. But I also know that I'm not alone. I have amazing people to help me, and that's why I have to say thank you to so many of you here today."

My voice locks up. No air, no words. I'm suffocating. I'm choking up right in the middle of my Bar Mitzvah speech. The audience shifts, and I can feel everyone looking at me.

I reach up to loosen my tie, and that's when my fingers make contact with something under my collar: RJ's shell necklace.

It suddenly feels tight; so tight it's constricting my oxygen flow. I fiddle with the clasp and loosen the loop.

It's not perfect, but it's better. I take a few deep, slow breaths and finish my speech.

"To start with," I say tentatively, "Max and Shirah, you're true, good friends. You each have gifts that I've tried to learn from. Max, you taught me the art of movement. Whenever I was stuck, you showed me how to run and leap and climb.

"And, Shirah, you taught me how to make a fist, how to beat a ball across a net, even when you're down ten points. If the heart is willing, you can climb up and fly out of any hole you're in.

"Ms. Kuper," I go on, glancing at her, "you taught me to fight for what I believe in. Some of those fights are visible, and some are invisible. Some of those fights you only win once, and some you have to fight again and again and again. In the future, should anyone ever try to do something bad to the Back 40, I'll be there, ready to fight."

I see Ms. Kuper make a subtle fist, a show of solidarity.

"Gwen," I continue, "besides helping me with this speech, you taught me that it's never a bad idea to risk loving someone. You also taught me that there are always people who know more than you do, even about the subjects where you already know everything."

There's a little jolt of laughter in the room, even though only she and I know what I'm talking about. I see her dab at her eyes with the tips of her pinkies, and Ms. Kuper hands her a tissue.

"Rabbi Harris," I say, looking behind me to where he's sitting in the big chair at the back of the *bimah*. "If RJ was the one who pushed me into the water, you're the one who led me to the shore. I didn't like what you were up to early on, but now I see that you had a sense of what I needed from the beginning. I'm lucky to have you in my life."

I pause and realize something. My speech is almost over. That means the whole thing is almost over: the speech, the Bar Mitzvah, the year leading up. The waiting, the stress, the nightmares, the wondering. It's all about to become a memory. But there are two more people to thank, and I'm swimming deep. Only the vast, deep blue below.

"Dad," I say, and stop. I touch my throat. Amazingly, there is no fear. Instead, there is an ocean of warmth and compassion and concern before me, keeping me afloat. "I used to be sad when I thought about you, but now I feel different. I feel connected, knowing how happy you'd be for me. Thank you—I love you. I miss you."

"Mom," I say. I look up, and there she is, looking at me, shining her smile at me, bright as a lighthouse. "You know me better than anyone in the world. And even when I tried as hard as I could to push you away, you never left my side. Your love was always stronger than my fear."

I thank everyone for coming, I shut my mouth, and everyone shouts "Mazel Tov!"

It's over.

• • •

After the service, there is lunch: pastrami on rye bread. I sit at a big round table with Max on my left, Shirah and Gwen on my right. I eat and feel the squiggly feelings of relief and satisfaction. Across from me are a few of Shirah's volleyball friends, and the kids from Thestrals. The group is named after the winged, skeletal horses from Harry Potter, creatures a person can only see if they've witnessed death. For a little while, though, we're like everybody else. We laugh and talk, and every time I take a bite, I sneak a peek at the flawless C shape I've bitten into my sandwich—beautiful layers of pink, yellow, and white, nothing falling, nothing landing in my lap.

The moment is perfect. Almost perfect. I can't shake the feeling: something remains unfinished, and I can't enter this new chapter of my life without completing it.

I need to finish the last task.

I need to swim in the ocean.

CHAPTER 70

IT'S JUNE 25. I'M IN NORTHWEST MAUI, IN AN AREA called Kapalua.

Yes, Maui. I'm in Hawaii.

On our first day, I put on the diving mask and went into the water—just wading out, waist-deep. I started to get anxious, so I stopped and went back to shore. Some old voice inside my head said, *You're done! It's good enough!* But I knew wading around and running for shore wasn't what RJ meant by "swimming in the ocean."

The next day, I tried several times to go deeper. I was wearing RJ's shell necklace, and whenever the water reached the necklace, I started breathing hard. I thrashed my way back to shore, disappointed in myself.

Each day, Mom brought a book to the beach and sat under an umbrella. After failing to swim, I would sit with her. We ate sandwiches and drank iced tea. We're not big talkers in general, but we've been working on that. We've been talking about fixing up the house. Maybe even moving to a new place in town. We've even talked about Dad, four or five times. Mom's told me some stories I've never heard.

I've also been spending time with RJ's headphones on, listening to music and playing the practice pad. I gaze at the horizon. Sometimes it's just deep, endless blue. Other times, the clouds stack up in these dramatic pillars. I've seen a few rainbows that stretch down to the water. They're so impossibly beautiful that I don't believe my own eyes. And yet, there they are.

Still, I didn't come all the way to Hawaii to practice drums or gaze at the scenery. I came to finish the bucket list.

"It's nearly time to go, Will," says Mom. "We need to head back to the hotel and pack; it's a long way to the airport."

"I'm going to try one more time," I say.

"Try what?" she says.

"Swimming," I say. I never did tell her about the bucket list. It always felt like something intensely personal, something private between RJ and me.

I take off Dad's hat and slide the snorkel and mask over my head.

"Have fun," Mom says, going back to her book.

"Beep," I say.

"Beep," she says.

I head for the water. This time, I grip RJ's necklace as the water reaches my neck, splashing my chin.

I turn and see Mom at the shore. She's blurry, but I see her waving.

"It's now or never, Will," I say out loud.

I crouch down in the water, put the snorkel into my mouth, and plunge my face through the surface. In front of me is dazzling color and motion—rocks, sand, and a handful of tiny fish glinting with the sun. Instantly, my breathing speeds up. This makes me panic a little, and I lift my face out of the water, my feet shuffling back to shore. I cough and sputter as salt water burns my mouth, nose, and throat.

Then I remember how Roxanne showed me how to breathe when I was panicking, way back when I stepped through RJ's door and he wasn't there.

One. Two. Three. Four.

Boom. Pack. Boom-boom pack. Boom. Pack. Boom-boom pack.

Slow and steady goes the rhythm, and it isn't long before the panic fades.

I put my face back into the water. I fold my body into the lapping waves and crouch-walk deeper and deeper, and soon I'm floating. I'm not touching the bottom. I'm swimming in the ocean.

As I swim deeper, I can see much farther without glasses than I can on land. Fish stream past, nipping one another's tails, nibbling at the rocks. I find myself moving my limbs, awkwardly at first, and increasingly relaxed, trailing after them. I recognize some of the species from the pictures on RJ's wall. Long, narrow white fish, delicate yellow fish with white stripes, and some bigger fish, with big mouths and tiny, sharp-looking teeth, chomping at the coral. They all move aside as I float past.

I realize that I'm really far from shore. Maybe it's dangerous. But when I lift my head, there's a handful of other swimmers. I'm not the only one out here, even if I'm the only one in here.

Soon I relax enough to let my mind drift. I try to think about RJ, how proud he would be of what I'm doing. I try to remember what he looked like and how he sounded—his face, his voice, his hospital room—but I can't. It's all so far away, I find that I can't do anything out here but float and swim and breathe and see, and maybe that's how RJ would want me to be.

WHAT WAS THAT?

A giant, terrifying shape moves past my peripheral vision. Some primitive, illogical part of my brain screams, *SHARK! I'm going to be eaten alive!* But it isn't a shark at all.

Chelonia mydas.

It's a giant green sea turtle.

A scared sound comes out of my mouth. "Oh!" piped loud into my ears by the snorkel, but then it's replaced by my own gentle breathing. *One . . . two . . . three . . . four.*

The sea turtle floats past me lazily, slowly moving its fins with minimal effort, and yet loaded with some sort of quiet, ancient power. It looks at me. It's not my imagination; it's actually looking at me. I lift my head above the surface, almost to see if I'm dreaming, but I'm not. I return my face to the water, and the turtle is still here, with its brown and green plates and its big black eyes. It's in no hurry.

Then, from below, a second, slightly smaller turtle drifts upward, sticks its beak above the water, and coasts along for a while. I can't believe this—two turtles! But it's not just two. I see a third a ways off, gliding like a shadow through the gray-blue murk. I'm surrounded by turtles, and my heart starts to pound. I know that this is the moment. I have reached a place where everything is perfection. I cannot stay here forever. But I can leave a piece of myself here.

I touch the string of shells around my neck, twisting the metal hook that keeps it closed. Once it's free, it hangs from my fingertips like a strand of seaweed.

"RJ," I say.

And with that, I loosen my grip, and the necklace slips past my fingers. It sinks into the water, in no hurry, like the turtles, and it swirls as it drops on its voyage. I watch it go. I gaze at the turtles one last time, until my eyes are blind with tears, and then I reposition my body and head for shore.

AUTHOR'S NOTE

Like Will's, my turtle face emerged slowly and then all at once. I didn't understand my classmates' cruel comments about my chin until one day, I grabbed a makeup mirror and looked at my face in profile. Suddenly, I saw myself how others saw me. I began to struggle with body dysmorphia, with being publicly reduced to a single body part. When I was fourteen, hospital orderlies wheeled me to an operating room as my mom and dad waved goodbye. Six hours later, I was no longer a turtle on the outside. Inside, however, I was the very same me: afraid of the world, afraid of myself.

I found refuge in music, in playing guitar and drums, in Judaism, in writing short stories—and like Will, I discovered that I was only in the first stages of picking up the pieces of who I am. My sense of self needed to go through a kind of breaking down and rebuilding. Therapy, travel, studies, and art—along with the love of family and friends—helped me to do the work I needed to do:

to discover myself on my own terms, not to crawl in shadows, but to step into the light.

Almost thirty years later, I returned to the "makeup mirror" and began writing an autobiographical comic strip—an origin story—about my journey from diagnosis to surgery to true transformation. That comic morphed into the fictional story of *Turtle Boy*.

RJ, on the other hand, is based not on a single person, but on an amalgamation of several close friends I've had throughout my life, all of them, like RJ, proud and determined, yet sensitive and also intolerant of excuses. They saw me for who I am and pushed me to be better. I also want to mention that RJ's condition, mitochondrial disease, is real, affecting one in every five thousand people. The range of symptoms is wide, and prognoses vary from patient to patient. For more information, investigate the excellent resources at North American Mitochondrial Disease Consortium and United Mitochondrial Disease Foundation.

I hope you enjoyed meeting Will, and I hope he inspired you to try something new. I wish you strength as you journey out of whatever shell in which you find yourself.

ACKNOWLEDGMENTS

Deep gratitude to my brilliant agent, Richard Abate, for believing in me, sticking by me, and helping me turn a ten-panel comic strip into this book. To Rachel Kim and Rebecca Gudelis, who helped guide this book along, from the rocky early drafts until it crossed the finish line. To my incredible editor, Beverly Horowitz, whose depth of understanding about what was hiding under Will's shell (and whose mastery of how to craft a great book) brought our protagonist into three living, breathing dimensions. Your judgment helped me to cut and cut, and your kindness helped it not to hurt.

Thank you to the amazing team that worked on *Turtle Boy:* Ken Crossland, Tamar Schwartz, Jonathan Morris, Colleen Fellingham (nothing gets past her eye!), and Bob Bianchini, whose jacket design made me laugh and cry.

To Meredith Arthur and Jeremy Moskowitz: thank you for reading early drafts, saying "yes!" and pointing me in the right direction. To Robin, who teaches me every day about saying "Yes, and!" To Sarah Lefton, whose real-life "Yo, Semite" design inspired Rabbi Harris's T-shirt. To Jenn Sturgill, mile by mile, hill by Fillmore hill, you were my constant *Turtle Boy* confidante. And speaking of hills, Shirah's motto, "Is the heart willing? Come what may!", comes from Israeli author David Grossman's novel *See Under: Love*. That simple call for courage has propelled me up many a mountain in my life.

A moment of appreciation for my colleagues and students at Jewish Community High School of the Bay: thank you for sitting next to and with me (literally and figuratively, Roni Ben-David), for allowing me to pitch you early "prototypes," for offering yourselves as sounding boards, and for cheering me on as I moved from gateway to gateway. You passed me the Kooshball and listened, whether I was griping or exulting. This book came alive and grew over the course of three academic years in the most wonderful school in the world.

To Joe, who has always known the real me.

To my parents, Alan and Kathy Wolkenstein, and my brother, Haran—your love and support helped me survive middle school, and it supported me in adulthood as *Turtle Boy* moved from a dream to reality.

Speaking of support, I cannot stress enough how essential the kind, compassionate, and positive guidance of Kristy Lin Billuni, my writing coach, was in picking me up when I was down, helping me find my way when I was lost.

To Larry Moskowitz and Ouisue Moskowitz, the best in-laws I could ever imagine.

Now, a few words to you, my beautiful, brilliant wife, Gabi. The story of my life would be incomplete without you—you planted a vision in my eye: a blog, a list, a comic strip, a dream, a book. You assured me with perfect faith that it would happen. Block by block, slice by slice, cup by cup, from the arc of Will's life to "nut loaf," there is no part of this book that does not bear the tender imprint of your fingertips.

And lastly, to Anna. May you grow up in a world where every child feels seen and loved for who they are. Sing, drum, dance, and run—may your home follow you anywhere and everywhere you go.